THE SEWING SISTERS' SOCIETY

THE PASTOR TAKES A WIFE
SECOND CHANCE CHRISTMAS
SECOND CHANCE AT LOVE
Copyrights 2015, 2016 in various anthologies.

Cover design: Beth Jamison, Jamison Editing

Interior Format

The *Sewing Sisters'* Society

Ruth Logan Herne

The Pastor Takes a Wife

A Sewing Sisters Society Story

Ruth Logan Herne

Dedication

THIS BOOK IS LOVINGLY DEDICATED to the earliest Americans in our family. Their courage and desire for religious freedom brought them to America's shores in the early 1600's. Thanking God… and them… for having the strength to make that leap of faith: The Soule and Vail families, and the Blodgett brothers. And I'd be remiss to overlook our later immigrants, the Logan, Hannon and Mack families, and most particularly Lena (Magdeline) Thumm Eichas, my husband's grandmother who came over from Germany as a child… and grew to be a wonderful woman who faced World Wars, a Depression, child loss, jobs, farming and raising eleven wonderful children to be hard-working, faith-filled adults. She set an example that has survived multiple generations with faith, hope and love.

Whosoever shall receive one of such children in my name, receiveth me: and whosoever shall receive me, receiveth not me, but him that sent me.

~ Matthew 9:37

Chapter One

IT WAS NOW OR NEVER, Macy Evers realized as she faced the dust-covered store-front of Hattie's Shirt Shop, Fine Goods Available by Order. Tucked north of Main Street in Second Chance, South Dakota, the small porch offered a covered entrance to the shop, but even the cornice work lay thick with dust above her. This town could use a good rain, but if it got one, the unimproved streets would be awash in mud.

Dust was better, she decided as she climbed the two steps.

Palms damp, she faced the door, half scared to death and Macy hadn't been afraid of much for a long time, but lying on paper to a potential benefactor— then repeating the sin in person— were reasons enough, she reckoned. And if Hattie McGillicuddy figured out she could barely thread a needle, much less sew men's shirts, all her careful planning might be for naught.

"Going in, Miss?"

The man's voice surprised her. She turned too fast and banged his left knee with her worn satchel. He rocked off balance, then pitched down the two narrow steps to the street below.

"Pa!" A school-age girl with a head full of golden brown ringlet curls hurried to the man's side. "I'll help you, Pa. No worries." And then the child made a great show out of helping her father up, as if the tall, square-shouldered, gentle-eyed man needed assistance. He didn't but he played along, letting her think she was helping, and oh! The joy on that little girl's face... Macy swallowed years of regret and heartache as she struggled to apologize, because she'd never known the joyful, gentle touch of a man, father or otherwise. But that was then and this was now. "I'm so sorry, I didn't hear you behind me. Are you all right?"

He made a show out of checking his arms, then his legs, amusing the child. "I appear to be." He grinned, the girl laughed, and their quick exchange ignited the tiniest flicker of belief in human nature. It would be dashed soon enough. Macy knew that from experience. Seeing the love flash between father and daughter made her wish all parents and children could share affection like the pair standing before her. But she knew better. She'd come here, hoping Second Chance was different. It had to be, or she'd just made the worst mistake of her life.

"So, Miss. Shall we begin again?" Holding tight to the child's hand, the man climbed the two steps, reached past Macy and pushed open the door. "After you. In interests of my safety and gentlemanly etiquette."

She stepped into the shop, and as soon as she did a woman bustled forward from the room beyond.

Macy tried to shrink back, but the man and the child were right behind her, so she couldn't.

The woman raised her brows, noted Macy's threadbare satchel, and gave her a quick look of appraisal. "I expect you're Macy Evers, and you just arrived on the twelve-o-seven and I was knee-deep in work and forgot to look at my watch. I'm Hattie McGillicuddy."

"I am Macy, yes." She answered carefully, because too many lies could trip a body up and when things of great importance were at stake, she couldn't afford mistakes.

"Reverend Barber!" Hattie waved the man in, spotted the girl and set her hands on broad hips. "Chickie, is that you back there?"

A giggle answered and the broad woman bent down. "I am always delighted to see you and your daddy, Chickie

Barber. Are you helping your daddy at the church?"

"We have been doing lots of things," the girl exclaimed. "So many, I forgot to count. We found a home over in De Smet for little John Collins."

"I heard about that and thanked God forthwith," Hattie declared, still bent low. "The Smiths are a fine and gentle family. Little John will do well there."

"I shall miss him," the girl— *"Chickie"*— replied. "But no sooner had the Smiths come to pick him up and take him home, than we found a basket baby on the side porch."

"No." Hattie straightened quickly and exchanged looks with the girl's father. "Oh, Will, that's a surprise, isn't it? No way of knowing who the little tyke belongs to?"

Macy held her breath, but made sure no one knew she was holding her breath. When the preacher answered, her heart started beating again.

"Just a name pinned to his blanket, same as mine as fate would have it, and no one saw a thing. 'Liza Beaucharde has him at the moment. We're trying to figure out a formula for him."

"My mama's recipe has always worked fine, I'm going to write it down for you. Simple and effective unless he's got sour stomach." Hattie frowned as if sour stomach was a really bad thing. Will Barber looked quite capable as he shrugged the notion off.

"I've walked the floor before. I can do it again."

"You've got a good heart, Will." Hattie scribbled down her recipe while Macy waited. She had to dip the pen-head multiple times. "Ink's low."

"And pricey," the reverend noted. "Shipping costs add to just about everything this far west, but Chickie and I have the garden in hand."

"And a lot of offers to help you put things up for the winter, I expect."

The man winced but still looked amused. "Coming in regular. But 'Liza doesn't mind lending a hand with no expectation of nuptials involved."

Hattie laughed. "Me and 'Liza are about the only single women in town who haven't set their cap for our pastor, here." Chagrined amusement marked her gaze, and gave more weight to her words. "More's the pity because we probably keep body and soul together better than our younger counterparts, but having said that…" She handed him the quickly written recipe. "I'm fine bein' independent, me and my Maker. I've got a shop to call my own, and I'm mighty glad to have help again, Miss Macy!"

Finally she turned full attention toward Macy, but Macy hadn't minded the quick back-and-forth between the seamstress and the reverend. A lot could be learned from seeing how folks spoke to one another, how they treated each other, and the friendly exchange said these were both good people. That was something to be grateful for, right there. "I'm glad to be here as well."

"Take your bag through there and I'll show you your room off to the side. And a cup of bracing tea would be lovely right now, even though it's blazing hot outside. Before we know it, ol' man winter will swoop in again, so we'll soak warmth into our bones to get ready. Just the one bag, Macy?"

"Yes, ma'am."

"Easy travel, then." Something in Hattie's expression said more than her simple words, but Macy couldn't read the emotion. "Will, are you after shirts?"

"Shirts, yes. And we need an everyday dress for Chickie and I'll need a Sunday dress by fall."

"She's growing like crazy," Hattie observed as she went to jot down a note, but when the pen wouldn't work, the pastor handed her a pencil from his pocket.

"Thank you, Will."

"Keep it, I have a box at home from old Mr. Singer. He left them to me in his will."

"Funny old duck, but beloved in his own way."

"Amen to that. And his place is open out there, still, and that's a worry." He looked actually concerned for his fellow man as Macy came back into the store area. "Someone will be getting a nice claim and a good, simple house, to boot, but after that long, harsh winter, a lot of folks are deciding to settle elsewhere."

"More opportunity for us," Hattie declared. She stuck the note to the wall with a pin. "Chickie, what color dresses would you like?" She turned her attention toward Will. "Do you have time to take her to the mercantile to pick fabric? Or should I?"

He shook his head. "I've got to get back to that baby, elsewise I'd do it."

"Macy." Hattie turned fully. "Let's put our tea off for a little. You don't mind, do you?"

Macy shook her head, because putting tea off meant putting questions off, and she was all right with that.

"You and I can take Chickie to the mercantile, get what we need, and I can introduce you to the shopkeepers. That way if you run an errand for me, folks'll know you."

"Of course." Macy smiled down at the little girl, because she could handle kids well enough. And she knew how to shop… and steal, but that was all in the past. She'd come here ready to start anew. And she would, too. She'd come to the West as a scarlet woman, but she had a new chance… a new hope.

"Thank you, ladies. I'll get back to the parsonage. Chickpea," he bent low and hugged the little girl. "I'll see you in a bit, okay? And no hornswaggling the ladies into a candy stick, okay?"

She peeked a smile at him and nodded. "But if they offer one, well… that's all right."

He laughed out loud, and Macy didn't think she'd ever heard such a nice man's laugh before. "If they offer first, it's fine. No begging."

"I won't!" She shook her dust-mop curls and grinned,

and Macy was pretty sure few merchants could resist spoiling her. Will walked out, Hattie followed, and Chickie reached up to take Macy's hand. "May I walk with you, Miss?"

She didn't wait for permission, she simply tucked her little fingers into Macy's much rougher hand, and when she did, she won a piece of Macy's heart.

Would the good reverend let his precious child hold your hand if he knew the truth, Macy Evers? Would he allow you to walk his child down Main Street for all to see?

He wouldn't, and probably shouldn't, but Macy pushed the harsh scolding aside. She knew who she was, and what she'd done, but she'd left that life behind long ago. Except...

She sighed, knowing the past could tread hard on the heels of the present, but she was strong. She'd had to be. And when opportunity flung its door wide, offering the chance to come west, she'd grabbed hold tight. She would learn to sew right quick and well, because a good respectable job like this was a huge improvement.

Dust kicked up as she and Hattie headed east on Main, with the reverend going west toward the church at the far end of town. They passed several small businesses. Hattie waved to the men at the lumber mill across the way, and when they mounted the steps to the well-kept mercantile, Chickie danced with excitement. "I love coming here to see the pretty things!"

"A fine store like this is a wonder, for sure," Hattie told her. She bustled through the door, called greetings this way and that, moved to the counter and smiled broad. "Ginny Beltry, this is my new helper Macy Evers. Macy, this is Ginny, she's great at fabrics and notions, and if I send you here for supplies, Ginny's the gal to see."

She shook Ginny's hand and when Ginny met her eyes with an easy smile, another wave of emotion hit low and hard. She wouldn't have been greeted like this back east, no one would have given her the respect of a smile, but Second Chance was different. There were no memories and pre-conceived opinions, and what a relief that was.

"So what do you think, Chickie? I think your new everyday dress should be sturdy. I know that might not meet your sensibilities," Hattie went on as Chickie lifted disappointed eyes her way. "But sensible we must be. The Sunday dress, well, that's different, and I'll take your opinion most seriously on that, my dear."

Macy pointed out a bank of green-and-gold shaded calicos on one table. "These would be beautiful with your pretty hazel eyes, Chickie."

"And perhaps yellow with blue for Sunday?" Hattie suggested.

"Well." Chickie stared hard at the green and gold, then moved to the right where plaids in similar colors were displayed. "I like these checkery-ones even better. Would that be okay?"

"Which ones are your favorites?"

"This and this. And this," Chickie pointed out three pretty plaids.

"It will be trickier to lay out, but for you Chickie Barber, I'm pleased to do it," Hattie announced. She plunked one of the bolts onto the cutting counter, ordered a dress length, and when Ginny added a calico bolt to the mix, Hattie looked up in surprise.

"Everyone one should have at least two daily dresses," Ginny whispered. "I'll cover the goods if you cover the sewing."

"Happy to oblige such an excellent idea!" Hattie turned back to the softer-toned goods farther down the table. "Chickie and Macy, what do you think of this?" She held up a soft yellow calico with tufts of forget-me-not toned flowers sprinkled in every direction.

"My ma had a dress like that, almost just like that," Chickie whispered. She trailed a hand across the soft, pale fabric. "It was so pretty, Miss Hattie, and I think if I wore a dress like that it might make Pa miss her even more."

"You are a thoughtful and caring child." Macy leaned down and gave her an impetuous hug. "What about pink?"

"Oh, do you think?" Chickie's eyes grew wide. "No one ever lets me wear pink because they always say green and yellow go better with my eyes, but I think pink is so very pretty, Miss Macy."

"If we do pink with yellow and green flowers, we've covered everything, haven't we?"

"Yes!" Chickie clapped her hands together. "Everyone will be happy then!"

"Oh, child." Hattie reached down a hand to cup Chickie's chin. "Everyone is pleased with you already. You've got nothing but admirers here in Second Chance, dear girl."

Chickie dipped her head as if embarrassed, and Macy looked from one to the other, puzzled. What would a child have to regret? And why would she worry about making others happy? Didn't the grace of a child make people happy naturally?

Remorse hit her hard. She fought the groundswell of emotions quickly, before anyone saw. *Focus, Macy. Remember Jochebed's journey, her choice to give her child the best life possible and spare him the Pharaoh's sword. A wise mother puts her child first, always. Moses went on to be a leader of men.*

"Then I think I like this pink the very best," whispered Chickie, as if admitting it was beyond the realm of possibilities. "It is the very best and prettiest by far. Don't you think so, Miss Macy?"

The girl's earnest question made Macy squat to meet her eye-to-eye. "I can't imagine anything prettier."

Delight chased shadows from Chickie's eyes, and when she threw herself into Macy's arms, she nearly bowled her over. A shelving unit prevented that, but the feel of the child in her arms, the softness of rampant curls pressed against Macy's cheek, heightened Macy's emotions again.

She'd been forced to make her way as best she could for many years. Here, holding Chickie, chasing away the girl's worries, made her remember the child she'd been, bereft and misbegotten. She'd read about the milk of human kindness, but it had been little more than ink on a page until the MacDonalds and Jean Ellen Crowley approached her about coming west to work in Hattie's shop.

If she could show this child that same consideration, maybe she could keep the flow of kindness going. She hugged her back, lugged the over-sized bolt to the counter and set it down carefully.

Hattie pointed things out to Ginny, spouting words like muslin, cotton, netting, hooks, eyes and lace.

Macy got the lace part, the rest was a jumble until she saw the pile of various goods on the counter. "It takes all this to make a dress?" Too late, she realized her question showed her ineptitude. She flinched, hoping the women didn't catch it, and to her surprise, they didn't seem to.

"Well, I'm going to make an underskirt as well, a petticoat but not too flouncy. Flouncy out here is a fire hazard in the winter."

Hattie's observation seemed wise. Macy wouldn't have given it thought, but the image of wide-skirted gowns and narrow rooms with fire box heaters made them impractical and possibly dangerous. "That makes so much sense."

"The three of us will take these things back to the shop when we're done," Hattie said as Ginny cut the fabric to the proper size. "And Ginny, I'll need three shirt lengths in white, light blue, dark blue and two-dozen three-eighth inch buttons."

"Threads too, Hattie? Or are you set on those?"

"I have more thread than any three seamstresses could possibly need in a lifetime, but I don't have the right shade of pink for Miss Chickie's gown," Hattie palmed the child's head, smiling, and Chickie lit up at the attention. "So perhaps a spool of light pink would do well."

"I'll grab it, Mother." A teen-age girl came across the room. She smiled a greeting at them, found the right shade of pink thread, and set it on the counter, then stretched a hand out in greeting. "I'm Samantha."

"Macy." Macy accepted the greeting and hoped her acting was up to snuff. "I'm working for Miss Hattie now."

"And plenty of work we have, too." Hattie accepted the bundles from Ginny, handed a small pack to Chickie and a larger one to Macy. "I'll be glad of the help, that's for certain!"

"With a new influx of train men going back and forth, business should be booming," said Ginny.

"And a blessing," Hattie replied. "Thank you ladies, I'll see you soon."

They called goodbyes as Hattie, Macy and Chickie walked through the heavy door to the porch front. As they headed back to Hattie's, the seamstress offered quick directions. "Now, Macy, I know you're somewhat new at sewing—"

New didn't do justice to her lack of experience, but she nodded.

"And I intend to start you out with cutting, marking, trimming and button work."

The thought of putting scissors to bolts of pricey fabric nearly did her in. "Cutting?" she squeaked. "Um, I might need a little practice, Miss Hattie. My skills most likely lie in other directions."

"Cutting it will be," Hattie persisted. "I'll show you how to pin the patterns, you'll cut and gather the panels and sleeves together, and we'll make quick work of all of this. And when I think you're ready, I'll have you put together Chickie's petticoat."

A petticoat? Layers and gathers and tucks?

"While a petticoat isn't an easy pattern for a beginner, it is hidden by virtue of its necessity and therefore hides mistakes with it."

"That seems quite logical."

"We try," Hattie agreed. She opened the door to her shop and stepped in. "Let's lay all of this in the back room. I'll get things put where they belong, and Macy, be a dear, and see our Chickie back to the parsonage, won't you?"

"Of course." Chickie took her hand again as they went through the door. "I'll be back soon."

"Wonderful! And then we'll have that promised tea."

The thought of tea sounded marvelous, but she could do without the inquiry that would most likely accompany the respite. Still, Hattie had extended a momentous opportunity. With Hattie, Macy needed to be mostly honest. She couldn't reveal all, not and be the woman she longed to be here, washed clean in the spirit. Christ had set the example for sacrificial love long ago and she intended to follow that example.

She'd failed long enough.

Now was the time of success.

She and Chickie walked up the hot, dusty street hand in hand. Some businesses had coverings over the board walk, some— newer, perhaps, or not as well-funded— had nothing but a narrow step separating the door from the street. But as they approached the parsonage, the sound of a baby crying pushed Macy's feet to hurry. She had to force herself to walk slowly, almost leisurely, as if the child's cries didn't call her to run.

"That's our new baby, Little Will." Chickie tugged her into a quicker pace. "Miss 'Liza calls him a sweet thing, but he doesn't smell sweet all the time."

"Well, he's a baby, so that's part of it."

Chickie drew her all the way up to the door. When she pulled it open, Macy was set to turn back, but Chickie had other ideas. "Oh, you must come see him!"

How could she? How could she walk into this parson's house and see someone walking her precious child?

"Pa! I'm here with Miss Macy, she brought me home."

Chickie's announcement left little chance for escape, and when the pastor appeared, one look at his face had her reaching out her hands for Will.

"He won't be comforted," the pastor confessed, and he looked quite pleased to pass the baby off in quick order. "Miss 'Liza said he'd grow used to the substitute given a little time, but it doesn't appear to agree with him."

"Oh, it might just be a bubble," Macy crooned as she accepted a piece of flannel from the pastor and draped it over her shoulder. "Babies get those, I hear, and they can be quite angry until they burp up the gas."

"Well, he's had gas, that's a fact." The pastor rubbed the back of his head, but then paused when the baby belched and then dropped a sleepy head to Macy's shoulder. "Will you look at that?"

Macy couldn't look, of course, because her precious son's head was tucked beneath her chin, but the appreciation on the pastor's face made her feel good.

"You have a knack with him, Miss Evers."

Dumb, Macy. What if he figures out who you are? "My friend in Pittsburgh used a slightly different formula for her baby when he wouldn't eat proper. Of course I suppose it's not proper talking about that with a pastor, is it?"

"If *he* sleeps, everyone gets a chance to sleep. Or get work done," the pastor supposed with a grin. "Which makes it proper enough. So tell me your recipe and 'Liza and I will try it out. Of course nothing is the same as having your very own mother care for you, but since that appears to be impossible, we'll muster along. He's a fine little fellow, isn't he?"

Oh, he was the very best of fine little fellows, but she mustn't seem too excited about it. "He's sweet enough, yes."

"You don't like babies, Miss Evers?" Curiosity crinkled the pastor's gaze. "And yet you handled him with an expert's touch."

"I expect it was more circumstance than skill," she told him as she bent to lay the sleeping boy in the dresser drawer tucked in a shaded corner. "Sometimes you just happen to be in the right place at the right time."

The pastor motioned her toward the kitchen at the back of the house, and when she stepped through the door, he indicated the baby. "I didn't want to wake him by talking out there."

"He'll sleep fine now that he's down," Macy said. No sooner had the words left her mouth, than she wished them back. Never had she realized how hard it would be to live a lie outright, to pretend all day, every day, and she was still on day one. She had to re-double her efforts and try harder. "Most do, according to my friend."

Fear of what she might see kept her eyes off his. Was he putting two and two together? Sensing her dishonesty? Her fingers tingled and her heart beat a harsh rhythm in her chest. She was doing this for the baby's sake, wasn't she? Or was it for her sake too, because a labeled woman bore her sin for all to see?

Maybe both, if she was honest, because no one would care that it wasn't her sin. They'd see what they wanted to see, a single woman with a child, and that would be enough to shrug her off. No one would care about the wickedness involved, and there was no reason her son should live in shadowed darkness. Not when other choices loomed.

Her child deserved better. No baby should grow up shunned by folks who claimed the love of Christ. This way the baby... William... would have a chance, the chance she never had, and by glory she'd do everything in her power to see he got that opportunity. Starting with pretending to be a seamstress. "I'd best get back, Hattie's got work."

"Thank you for seeing Chickie home, Miss Evers."

It was the simplest of phrases, so why did her heart beat furiously? What quality of voice sent her silly pulse into a tailspin? This wasn't some child's tale of love and serenity. This was real life, a fallen woman, a helpless child and the harsh choices that came from both. "I was happy to do it, Pastor."

She slipped through the door, chin tipped down, avoiding his gaze. She'd keep her secrets close, but with the kind-hearted pastor around, that might be easier said than done.

Chapter Two

A BSOLUTELY BEAUTIFUL.
       Will Barber tipped the curtain aside as the new-
comer retraced her steps to Hattie's shop. When was the
last time he thought a woman beautiful?

That thought took him back over a decade when he met
his late wife. She'd been beautiful in a different way, the
kind of beauty that drew a young man's way of thinking.
He realized too late he'd been foolish. The last thing Elissa
wanted was to live a life of service as a wife and mother.

He almost sighed, then got hold of himself. The baby…
Little Will… would waken soon, and then he'd have no time,
so a smart man wouldn't stand around thinking thoughts
that couldn't be changed. He'd busy his hands changing
what could, same as he decided five long years ago, when
he buried his wife and baby boy. He and Chickie carved a
life for themselves, a good life, too. He grabbed a hoe and
called Chickie's name.

"Coming, Pa!" She hurried down the back stairs, saw the
hoe and reached for her apron. "I'll help you, okay? I can
do the weeding. You'll hoe faster that way."

"I'd be obliged." She trotted outside with him, sunlight
glancing off wisps of golden curl. "You made out all right
with Miss Hattie, I take it?"

"Oh, it was wonderful!" She weeded as she talked and
that made the work seem quicker and lighter despite the
heat of the late-day sun. "Miss Hattie said serviceable was
important for my everyday dresses—"

Will raised a brow. "I believe I ordered one everyday dress."

"You did!" She exclaimed as if this was the best thing of all. "But Miss Ginny and Miss Hattie thought two were better, and then Miss Macy said what about pink and I couldn't even really hardly believe it, it was so pretty."

"I'm confused, but that seems to be our normal state of affairs these days, Chickie. What exactly is pink?"

"My Sunday dress." This time she paused in her earnest ministrations and gazed up at him. "Oh, Pa, it is the prettiest of pretty goods and Miss Macy said every little girl should wear pink if she's a mind to do it."

Macy that just walked back to Hattie's place wearing a very serviceable, un-notable brown. "I expect it will be lovely."

"Oh, it will! And then Miss Macy let me hold her hand all the way back to the shop and then she walked me over here and she smelled so soft and sweet, like one of those lemon cookies 'Liza makes sometimes."

Lemon and cream.

He'd caught the faintest whiff when she moved through the room, just enough to blend scent and sight. Soft sunlight streaming through the west-facing windows, and the sweet, clean lemony scent of ladies' soap. "I like lemon cookies myself."

"Well I can't make them, and you don't have time, so how about we tell folks we'd like some?" Chickie wondered. "When you said you had a taste for apple cake, lots of people stopped by that week. Remember, Pa?"

Oh, he remembered all right. Every single woman and mother of a single woman made sure they dropped off some version of apple cake as if the parsonage was the local fair grounds and him the appointed food judge. "I don't think we need that many cookies, Chickie. A few would do for just you and me." A noise came through the tacked-on screening, and Will turned, startled. "I forgot we had a baby in there."

"I don't think he'll let you forget for too long, Pa." Chickie put her hands up to her ears. "He's powerful loud."

"God made him that way on purpose," he told her as he set away the hoe and moved to the pump to wash his hands. "There's no ignoring a baby's cry, it's nature's way. They're set to squall and we're meant to appease. Just the way the good Lord planned it."

"I bet my mama took real good care of me when I was a baby."

He turned at the top step and cupped his beautiful daughter's cheek. "You were beloved from before we knew you." It was a half-truth, but Chickie didn't need to know more. No child should know that her mother shrugged her off like an ill-used doll.

"I wish I remembered." Chickie turned her gaze out to the gently rolling plains, her hazel eyes unusually somber.

Will was glad she didn't remember, but he couldn't say that out loud. "You come watch how I handle Little Will and make a memory of that because that's how we cared for you." Would God hold him guilty for his fib?

He decided He wouldn't. God was bigger than that, bigger than anything. God would see the self-worth of a child as more important than the mother who never wanted her or the brother that followed three years later. He hurried into the small parsonage, lifted the baby from the padded drawer and cooed words of comfort to the angry infant. "Sorry, little fella, I've got your bottle right here, we'll see how well you handle this mix, won't we? And then we'll see about your other end."

"I don't see more nappies, Pa," Chickie announced from the other side of the room. She pulled out the worn blanket Little Will had been bundled in and shook her head. "Unless we use the blanket here."

It seemed a shame to cut up the blanket, even though it had seen better days. "'Liza washed two. I think we'd be smart to grab some flannel from the mercantile and cut a few more."

"Is it pricey, Pa?" Chickie asked. "Maybe I could do some work for Miss Hattie and earn a little money. That would help us get by."

"We're getting by just fine," he told her, and they were. He had his father's money tucked away, and while the church coffers weren't overflowing, they had plenty as long as folks supplied him with wood and winter meat. "We're blessed to have such good folks looking out for us."

"Will they care if we have a baby here, Pa?"

Will did sigh this time. A few folks didn't take kindly to his open door policy for orphans, but then they didn't know what it was like to watch a mother cast aside a child. Will knew it first-hand and he'd decided to pull good from bad. Wasn't that what Jesus did on the cross? From bad came wondrous good? How could anyone fault him for following that example? "Most won't and the ones that do will let us know, but this little fellow is one of God's children, Chickie. Just like you and me. And whatever made his mother leave him at our door, he deserves the best chance we can give him at a good life. Beloved and raised up right." He settled into a chair with the baby, and soothed him with the bottle. Tiny gasps turned into slurps of satisfaction. Will stared into the face of the small boy, his namesake, and remembered another boy, another day, long ago. He'd lost so much that day. His dignity, his heart and maybe even some of his soul because he should have seen what was coming. He was a learned man, with degrees to his credit, yet he'd been blindsided by what seemed so clear in retrospect.

He'd made a grievous error, and no matter what happened, he would work tirelessly for atonement, one blessed child at a time. He'd been too late and too blind to save his own child, but he'd be man enough to save others.

"He is mighty cute, Pa." Chickie whispered as she came

up alongside. "And when he smiles at me, it's like I can't help but smile back."

"That's how it is," answered Will. "Fetch those triangles off the line out back, will you Chickie? Hopefully they'll get us through the night and we'll head up the road to get more tomorrow."

She skipped off, humming, her sweet nature a blessing. As the baby boy blinked, burped, then yawned, arms stretching, Will gazed upon the miracle of life. Each child a blessing, a gift from God. Why then was he foolish enough to trust his newborn son to his half-addled wife?

Regret stabbed deep and fierce, but the wee boy reached up a hand right then, reached it straight up to his face and touched Will's cheek. And then he smiled, a big, wide, toothless baby smile, two tiny dark brows thrust up high and eyes crinkled half-shut.

A benediction.

The baby's touch and smile felt like a blessing, as if God himself was telling Will it would be all right. *Forgive us our trespasses as we forgive those who trespass against us...*

Easy words. So much more difficult to do, and truthfully, it was far more difficult to forgive himself than others.

Forgive us our trespasses...

Christ's instruction, and a good one. Now if he could only learn to use it on himself.

Chapter Three

"I NEVER THOUGHT I'D SLEEP SO much." Macy exclaimed as she hurried in from the necessary the next morning. "I thought we'd have time to get to know one another, Miss Hattie, but then…" she shrugged in frustration. "I don't remember a thing."

"You dozed off sittin' in that needlework chair and I laughed to myself because I forgot about time changes an' all," Hattie told her. "I sent you right off to bed, and a good thing, too! And it's Hattie, dear, plain and simple."

"But you're my boss." Macy frowned. "It doesn't seem right to pretend we're equals, ma'am."

"We *are* equals which doesn't make me any less your boss, it just makes us women with a mission," Hattie answered. "To help bring peace and joy and gentleness to a land that could be wild if we let it, and I've got no intention of seeing that happen."

Macy had heard tales of Western wildness, but she didn't see signs of that in Second Chance. She'd noted the lack of saloons right away and considered that a plus. If she never set foot in or near another saloon, she'd consider herself a fortunate woman.

"There's a coffee pot brewing."

"That's what woke me, for certain, the perfect smell."

Hattie smiled. "Help yourself and let's see about breakfast for you."

"Not this late," Macy insisted. "My time should be spent working, so I'll pour coffee if it's ready. Working now will give me a hefty appetite come lunch."

Hattie glanced at the watch around her neck. "Well, you do make sense, Macy. All right, let's get to work, teaching is always a longer prospect than you expect, so I'm going to start with buttons and buttonholes. The buttons are easy enough, buttonholes are not, and you need to practice tiny, symmetrical stitches to get them just right."

The thought of tiny symmetrical stitches was enough to send Macy into panic mode, but if it could be learned, she'd do it.

An hour later she realized she was hopelessly inept and destined to be fired.

"How are we coming?" Miss Hattie wondered just then. "I meant to come over and check your practice piece, but then I got whirring away on that amazing machine and lost track of time. But there are three white men's shirts put together, and that's one for the record books."

Macy extended her practice piece and fought hot, angry tears. "It's terrible, Miss Hattie. I mean, Hattie," she corrected herself quickly. "I keep working that needle in and around like you said, and it will look fine for a stitch or two, and then it looks all out of kilter."

"But look at your button work!" Hattie exclaimed. "Macy, those are just fine after the first two. Now I expect you sat here thinking the buttonhole whipstitch would go along just as smooth, even though I do recall saying they're hard to learn and take some practice."

Macy grimaced. "You did say that."

"And now you're all worked up in a tizzy thinking you should have been able to do them by now."

She'd hit the nail on the head again, so Macy nodded.

"Landsakes, child, it took me years to get proper buttonholes as a child, and I've watched grown men and women work for months to get the balance just so. This was practice, so you'll keep on practicing on your own, but at least now you know how it's done. After lunch I'm going to train you on cutting, and wipe that look of fear right off your face. If you can lay paper straight and measure with a ruler, you can pin patterns and cut on the line."

"I'm actually good at math and numbers," Macy told her and she felt better when Hattie's smile went wide.

"Good! Learning to place the patterns just so should be a fairly easy lesson, until we get to Miss Chickie's plaid. Plaids and checks are a little different, so I'll set the pattern on that one. And speaking of Miss Chickie Barber," the older woman looked up, grinning, as the door swung open. "Here she is, and she and the pastor have brought a little friend along, I see."

"It's Little Will," crowed Chickie, then she clapped a hand to her mouth. "Oh, Pa, I'm sorry. Did I wake him?"

"Not that time," Will answered in a tone that said she might have wakened the wee boy prior to that. "Ladies, good morning."

"Good morning, Pastor." Hattie smiled up at him, then down at the baby. "Oh, Will, isn't he just the cutest thing?"

"He's cute, all right."

"Is he sleeping at night?"

"Not so's you'd notice." The pastor yawned and shrugged it off as if sleepless nights were no big deal. Macy knew better. "We'll get by. We always do. I stopped by the mercantile for flannel and Ginny said you grabbed some yesterday to cut nappies for Will. You didn't have to do that, Hattie."

"I was glad to be of help." She waved Macy toward their sitting room behind the store. "Macy, be a dear and fetch that stack of cut flannel near my machine, won't you?"

Macy found the flannel and brought the stack up to the store front. "May I wrap these for you, Reverend?"

His grateful smile touched her, the kind of smile that said he appreciated the smallest gesture, and wasn't that a difference? "That would make carrying them easier. I never thought to bring a basket along."

Hattie had shown her how to pull the paper down, center the item, then wrap the garment and tie it with white, cotton string on the flat, board counter. She fumbled a bit with the string, but in the end she got it done and handed it to him. "Here you go."

He started to take it, but the baby fussed and when he adjusted him to a better position, he couldn't spare a hand for the package, and Chickie was licking sticky sweetness from a peppermint stick.

"Macy, do you mind walking Pastor home? That way no one drops the baby, the nappies make it in one piece and Miss Chickie's sticky fingers don't get all over things."

"I'd be beholding," Pastor Barber said, and when Macy looked up, he locked that clear, sweet gaze on her and for the longest time, they just stood there, staring.

"Hmm," buzzed Hattie as she stepped forward to open the screen door. "Let me get the door for you. Macy, we'll grab a bite when you get back."

"All right." She ducked her chin because the sight of the bright-eyed, kindly pastor carrying her son grabbed hold of her heart and didn't aim to let go.

Wasn't that the image she'd dreamed long ago? To grow up and be someone's treasured wife, and see pride shine in his eyes as he held their child? Oh, it was a silly notion then, and sillier now, but for that split second, she felt like she tucked herself right into that dream.

Except she had no right to dream like that, so she dropped her attention to the dusty road surface beneath their feet, determined to be silent. That lasted all of about five seconds, until Chickie's toe hit a rough spot and she sprawled, face-first, into the heated dust. "Oh, oh, oh!" Macy stooped instantly, helping the girl up and brushing dust and dirt from her as quick as she could, but the stickiness of the peppermint stick made the dirt stick as if glued to Chickie's skin. "Come on, darling," she soothed through Chickie's quick tears, and who wouldn't cry under such a circumstance? "We'll get you home and cleaned up with some quick wash-water, and it will all be fine, I promise." She used her apron to wipe the worst of the tacky dirt from Chickie's face, and when Will saw the dark smudges, he looked concerned.

"Miss Evers, you don't have to do that, look at your apron. How can you sew with dirt all over your apron?"

"Dirt washes out," she explained cheerfully, as if it didn't matter, and it didn't. What mattered was making Chickie feel better, and as soon as they drew up to the parsonage, she asked for a rag to use by the water pump. "A well is a marvelous thing," she told him when Will came back out with the cotton square. "The baby went down all right? He's still asleep?" She hoped she asked the question with nonchalance, as if making a polite inquiry, and when Will nodded, her heart sighed… but she smiled, relieved. Little Will was making the adjustment well, and that was the most important thing of all, despite how her arms ached to hold him. Rock him. Croon to him. Knowing he was safe and sound, unfettered by the labels some would put on him, balanced things. Her broken heart was of little consequence if Little Will's future was restored. *"Do not fear, and do not be ashamed, for I am with you…"*

Isaiah's verse from long ago. The passage touched her. She believed God to be good, but God's people weren't all that nice. Not in her experience, at least, but when she was in the brightness of Pastor Will's smile, she sensed God's love shining through him. A silly notion, for sure, but she knew what she felt, didn't she? And as long as Little Will was safe and sound, nothing else mattered.

You can do this, she scolded herself as she washed Chickie's face with a gentle touch. *You must do this.*

"Will my dress be ruined?" Chickie's worried whisper pulled Macy back to the moment at hand.

"No, it will wash out fine. And it's mostly the apron, anyway, so if you take that off, I'll wash yours and mine quick, and we can hang them on the line and all will be well."

"Oh, thank you, Miss Macy!" Chickie launched herself at Macy, and because she was already off-balance, Chickie's excitement bowled her over.

"Oh, Miss Macy!" Chickie backed off, her hands to her face, surprised and chagrined. "Oh, no!"

"I've got this," Will said softly. He reached down with two strong hands and gently brought her to her feet. "There we go. Are you all right? Are you hurt or shaken up?"

Oh, she was shaken up, all right, but not because of a little tumble.

The firm but gentle grip of his hands on her arms. His eyes, on hers. The warmth and concern in his gaze, sincere and kind. Her heart tumbled.

She righted it instantly, because if this man of God knew her story, he'd likely banish her from the church pews and lock the doors against her.

But maybe he wouldn't, a soft nudge of her conscience offered. *Maybe he's different than those pastors of long ago, the ones who cast your mother out. Maybe he lives as he says to live.*

Macy didn't dare take a chance on that, so she pulled back, and gave a swift nod. "Just fine, of course, and Chickie, don't fret. I love your enthusiasm and find it most refreshing."

"You do?"

"Yes." She smiled down at the girl purposely, because looking up at the handsome father would get her nothing but trouble. "I must get back. Hand over your apron and we'll wash them both at the shop."

"I can wash it here," Will protested, but Macy shook her head.

"I promised, and there's something special about keeping one's promise to a child, isn't there?"

"There is," he agreed, and the solemnity of his voice said promises meant something.

She took the girl's apron, said goodbye, and hurried up the road. Hattie would think less of her if she couldn't do a simple task like see a child home, or help a customer and get back in a timely fashion. Time was money, and she'd had her share of tough reminders back east. She took a deep breath, enjoying the heat and quiet of the wide open spaces surrounding her. Just being able to see from here to there, to breathe fresh air, to stretch her arms out from side to side and not touch another person...

Like Moses' mother, she was close enough to keep an eye on her precious child, but smart enough to protect him. There was no evil king after him, but the sharp tongue of folks who should know better could cut deep, too, and she didn't want that for her tiny son.

Chapter Four

"WILL, HOW'S THAT BABY DOING?" 'Liza called through Will's screen door the next morning. "I brought some fresh bread by, along with a tub of butter. Mort Jensen found a lovely honeycomb the other day, and sent along a nice piece."

"Bread and honey." Will balanced the baby in one arm, the Good Book in the other and nudged open the screen door with his toe. "Chickie's gone down to Hattie's for a fitting, so I'm on my own here."

"Well, let's trade," said 'Liza. She set her things on the smooth table and moved to the rocker nearby. "He seems more content, doesn't he?"

"He does," Will admitted. "I think that new recipe suits him, which means he's more comfortable and everybody sleeps more."

"A fine prescription for happiness right there!" 'Liza agreed as she sank into the broad-backed chair and held out her arms. Will handed over the baby and the half-filled bottle. "There we go, sweetie-pie. It's been too long since these old arms have had the pleasure of doin' for one so young, so this is a treat, Will."

"I'm beyond grateful for the help, 'Liza." He smiled, palmed the boys' head and tapped his watch. "If you don't mind taking over for a little while, I'd like to get my sermon done for Sunday and Mrs. Gruber's service."

"I'm sorry she's gone," 'Liza told him. "But she took to suffering these past few weeks and it hurts me to see that.

When I look up at the stars at night, and I see all that heaven holds dear, I wonder why pain and suffering come into it at all? But then I look around and see the pain folks cause one another on purpose, and my heart goes a little sour." She cooed to the baby, then raised her gaze to Will's. "How do you do it, Will? Keep from going sour or doubting God's goodness? You see the good and bad of folks every day. Don't it wear on you from time to time?"

He thought back to Maryland and the double grave there. A grave that wouldn't exist except for his laxness. "It does. But then I say to myself Will? You're human, and you think in human terms. But God is GOD, in capital letters, like a big, bold sign, plain as can be and He's got so much more to offer."

"And that helps?" 'Liza asked.

He took the seat across from her. "It helps immensely because I stumble when I think of myself in God-terms. Why can't I be this, that or the other thing? But God made us human, He allows our choices, and good or bad, He must think highly of us because He created us."

"Sounds a little simple to me, Pastor." She arched a brow that said he might be thinking too broad or too narrow, one or the other, and he laughed.

"Sometimes simple is best," he proclaimed. "That simple faith of a child. Heartfelt belief. That's what I grab hold of when bad things happen, like that blizzard taking so many and fires burning down whole towns in the course of a night. Believing when there's reason to doubt. That's what gets me through."

"Well you've got a heart of gold, that's for certain." She waved him off with a smile. "You go get your work done. Does Chickie need to be fetched or will Hattie see her back?"

"Hattie or her new assistant will bring her back up the road when she's done. And you know Chickie, she'll most likely get a few cookies or a sweet stick out of the deal."

"A sweeter child I never did see," 'Liza declared, "and I've seen my share with all the years I've got to my credit. I'll keep an eye out for her."

"Then I'll head over to the church for a little contemplation time." He shut the screen door quietly so the slap wouldn't disturb his namesake, and veered toward the board-and-batten church. As he cut across the road, temptation pulled him in the other direction. He had to stop himself from turning right and walking straight down to Hattie's place, because it wasn't concern for Chickie that drew his interest.

It was the wish to see what Macy was up to, how she was getting on, and wouldn't that put him in a fine pickle? He'd been warding off invites and potlucks from the first day he rode into town nearly three years back. The minute women realized he was a widowed father, they set their caps to make things right, and by 'right' they meant a mother for his child and a wife for him.

He'd had no interest, then.

Now his awareness was piqued, but he made a firm turn to the left and headed for the church. If there was something to come from this attraction, it would come in its own time. Work, first.

An hour later he'd written one foolish sentence five different ways, and couldn't think of anything other than the kind way Macy took charge of Chickie the previous day. And there was the matter of her smile, soft and perfect. The sincerity of her words and the directness of her gaze.

He balled up the latest sheet of paper, scolded his foolish extravagance, and rolled his desk chair toward the window. Bright sun shone down on the growing town, the summer heat moving the air in thick waves. 'Liza had moved to the small porch with the baby, and as he watched her care for the orphaned child, a verse came to him, the promise of God's love, fulfilled.

He sat back down, grabbed new paper, and in fifteen

minutes had written a strong, stirring sermon about a subject he knew little about: motherly love.

And when he set his pen aside, he knew he'd done a
good job of explaining God's word in uplifting verse. He
stood, stretched, opened the front door and almost walked
straight into Macy Evers' arms. "Whoa!"

He grabbed hold as she wobbled on the edge of the
step and Chickie burst out laughing. "You two are always
knocking each other over! It's so funny, Pa!"

"I'm not sure my clumsiness is a source of amusement
for Miss Evers," Will argued, but he let his eyes twinkle
into hers, and by Jove if he didn't see a hint of twinkle
come right back his way. She squelched it quickly, but Will
knew what he saw… and with his hands on her arms, he
could feel her pulse ramp up to match his, so that was a
mighty nice sign. He stepped back, released her arms and
smiled. "Did you two come to fetch me?"

"Yes!" Chickie grabbed Macy's hand in excitement. "I
got to try on my new dress for a proper fitting and it is so
very beautiful, Pa!" She clapped her hands together and
tipped her smile up to him. He bent and hugged her.

"Do you love it, Chick-pea?"

She nodded, excited. "Oh, I do. And I'll love the other
one, and when they're done with those two, then Miss
Hattie will begin the pink dress!"

"Miss Hattie doesn't want to waste two months of summer growth time, so she's waiting on the pink for a few
solid weeks, yet," Macy explained.

"It's good of Hattie to think of budgets," Will noted.
"Mine and everyone else's. She's a good lady and a fine
neighbor."

"Indeed she is." Macy moved down the three narrow
steps and turned. "You're home safe, Miss Chickie, and
thank you for being such a good girl."

"You're welcome!"

A cry sounded from across the way. Macy turned full

around. "Oh, it's the baby." Her voice had that soft sound he'd once thought intrinsic to women, but he'd been proven wrong years before.

"Well, I got the sermon done." Will aimed a grin at the porch as he started to cross the road back to the little rectory. "Seems like that's all the time a little guy can handle."

"I can keep on with our weeding, Pa."

"I'd appreciate it, Chickie. And this weekend we'll put the word out about Little Will."

"Put the word out?" Macy sounded surprised. "What does that mean?"

"At church on Sunday," Will explained. "I'll let everyone know he's available."

"Available?" He didn't think her brows could go higher, but they did.

Will nodded. "For adoption, yes. I don't do that from the pulpit often, but in this case it would be best to get the little guy settled with a family as quick as possible. That way he's got his own mom to care for him."

"But—"

She looked concerned and confused, but why?

"I thought he was going to stay here," she explained. "With you. Don't you think that's what his mother intended?"

"Forever?" The thought of raising a tiny little guy was tempting, but how could he undertake a major responsibility like that and maintain his dedication to the town? Already they'd buried too many after a sparse growing season and a worse winter. New folks headed their way every day, folks that needed a church to welcome them to a harsh and sometimes inhospitable country.

She nodded.

Of course the notion was impossible. "I wish I could keep him, he's a likely little fellow, isn't he?"

"Oh, yes!"

"But I can't," he explained, and he truly regretted his

answer. "I'm alone here with Chickie, and there's work to be done. Things are quiet right now because it's summer. Everyone is cutting and raking hay, coaxing winter food out of gardens. By fall we'll busy right up again and I can't rightly take care of a baby on my own."

"Who might take him?" She glanced around the sparse town as if measuring. "Someone in town?"

Will swept the town a doubtful look. "I can't see anyone living in town taking in a baby. Of course folks come a distance for Sunday service and those that don't come will likely get word passed. That's not always a winter option, but this time of year, word spreads. No doubt someone will be longing to hold a sweet boy like Will in their arms."

Chapter Five

MACY WORKED TO CONTROL HER first impulse, which was to grab up that baby from the older woman's hands and claim him outright. Why hadn't she considered this possibility? She'd set up an old-time image in her head, the sacrificial mother watching her child grow in strength and beauty, but that might not be the case at all. At any time the pastor could find a family to take her child, and he'd be lost to her forever.

Macy hadn't bargained for that.

Regret stabbed deep, so deep she wasn't sure she could draw a breath, her ribs hurt so. She didn't dare go up those stairs with Will and Chickie. She couldn't trust herself to hold back from the tiny boy's plaintive cries.

She turned abruptly, making her way back to Hattie's shop. The bright-eyed pastor might think her rude, and Chickie's tender feelings might be hurt, but her own heart felt seared, and it was nothing to do with the hot, July sun.

Gone from her.

After all this, the tiny boy she'd carried, birthed and nurtured might disappear from her life forever.

Could she handle that?

You have no choice. You must handle it. If you love him, that is.

I will never forget you or leave you orphaned. That was God's promise, but hadn't she just left her wee boy orphaned on purpose? Sure, she'd done it to save him being ostracized, and she knew that church-going folk could be the most judgmental. She'd lived that truth.

She swiped her hands to her face as she approached Hattie's door. If the kindly seamstress saw her upset, she'd want to help, and there was nothing she could do. Nothing anyone could do, and the truth in that broke Macy's heart a little more.

"Macy!" Samantha called her name as she hurried around the corner. "Ma sent me over here to leave this mail for Hattie. Can you see she gets it? I'd run in, but Ma's on her own at the store."

"Of course."

"And maybe you can come over for a bite later? When your work day's done?" Samantha looked excited by the prospect, but that's because Macy was living a lie. A fallen woman wouldn't be welcomed the same way, she was certain of that. "There are no other young women in town and everyone's so busy on their claims this time of year that I don't get to see anyone. Do you think there's time?"

Macy didn't know how to say no, so she had to say yes. "After six?"

"Yes! And tell Hattie that Ma's got a pot of beans on and she's welcome to come, too. With Pa gone to the city for supplies, it would be nice to have a ladies' night!"

Samantha's word choice reminded Macy of the obvious, but she hid her misgivings beneath a smile. "I would like that so much."

"Us, too." Samantha hurried back around the corner as Macy went through Hattie's door.

"I'm back, Hattie."

"And in time for tea and biscuits," Hattie declared. "I have a tin I keep for special, and having you here has made things quite special, Macy. You got Chickie home okay?"

"Yes."

Hattie aimed a sharp look her way. "Are you all right, child?"

She had to be, so she nodded.

"Did someone upset you?" Hattie set down the cuff

she was turning and frowned. "Tell me who and I'll settle them down right quick."

Macy had never had anyone leap to her defense, and Hattie's quick sincerity made it nicer yet. "I'm fine. Samantha stopped me and wondered if we'd like to come by this evening for beans and tea. A ladies' night."

"With Hi out of town, that's a fine idea! I'll be too tired to sew a straight line by evening, the heat and humidity wear me out more than they did when I was younger. And lighter," she added with a wry glance down. "And I must tend the vegetable garden first thing in the morning before the heat builds. The drought keeps weeds down, but it's a mean trade-off."

"I'll do the garden," Macy insisted, and when Hattie started to voice an objection, she refused to hear it. "You've given me a wonderful opportunity here. Marvelous, really. And getting up and down in the dirt is easier for me."

"Then I'll take garden work in place of room rent," Hattie decided. "There's no sense arguing," she scolded happily when Macy opened her mouth to protest. "I love having the company, and you work hard at everything you do. I'm hopeful for a good, soaking rain to give things some size. Life-giving water is a wonderful thing, the Bible makes that clear across generations, and it's just as true today." She set two glasses out, filled them with tea and handed one to Macy. "Let's take these out on the back stoop in the shade. If anyone comes in, they'll know where to look. Can you bring the tin along?"

"Of course." She followed Hattie to the narrow, covered stoop, and breathed deep. "Funny how that little bit of shade makes such a difference, isn't it?"

"A body needs respite for certain." Hattie sank onto a broad chair and set the tea glasses on a sturdy wooden table. "But after a rough winter, I'm determined to welcome summer with open arms. I know it got mighty hot by you, too."

"Heat like this is a suffocation in the city," Macy admitted.

"Do you miss the busy?"

Macy didn't miss it one bit, but she kept her voice mild. "Not at all." She leaned the cool cup against her forehead. "Heat will come and go, same as cold and snow, but so many people, and not all of them kind, well…" She set down her glass of tea. "I'm mighty thankful for this opportunity, Hattie."

"Serves us both." Hattie opened the tin of cookies and handed it over. "Rosemary shortbread cookies, an old recipe from my mother, God rest her soul. Tender and refreshing and they keep so nice in a good tin."

"They're delicious." Macy let the buttery cookie melt in her mouth. Cookies and cakes were a luxury she hadn't been able to afford. "I've never had better."

"So about that baby," Hattie began, and Macy like to fell off her chair before Hattie went on, because how could she know about Little Will? Hattie's next words put her heart on a steady course again. "I think we should make him a few gowns, don't you? I'd say it's the least we can do, but I've got more shirt orders with that new group of railroaders coming into town and I think they'd be good practice for you. Simple, too, just a drawstring bottom and same on top."

With the conversation to simple sewing, Macy let out a breath. "I'd be glad to. It's a good skill learned."

"It is, and I've got a pattern I've shared with many a young mother," Hattie told her. "I'll give it to you tomorrow. On that top shelf in the back room there's a stack of leftover cotton scraps I keep for quilting. Some pieces are big enough for baby gowns. I'll let you go through and see what might work. Will Barber's got a heart of gold, but he is a man and the thought of a baby needing fresh gowns might not occur to him as fast as it would to you and me."

"Well, we're—" she almost said 'mothers', but caught

herself in the nick of time. "Women," she finished, as if planning a baby's clothing was a particularly feminine skill. "Although I've never seen a man better with children. The pastor is so good with Chickie, and the baby doesn't make him a bit nervous." She'd been plenty nervous when Little Will was born, so the thought of plucking a baby off the doorstep with Pastor Will's ease amazed her.

"He's got the knack, and that's a fine quality, man or woman. Are you from a big family, Macy?"

A dreaded question that scored deep. How could she explain her family to a caring person like Hattie? "I separated from my family some time back and I'm not sure who's where anymore."

Hattie stayed looking straight out. "There's a hardship in broke families, but sometimes a child does best looking after his or her own. It can build or break character, that's certain."

"Yes, ma'am." She'd like to think it built hers, but her situation with Little Will would make others think different. A long time back she didn't care much what folks thought. She was a 'spit in their eye' kind of young woman. Now, with some years to her credit, and a perfect son, she wanted that respectability, she wanted it so bad she woke up tasting it some days. But gaining that deference meant living a lie, and the conundrum of that hit her hard. "I never knew my father, who he was or where he was, so seeing a man like the pastor be so kind and loving with children brings me joy. That's how it should be for a child, don't you think? Parents that love them, that smile for the pleasure of having them."

"I think exactly the same," Hattie declared, "and I'm sorry for those who can't look back on a sweet childhood, but I lived in cities long enough to know how tough things get. Out here, too, but it's a different kind of hardship here, maybe easier because it's shared by so many. Caught in the city where lots of folks have plenty, it's awful hard to be a have-not. And a woman down on her luck in the city can be a dangerous circumstance."

Macy had found that out the hardest way possible. She swallowed past the thick lump in her throat and shoved those memories aside.

"But here, we've got choices, Macy." Hattie's voice softened. "And wide open spaces. There are even women homesteading here, all on their own."

"No." Macy stared at her and Hattie bobbed her head in assent.

"I know of several, and it's hard, hard as hard can be, but they have the right to do it and they're doing it. Women of courage will do just as much as any man to make this country great."

"Homesteading. Alone." Macy couldn't hide the wonder in her tone, because how could one person do the work required to maintain a claim and a shack and stay warm and fed and dry?

"Well, they give each other help now and again, and the nice thing out here is that neighbors can be downright neighborly, when the weather's not foul. While I prefer being here in town, closer to neighbors and helpin' them, I think our long, hard winter showed folks we need to look out for each other. If we want this settlement to work, that is."

The thought of a claim made Macy nervous. "I agree about living in town," she confessed. "I don't miss the city one lick, but the thought of running a claim on my own would scare me."

"Good to know that about ourselves, I reckon." Hattie took another draw on her tea, then stood. "Well, we'd best get back at it. I'll get you that pattern for the baby clothes, then I'm going to have you practice buttonholes for an hour. Honestly, once I get you trained on them, I can rest easy, Macy, because whip-stitching is not easy on old fingers."

"Then I'm going to work hard to get good," Macy promised. "If that takes some trouble off your hands, I'm happy to do it."

Hattie brought out a basket of scraps, withdrew four sturdy, matching pieces, and handed them over. "You'll want to press them first, then pin this pattern to a doubled piece. I'll show you how to turn the edges for the draw-string, then how to sew the sides and sleeves. Quick as a wink we can have a few new gowns made for that precious child."

It wasn't quick as a wink, but Macy got them done. Three sessions of buttonhole practice showed improvement on her part, and she weeded the garden from end to end.

"Landsakes, you are a worker!" Hattie exclaimed. "And such a blessing to me. I can't remember the last time I was able to catch my breath like this. Now here," she set the garments and a jelly jar into Macy's hands mid-morning. "I want you to take a break and deliver these to the par-sonage. I expect Miss Chickie will help her daddy to some bread and jam for supper. You don't mind running over there, do you?"

"Not at all." Macy had to keep excitement out of her voice, because she'd been itching to see how Little Will was getting on. "Should I say that Chickie's first dress will be ready soon?"

"Yes, indeed! And tell Will if he needs help with the children for services, we'll be glad to take charge of both. 'Liza's come down with a summer cold. I thought to give her time to rest, and you have such a knack with children."

"Do I?" The compliment made Macy stand taller. "You really think so?"

"I'm not one to sugar coat, and I do like to speak my mind, so if I say it?" Hattie tipped her spectacles down and peered at Macy. "I mean it."

"Do you think someone will claim the baby on Sun-day?" The reality of that possibility soured her stomach.

Hattie had gone back to threading her machine, but Macy's question brought her eyes up quickly. "Whatever do you mean?"

"Pastor Barber said he was going to make an announcement about the baby on Sunday, to find him a home." She tried to keep her voice even, but if a hint of desperation crept in, would Hattie notice? Surely not.

Hattie frowned in surprise. "Will said this?"

Macy nodded.

"Well, that's a bend in the road." Hattie pressed her lips together, then waved her on.

She noticed Macy's wondering expression and shrugged. "You go on ahead and I'll get this last shirt finished up for that nice railroader that stopped by last week. We'll see what kind of help Will needs as he needs it."

Macy made sure the door latched behind her, moved to Main Street and turned right. She would opt for the shady side if there was one, and that was one thing she *did* miss about the east. Trees were abundant in and around Pittsburgh, the state's name even meant "woods". Out here the sun and wind met with little resistance. If she ever got a place of her own, she'd plant some trees, tiny ones, if that was all she could find. And then she'd give them the tender, loving care they'd need, just to see the shadow of a tree cast on the ground.

She crossed the road kitty-corner and walked up the worn side of the modest parsonage. The house was quiet, so she walked out back.

"Miss Macy!" Chickie called to her from where the creek edged the yard and raced her way. "We were just gathering eggs from Feather and Goldie! And I wanted to get the ones under Sunshine but Pa said the look in her eye meant 'come back later'."

The girl's delight shined through bright eyes and a happy attitude.

"Macy."

Will came up behind his daughter. She looked up.

Big mistake.

Once she looked up, she couldn't bring herself to look down again. And when he smiled right into her eyes, it was as if her heart tripped and refused to re-settle. "Hattie sent some things." She went to hand them off, but Will raised his hands.

"I'm dirty, how about if we go wash up? Then we can see what you've brought."

"All right." She worked to make her voice sound calm.

She was anything but calm. When she was in Will's company, she longed to dance and sing, and talk to him about everything there was in the world, at least the world she'd known. A part of her believed he might understand, but another part— the part that understood how quickly people turned against one another— knew a man as good and kind as Will Barber could never understand the prospects of evil surrounding a lost soul in the big city. And if she told him, what then? Wasn't it better to hold her secrets clutched tight to her heart? Surely they would get better in time.

Then the baby let out a squawk from a netted basket in the shade, and she knew she was wrong. How could her longing for her little boy ever get better? "I'll get him." She set the gowns and jam down on the back stoop and hurried to the basket. "Hey, little man. How are you? How are you, precious boy?"

Her voice calmed him. He turned in her direction and when she lifted him out of the basket, he rewarded her with a smile so wide with delight, it seemed like his little self was too small to hold so much joy. And yet he did. "There, there." She crooned into the softness of his neck and cheek. "Should we have a look at your other end about now? Get you cleaned up before you get hungry again?"

"That will be a trick because he's always hungry." Will shook his damp hands while Chickie carried the precious eggs inside. "And it looks like he's taken a shine to you, Macy. Just look at that smile!" He grinned back at the baby. "You've got a way with him, that's certain."

She didn't want to raise suspicions by being too good with Little Will, but once again the compliment made her proud. "I've had the chance to watch lots of mothers in the city," she told him. "I expect when you see enough mothers and babies, you learn a thing or two." It wasn't a lie, she had learned by watching until William and Bonnie MacDonald offered their help. She went to hand him the baby, but he picked up the pile of gowns and the jam jar, leaving her to snuggle the boy. She should exchange tasks. She should have Will tuck the boy into his strong, muscular arms and keep her at a distance, but she couldn't.

"I've got some tea steeping," Will told her. "Stay for a glass, won't you? We can sit on the front porch and watch folks pass by."

Macy laughed because not too many passed by this end of town. The trail west forked off mid-way past the mercantile, so Will's end of town had been fairly serene since she'd arrived in town. "I'd enjoy a glass of tea."

Will pulled the tacked screen door open, let her precede him, then followed her in. "You brought baby clothes."

"Hattie's idea, aren't they marvelous? And so easy, I was surprised that I could handle them as well as I did."

"You made these?" Was it the gratitude in his eyes or the look of happy pride in his smile that set her heart jerking around again?

"I did. Hattie had the pattern of course, and other than setting the sleeve cuffs, it's pretty basic. But, yes." She smiled, happy to have done something nice for her son. "I made them."

"Formed with grace and stitched with love."

His words painted a picture of what mother's love should be. "I expect you're good in the pulpit."

"I hope so!" He gave her that cheerful grin again. "That

was a phrase my mother used to describe her kinship with God when it came to raising seven boys."

"Seven boys?" Macy half-squeaked the words, because the thought of raising one child seemed daunting. So much could go wrong!

"And all turned out to be law-abiding, successful citizens," Will told her. He set out a new nappy for the baby. "I can change him if you like. I've gotten good at this."

"I don't mind doing it." Quick as a wink she cleaned up the wee fellow, and had his lower end set to rights in no time.

"You must have had little brothers and sisters," Will noted as she stood.

She did, but she couldn't tell him where they were. She hadn't seen them in well over a decade. "Yes."

"You must miss them."

She didn't miss them. She didn't know her younger brother and sister, so how could she miss something she hadn't seen in so many years? "We're the sort that don't mind being on our own," she told him, and then shrugged. "It suits, most days." But when she turned his way, his expression had saddened, as if not missing kin was wrong.

It wasn't wrong, it was simply how things were when children were separated at a young age, but a man with six beloved brothers wouldn't understand that.

Chapter Six

D ID IT, WILL WONDERED?
    No, he decided, because he read the longing in her
eyes when she talked of family. The look deepened when
she was around Little Will or Chickie, as if being with the
children filled a need. That's how he'd always felt about
God, that being one with spirit and grace filled that yawn-
ing hole inside him. He'd just handed her a glass of tea
when a voice bellowed out front. "Pastor, you in there? I
came to fetch you out to Buck Hardy's place, if you will.
He's in a bad way."

"Bad way?" Will hurried to the front door and swung it
wide. "How? What does that mean exactly?"

"His leg met the business end of the scythe," Brian John-
son went on. "I stopped by the sewin' shop to get hold of
Hattie. Didn't think the little one should come along, if
you get my drift."

Will got it all right, and more than Brian or Buck would
have imagined.

Blood loss. Trauma. Shock. Will was familiar with all the
elements of a deep wound, and then if the wound went
septic...

Noise buzzed between his ears. He barely heard Brian's
words, right until he realized Brian wasn't looking for Will
Barber, the doctor. He'd come to find a pastor to give last
rites. "Him bein' Catholic and no priest here-abouts, he
wanted to see a man of God. Do you mind, Will?"

Hattie bustled up the street. "Macy, can you go with

Will? Give him a hand? I'll watch the little ones."

Will didn't wait for an answer. He reached up on a high shelf, grasped a leather travel bag and thrust it into her hands as he hurried outside. Brian followed and unhitched his horse. "Take Beauty, preacher, it's not far and saves you the trouble of saddlin' up. I'll follow once I get your mare to rights."

"Thanks, Brian." He swung himself into the saddle, then reached out a hand to Macy.

She stared at him, then his hand. She handed up the parcel he gave her, then took his hand and let him pull her onto the saddle behind him.

"Hang on."

She did, and the way she did told him she'd never rode double before. Will was pretty sure she'd squeeze the breath right out of him before they got to the claim, but with the feel of her tucked tight against him, he might just lose his breath anyway. Mary Dupre waved as they rode past, and then the swell of the Hardy place came into view. He rode hard and when he pulled the horse up in front of Buck's claim shack, he jumped off the horse, hauled Macy down with one hand and the pouch with the other and hurried inside.

The stench of blood hit him like a sack of bricks. He wanted to pull back, he wanted to turn and run, hard and fast, as fast as his legs would carry him.

Then Buck's wife looked up at him. Fear and grief filled her gaze, and Will didn't stay because he thought he might make a difference. He stayed because he already had enough on his conscience. There was no room for Adeline Hardy's grief on top of his own. The two oldest daughters had flanked Buck's far side, and he felt their worry clear across the room. "Felicity, clear that table. Aggie, you help her, then get me a clean sheet and cover it up."

The girls fulfilled his request in quick order, then waited for further instruction. "Felicity, you go care for the younger ones outside, okay? And no matter what you hear, don't let them in here. Aggie, I need you and your mom to help me hoist your dad onto this table. Macy," he moved to Buck's left, "Can you help with the right shoulder?"

She hesitated, then did as he asked.

"We'll lift him on three." Will counted, they all lifted, and got Buck up, off the floor. He gave Adeline a litany of instructions as he yanked open his leather bag and pulled a length of cord from inside. "You got alcohol, Adeline? The cleanin' kind?"

"In the barn."

"Get it. You got any fresh-brewed tea around?"

She nodded.

"Bring that too. Aggie, get me a wooden spoon."

She dashed off as he pulled off his shirt and wrapped it around Buck's upper leg to staunch the blood, using the wooden spoon as a lever. "Macy, there are stitching needles in my bag. Get me the smallest, run it through the flame from that fire outside, then bring it back to me without touching the end."

She didn't argue, and right there he had more reason to like her. She fumbled in his bag, then left for the cooking fire outside. She came back quickly and handed him the needle.

"A strand of your hair, please."

"You can use mine, preacher!" Aggie stepped forward, anxious to help her father.

"Sure is pretty, but it's too long, Agatha. Miss Evers here has just the right length." He flushed the wound with the tea repeatedly. He knew a good stitching job might put Buck to rights, but a deep cut like this could go septic. If it did, he'd lose either Buck or Buck would lose the leg, and either way would send a man to heaven way too soon and yet another family scrambling back east. He owed it to the west to save this man's life.

Eyes wide, Macy handed him a strand of her hair. He

threaded the needle, then worked to stitch Buck back together. Eight strands, forty stitches and nearly an hour later, he sighed. "Done." He set the needle aside, and gently undid the tourniquet knot. He went slowly when he wanted to go fast. Buck's lower leg had been cut off from blood flow for longer than he liked, but if a darn fool will manage to cut through major blood vessels with a scythe, then the treatment takes a bit more. Loosening the fabric's grip on the leverage stick, he watched, and when Buck's lower leg began to show the healthy tinge of pink, Will hauled in a deep breath.

"You sewed him up."

He turned, almost surprised to hear Macy's voice. "I did."

"You're not a preacher. You're a doctor." She stared at him as if there was something wrong with being both.

"I was a doctor, a long time ago. Now I take more peace in mending souls than skin."

Buck started moving just then, and when he blinked open his eyes, he reached out to grip Will's hand. "I know you ain't a priest, pastor, but if you could give me a prayer and absolution, I'd be grateful."

"Buck, you can bet I'll hear your confession since there's no priest here in town, but you might want to think twice because you just might live."

Buck's eyes went wide, then he made a face. "I saw that cut, Will, I know when serious damage has been done, and I should be meetin' the Almighty on the golden streets of heaven about now."

"Not unless that wound goes bad." Will moved to the basin of warmed water he ordered and started scrubbing up his hands. It was then he noticed he wasn't wearing a shirt, and the look on Macy's face said she'd noticed right off. "Adeline, can I borrow a shirt of Buck's please?"

"Of course." She hurried out to the line and brought in a sun-warmed work shirt. "Pastor, you think he's going to be okay? Really?"

"I can't make promises. If it gets infected, then we're in trouble. Bad trouble because then the infection is inside Buck and there's no way to fight it. But if it doesn't, we've got a real good chance of him being fine. But Buck, you've got to lay low for a good week, maybe more."

A sturdy boy moved to Aggie's side. "Aggie and I can finish the hay, Pa. I ain't quick but I know what to do and we'll work without fighting, I promise."

"A week at least," Will repeated. "If that wound opens up, there's more chance of it going bad. You've got to give the body time to heal itself, Buck. You hear me?"

"Oh, he hears all right." Adeline came up alongside Will with a cup of soup broth. She fed her husband a spoonful and looked up at Will. "He might be stubborn as all get out, Will, but Buck Hardy knows better than to cross his wife, or he might get to meet his Maker after all."

She nailed her big, strong husband a fierce look, and Buck almost quaked. "I know better than to cross you, darlin', though it was a blame fool time to be having an accident like that."

"There's never a good time, Buck," she told him as she offered him another spoon of broth. "As long as you heal up proper, we'll be fine. Just fine."

Will set a small, corked jug onto the table. "Now, Adeline, if he needs a drop of spirits against the pain these next two days, go ahead and administer them. But if he wants them on the third day, you have my permission to cause him more pain."

She smiled up at Will. "I'll give back whatever doesn't get used. That way you have it for the next time."

"I'd be beholding." He went to gather up his supplies, but Macy beat him to it. She didn't put the blood-soiled shirt into the bag with the implements. She folded the stained side in and curled it up, around itself, then followed him out to his horse.

"You did well, Macy." He swung himself up, then hauled

her up behind him. He checked the sun's angle and decided it was well past both tea-time and supper time. A tiredness swept him, an old sort of weary, but it disappeared quick when Macy's arms laced around his middle.

"You did, too." She sounded respectful. "I've never seen a doctor work like that. Did you really use my hair to stitch him up or was I dreaming that part?"

"Easier on the body than thread, and I can use the tiniest needle that way."

"You saved his life, pastor."

"Will. Please."

"You saved his life."

"I didn't want to."

She took a sharp breath.

"Not because of him. Because of me," Will confessed as he urged the mare into an easy walk. "Buck's a good man and a good father. He loves God with his heart and soul, and when he's had a drink or two too many, he sings the Lord's praises mightily no matter what time of day it might be. So if we saved him, it was the right thing to do, Macy." He paused the horse and sighed. "But I didn't want to be the one to do it."

"Why?" She leaned up around him to try and catch his eye, but he turned his head. "Why wouldn't you want to help folks all you can?"

"Because you can't always help them. Some of them don't come around, and I realized I'm no good at losing patients."

"Is losing their body to illness more grievous than losing their souls?" she asked, and Will had a ready answer for that question.

"If I lose their souls, they can still wake up the next morning. That gives me a second chance. And maybe a third and a fourth." He sighed hard. "I don't get any second chances if they die, Macy. And that comes back to my door, each time."

"That's taking a high and mighty role, Will."

Her words surprised him.

"When we start to figure everything's in our control, isn't that putting ourselves in God's place?"

Was he doing that, Will wondered? No. Of course not. But her question niggled. "Medicine lacks a lot of answers," he told her. "I guess I always wish I could do more."

"Wishing we could do more is different than taking the whole world on our shoulders," she replied. "There are some folks you can't help whether they're touched in the head or grievous ill or just plain rotten mean. We've got our limits, I expect."

She made it sound simple. It was anything but.

"Of course good folks want to do their best, and you're a good man, Will."

When she said it, he suddenly felt like a good man, and he hadn't felt that way in a bunch of years. "Thank you, Macy."

He let the mare lead them into the back yard of the small parsonage. He climbed off, came around and lifted his arms to her. She leaned his way and half-tumbled into his arms, and right then Will realized that was exactly where he wanted her to be, snug in the curve of his arm with the sun just starting to ease its way west.

He stared down. She stared up. The feel of his hands at her waist seemed just right. Then he glanced at her mouth. He meant it to be a quick glance, but found he couldn't shift his gaze, wondering what it would be like to kiss Macy Evers and maybe just keep on kissing her. "Macy."

"Pa, you're back!" Chickie raced forward from the back yard. Hattie followed more slowly, carrying the baby.

Macy's eyes sombered. She pulled back, and it was only then he realized she'd gotten blood on her apron. "Macy, I didn't realize you got soiled. I'm so sorry."

"It will wash." She untied the apron and set it on the bottom step.

It wouldn't, not after setting this long, but her expression and her tone said she wanted distance. When she moved several feet away, Will figured the attraction was one-sided, which made him more determined to make it two-sided.

"How's Mr. Hardy, Pa?"

"All right for the moment. We need to pray the wound heals clean, and then we'll see."

"I'll pray!" Chickie grabbed his hands. "I'll pray real hard, Pa, because Sadie would be so sad to lose her pa."

"Sadie's the youngest Hardy," Will explained. "She was outside with Felicity."

"Ah." She was looking beyond him, at Hattie and the baby, and when Hattie plunked that little boy into Macy's arms, a wide smile reclaimed her features. "Hey, little fellow, how are we doing? Such a handsome boy, aren't you?"

The baby grinned back, then reached up a plump arm to touch her face. He smiled up, she smiled down, and when the baby burbled little cooing sounds, Macy answered in kind. And then they both smiled more, if such a thing was possible, and seeing how good she was with children just made her more attractive. And when she planted a natural kiss to the baby's temple, Will's heart opened wider. He could imagine her at his side, holding their child, teaching Chickie the ways of goodness and righteousness, the way a virtuous woman would.

"Pa, you're not listening."

Chickie was right, he hadn't heard a word she said, so he squatted alongside her. "Guilty as charged, Chick-pea. What's up?"

"Can Miss Macy and Miss Hattie stay for supper?"

"They could if we were having supper," Will contended. "But it's a tough road to be treating a friend in the country and cooking supper at home, darlin'."

"I've got a ham hank simmering," Hattie told him. "If we throw some new peas and stored carrots and potatoes into the pot, we'd have a right nice soup to go with the bread 'Liza sent by and the jam."

"My mouth's watering, thinking of it, Hattie." Will smiled her way. "I'm going to go have a wash with strong soap, then I'll fetch the vegetables."

"You go wash, but show me the way to the bin and I'll get the vegetables," she told him, so he did. Will had learned early on that agreeing with Hattie was smarter than not. "And Will, Macy was telling me you were thinking of announcing the baby this weekend, and I'm going to come right out and ask you not to do that."

He'd started forward, toward the house to point out the vegetable bin around back, but now he paused. "I thought the sooner the better, Hattie. Get the little guy settled in a home."

"There's sense in what you say, of course, but early summer like this is a rough time to put a baby in the mix for any family. A few weeks here, if you can manage it," she hastened to add. "That gives folks time to get the first hay in shocks and the gardens well begun before they start drying or storing roots for the winter. My thought is to avoid adding stress to families whose work load is already overflowing."

"I hadn't thought of it that way," Will admitted, and he saw the sense in Hattie's words right off. Stress and worry could drag a body down so far, they could hardly lift themselves out of the depths. Will had seen the truth of that, first-hand. "You're right, as usual, Hattie. We'll keep the little guy here and give folks time to get this new season under their feet."

Chapter Seven

MACY'S HEART SOARED.
Little Will wasn't going anywhere, at least not for a while, and that would give her time with him. She breathed deep of her son, loving the scent of his baby skin, the softness of his downy hair. Yes, she wanted what was best for him, but the thought of fully letting go was a chasm. Could she make herself strong enough to cross it?

She'd thought so, but with the pastor's sweet smiles, and those long, lingering looks that set her heart to pumping harder, she wasn't sure. Maybe she'd have been smarter to make a clean break from the beginning.

"Macy, I'm going to see to these vegetables. Why don't you take a breather and rock that baby on the front porch? I expect you could use a little quiet time about now."

"I'll come with you!" Chickie squealed. "Oh, that will be fun, won't it?"

"Rocking on the porch is fun?" Macy smiled down at her as she crossed the worn drive and climbed the porch steps. "I would think playing tag, skipping beans or rolling marbles would be more to your liking, Miss Chickie Barber."

"I like all of those," Chickie admitted. "But sitting up here, rocking with you and Little Will is like pretending we're a real family. Like when I play with my doll and I'm the ma and she's the baby and it's okay, but something's missing because there's no one to be the pa. So today, sitting here, I can pretend Pa's inside, you're the ma, I'm the little girl, and this is our new baby! Like a real family."

Chickie's innocence painted a perfect picture, and when Will strode up the porch, drying his hands on an old towel, he completed the scene.

Macy's heart skipped, but she shushed it right quick. Will was a man of God and education, she'd seen that today. She was a fallen woman. God might forgive, she believed in His grace, but she understood people better than most, and she was willing to sacrifice anything to spare Little Will that embarrassment and rejection. He deserved the best life could offer, and that was more important than anything. "You pretend all you want, dear girl." A little make believe couldn't bring harm, but when Will lifted Chickie up and sat down in the rocker next to hers, she thought how easy it would be to stay there forever, rocking a quiet afternoon away.

"Pretty nice, this." Will cuddled Chickie on his lap, then smiled a few minutes later. "I don't think Chickie's going to make it for supper," he whispered.

"She fell asleep that quick?"

"Mighty close." He kept rocking, nice and easy, until Chickie's head lolled against his shoulder. "She was up early, wanting to work on numbers and letters and reading, I expect the heat of the day took its toll."

"She's a precious little thing." Macy kept her voice soft, too. "And we thought we'd have her first dress done, but it's likely a day or two more now with Hattie over here for the afternoon."

"Hattie said she'd be glad to watch the kids during service on Sunday. And then you'll come by with the dress on Monday."

"I can," Macy replied.

"Which means I get to see you two days in a row, Macy."

She pretended to misunderstand on purpose. "I am only a few hundred feet up the road, Pastor. Of course we'll run into one another."

"And even more if we plan it."

She couldn't miss the note of cheer although he spoke softly, but they couldn't plan meeting each other or any other thing because she was living a lie. "I expect Hattie will keep me too busy to do much visiting, what with all the railroad shirt orders we've got coming in."

"Some moments are best left unplanned."

She turned his way, exasperated, but when he met her gaze— when he smiled for her, at her, warm emotion made her long to be the kind of woman Will deserved. She wasn't, so there was no use pretending. "Will, you don't know me."

"I plan to."

A strange mix of anticipation and aggravation rose inside her. "You can't, Will. You just can't."

"I can quote you chapter and verse that says I can, and I'm pretty good at quoting," he promised.

She paused the rocker and stood, careful not to disturb the baby. "I mean it, Will. I know what you're saying, and I see that gleam in your eyes, and my heart beats harder and stronger whenever you're around, but you have to trust me on this. There can't be anything between us, not ever."

"Are you engaged, Macy?"

"No."

"Promised in any way?"

The man was irritation, pure and simple. "No, and that's all I'm saying."

"Determined to be a spinster all your days?"

She hadn't planned on that, no, but that didn't mean she could fall head over heels in love with a man of God. Wouldn't that be the model of ironies? "I'm not saying another thing."

"From the looks of Little Will's face, you won't have time to."

She looked down. Intensity knit the baby's face as he went about filling his padded bottom. "I'll go get a nappy."

She toted the baby into the house, found the stack of bottom wrappers on the table next to the narrow stairway, and cleaned up the little fellow. By the time she was done and washed up, Will had tucked Chickie into bed, Hattie'd prepared a bottle for the baby and Will had gone up the road to fetch the soup pot from Hattie's stove with two thick, stout towels in hand.

"It is so sensible to move a stove out back for the summer." Macy resettled herself into the rocker and snuggled the baby as Will settled the soup pot onto his outdoor stove. "I wonder why more folks don't think of it."

"It's a job, moving them," said Hattie as she took a seat on the top step. "But I can't see spending months cooking inside when it's so much more sensible to cook outside with the heat. The house gets hot enough without adding a wood stove to the mix. My parents had a summer kitchen on their back porch outside Boston, and it was a pleasure during the hot months. And with a family, cooking isn't a choice, it's a must."

"Do you miss the sea, Hattie?" Will wondered.

Hattie stared east. Her eyes said yes. Her words said something else. "I miss the idea of the sea from time to time. But while I loved being part of our family, I didn't like that men wielded power so freely in Massachusetts. I like to take a stand now and again, and I don't take rightly to men looking down on women. There were too many men who thought every which way about a woman, and I wanted to be well-rid of them."

"You like your independence," Will noted. "Nothing wrong with that, Hattie. Jesus made it clear that women were very special to him and to his Father."

"There's a good share of the men folk who forget that, Will. You're not one of them, and that's why we get along, but when I lost my husband, there was no shortage of men willing to access my property, my money and me in his wake. I moved out here because the gossip mongers and the laws there like to restrict a woman."

"I can't imagine any sane person trying to restrict you, Hattie."

"Never said they were sane."

Will laughed, then sobered. "I know what you're saying. Folks come here from all over the world to avoid persecution and to gain a new chance at land and life, but we carry some of the same old rules along with us."

"Out here I can own property and breathe fresh air. And if I speak my mind, no town elder is going to drop by and try and shush me."

"They wouldn't dare." Will winked at Macy, and she had to smile because he was right. Few would dare to cross Hattie. She knew her mind and spoke it. "It's funny that folks risked their life to come here for freedom, and there are still power-hungry people who want to restrict it."

"Still a man's world in many ways, but I see change coming," Hattie told them. "Women are making their presence known, and Godly men will grant them the rights they deserve. Some won't like it," she added. Her droll tone said that was a given. "But in the end, they'll do it."

"What makes you think that?" Macy adjusted Little Will's bottle, then looked up. The thought of women choosing freely… of being able to chart her own destiny… seemed both scary and wonderful. But mostly wonderful.

"Because once women have the vote, they share the power. Getting elected will take pleasing *us* as well as them." Hattie indicated Will with a look. "And that will change history."

"I hope it happens in my lifetime," Will agreed. "Chickie should grow up having the same rights as anyone, and I have to say I never thought much about it until I had a daughter. Looking ahead at how many doors swing shut on women put me in mind of your words. I want equality on all levels."

"It's funny how our perceptions change when our children are involved."

"Do you have children, Hattie?" Macy hadn't felt right about asking, but this seemed like an okay time to broach the subject.

"I did." Hattie settled a hand atop the baby's soft head. "Two girls and a boy. They were little and so precious. First a girl, Adelia, a robust little thing, and such a joy to her father and me." Her features went quiet and still, like incense with an evening prayer. "Then twins, a boy and a girl, Lester and Abigail." She studied something off in the distance, or maybe it was nothing at all, then patted Macy's shoulder. "A wave of sickness came through when they were three and five. Took all three within a week."

"No."

Grim-faced, Hattie nodded. "It was a long time before I commenced to breathing again, to say nothing of thinking. And the hardest part about coming here was leaving those graves behind, Chester's and the children, but I see a future out here, Macy. A future for women, a future for families, a chance to make something special. After so much sadness, I wanted to be part of something special again."

"That's how it is," Will said softly. "Building a country, building faith, being pioneers. We've got a chance to be that first wave, long as we don't turn back. And then each wave that comes goes a little farther and does a little better." He stood. "I expect that soup's done, ladies, and I'm about as hungry as a man can get. I'll ladle some up in three bowls and let it cool."

"Thank you, Will." He went in through the front door, whistling softly. Macy thought those were sounds she could get used to with no real effort. Will's firm footfall, and the gentle whistle of nothing in particular.

"He's a good man, our Will." Hattie observed softly. "He's seen the good and bad of life and weathered both. I like that in a body. Makes me feel a kinship with folks who might fall down but work to get back up."

Hattie's words stirred something inside Macy, something strong. She'd fallen in many ways, but she'd always struggled back on her feet. Hearing Hattie talk ignited hope inside her. All her life she'd been judged and found wanting. She'd been treated as less by folks who should know better, who preached better. On the broad, open prairie she wasn't an outcast, but of course the folks here saw what she wanted them to see, an upright young woman, ready to work. Would they cast her out if they knew more? After meeting some of the locals, she'd like to think not, but who knew? "Life has a way of handing things sideways at times."

"It surely does. But once I saw the opportunity knocking to come west and no good reason to stay east, I packed up my belongings, shipped my goods and followed on the train. Out here, Harriet Beth McGillicuddy wasn't a sad, childless widow. She was a smart and savvy businesswoman and no one knew any better."

"So it's not a lie to change up your life and start fresh?"

"Putting our best foot forward is never bad," Hattie replied. "And using God's word for guidance is a powerful thing."

Macy's heart hit a misstep.

Did Hattie say that for a reason? No, of course not. There was no way Hattie could know of her relationship to Little Will, or how she used the story of Moses in the reeds to tuck her baby onto Will Barber's porch. Unless Mrs. Crowley had said something. She'd set Macy up with Hattie, and she knew about the baby. "You mean like the Lord's Prayer?" Macy thought her voice would squeak. When it didn't she was surprised and pleased.

"Exactly that, dear. Forgiving trespasses, being grateful for our daily bread."

A sigh of relief escaped from Macy. "True words."

"And of course the stories of old. Ruth, staying by Naomi's side, meeting her beloved Boaz. Noah, braving scrutiny, building a boat on dry land, expecting rains no one thought would come."

Macy nodded, because being mocked and scorned for doing what he could, well— she sympathized with Noah.

"And Moses' mother, tucking his basket in the river, praying the Pharaoh's daughter would find her precious son and take pity on a child of Israel."

Chapter Eight

THIS TIME MACY'S HEART DIDN'T misstep. It stopped. She peeked up and saw Hattie's kind, clear gaze and didn't know what to say. In the end she didn't have to say anything. Hattie put a hand on her knee, squeezed lightly and smiled. "As I said, using the Good Book for guidance in God's ways is a good thing."

Macy gulped. She wanted to ask Hattie how she knew, but Will's voice came through from inside. "Ladies, the soup's cool enough to eat. Here." He stepped through the door, lifted Little Will like he'd been toting infants around daily, and held the door wide. "Come on in. It's hot in there, but there are no flies. Well." He frowned as one buzzed right past him. "Except that one."

Hattie knew, and didn't hate her.

Macy moved into the tidy kitchen— Hattie's hand, she knew, because it hadn't been all that tidy when she first arrived that afternoon— swamped with mixed emotion. Sharing the secret helped her, but was she encouraging her mentor to lie? If she was, then all her new-found promises of goodness were for nothing.

"Will, this smells just wonderful," Hattie declared. She loosened her hat and set it aside after fanning herself with it. "I won't object to the heat because this winter I'll be praying for it, but the older I get, the more I like the middle. Not too hot, not too cold."

"You might be in the wrong place, Hattie," Will joked as he pulled out Macy's chair, then repeated the gesture with

Hattie. "I think the Dakota territory is the definition of extremes."

"All the better reason to gentle this land," Hattie told him. "Enough folks, enough imagination, things can be changed, or managed, anyway. I'm all for managing what needs to be done."

"That's not exactly a secret, Hattie."

She flushed and laughed. "I suppose not. So, Will, we'll take charge of the little ones at service, and then I'd like to talk to you about Bert Singer's claim."

"We can't talk now?" Will wondered, but Hattie shook her head.

"I expect you're tired after your session this afternoon."

His features stilled as he met Hattie's gaze.

"So I was thinking of putting on a pork pot out back tomorrow if the rain holds off. We can do a spicy sauce to go with, and I've got new peas to shell and some pearl potatoes."

"That sounds like a feast."

"It sounds like Sunday dinner back home," she corrected him with a smile. "I expect as more folks come and we find more ways to get around the wind and sun, we'll have more choices. With things comin' in by rail, our speed won't surprise me at all, as fast as they move now."

"You see change."

"I see opportunity, and that's what we'll talk about. Right now, I'm going to finish this soup and take Macy home. We'll get all cleaned up and ready for a proper Sunday."

A proper Sunday.

The very words appealed to Macy, like a long-awaited holiday. "I like the sound of that, Hattie."

"Good." Hattie waited as Will pronounced a blessing, then ate. "We might be a wild west, but with enough preachers and women around, we'll tame this land yet."

Macy had wondered about that. She'd read the stories of wild men and gunfights and women in saloons. She'd seen enough in Pittsburgh to know rough elements by a first-name basis, so the thought of subduing the west seemed unlikely as she'd carried a small child aboard the train the week before.

Now she could see it. A blend of Hattie's wisdom, Will's faith and her own common sense offered new hope of second chances. A new life for her, and her child. Separate, but together, at least as long as Little Will stayed with Will Barber. She realized Hattie bought her time on purpose.

Had Hattie known all along? Or strung the puzzle pieces together? Either way, they'd have to talk about it.

She should send you packing. You lied, you connived, you abandoned your child. No good person does these things. What makes you think she can forgive and forget your indiscretions? Why should she, when you misrepresented yourself to her?

Dread built within her chest as she and Hattie walked back to the sewing shop a little while later. She'd loved the smell of the soup, but the thought of their looming conversation killed her appetite. By the time they reached the house and Hattie opened the door, Macy was ready to burst. "I know we need to talk," she exclaimed as she closed the inside door behind her. "And if you need for me to leave, Hattie, I'll understand completely because I came to you under false pretenses and I don't want to leave the same way."

Hattie stared at her, right at her, then waved a hand as if bothered. "Oh, my dear child, do you think you're the first young woman to find herself in such circumstances?"

Pregnant? Single? Alone? Ostracized? Macy frowned. "It's not about the circumstances of pregnancy," she told her, and hated admitting the words out loud. "But in pretending to be something other than I am. I knew nothing about sewing."

"Many don't," Hattie confirmed as she set away her hat on the uppermost shelf.

"And little about fabrics and notions."

"All learnable."

"And I believe Mrs. Crowley let you think I was more skilled than I am."

"Well, that's where you're mistaken." Hattie loosened her big apron and hung it on a nail inside the back door.

"Huh?" Macy dunked her own apron into a small tub of water, then scrubbed at the blood-stains with a bar of stout soap. "I don't understand."

"Come sit once you're done there, but I fear it's a lost cause. Although hanging it out in the sun might fade the stains just enough to keep it usable." Hattie sat at the small, square table and waited until Macy did the same. "I may or may not have my own motives for tempting you west."

"Motives?" Macy stared at her. "I don't understand."

Hattie met her gaze. "Well, here's the point. When I got out here and started setting up my own business, and doing quite well for myself, I knew I needed help. Now there are plenty of local girls on the claims and a few here in town, but one night as I said my prayers, I saw the most wonderful thing. It was a train, all decked out like for an Independence Day parade. Red, white and blue bunting, folks waving flags, people clapping and I saw young women climbing on that train, smiling and happy, ready to head west. I thought I might have been a little touched by fever, what with colds going around, but the same sight came to me in church the following Sunday, and that's when I knew."

"You knew?" Macy leaned forward. "What did you know, Hattie?"

"That my vision for women should become a mission," she told her crisply. "A mission to bring women out of the darkness of the cities, out of circumstances beyond their control and give them a new day. A second chance in Second Chance."

"So you planned for Mrs. Crowley to help me?"

"I most certainly did, and when I have you safely tucked

in a new life, Jean Ellen will send me another assistant. And then another. Because women helping women is a good thing, Macy Evers."

"So you knew. All along, you knew about me, my life. The baby, too?"

Hattie's face went dark. "Jean Ellen was fighting mad about that, and that's why you were picked first. She heard what that old boss did to you. She never once believed you were sweet-talked by some steel worker, like some said. She told me you weren't afraid to speak out for women's rights in the factories, even at the cost of your job."

"If I'd stayed silent, he wouldn't have singled me out," Macy said softly. "If I'd just gone along and pretended it was okay to be treated like animals, I might have walked away clean."

"And that's just the kind of thinking we're going to erase, Macy, my girl." Hattie grabbed up her hand and her grip said the older woman meant business. "One woman at a time, we shall bring them out of those situations. Why, when I saw what young Nellie Bly was able to do with the written word, I realized I can do a similar good with my shop. We reach out a hand, one at a time, and we bring women to a new beginning, here in Second Chance."

Tears smarted Macy's eyes. "But what if folks find out? What if they scorn me? Or worse, they put labels on my baby son? I can't bear the thought of him being singled out. Taunted. I can't do that, Hattie, no matter who it might help. Not if Little Will's involved."

"And who's asking you to?" Hattie asked. "I say we keep that matter between ourselves and trust in the good Lord to sort through. He's gotten me this far, I expect He can do it again. What I'm asking of you, Macy, is to hold tight and let prayer, hope and faith work around us. No running off. You stay here and create a new place for yourself. And who knows what might happen?"

"Happen?"

Hattie sighed and rolled her eyes. "Honey, it would take a person older and less-sighted than me to miss the looks you and Pastor Will dart this way and that."

"Hattie." Macy put cool hands to her warm cheeks. "Hattie, he's a man of God. He's got so much to offer so many, with his hard work, his faith, his doctoring skills. I can't presume to even think along those lines."

"We'll let faith do the thinking for both of you," Hattie told her. "That's more solid than all of us put together. Most have come to Second Chance with some sort of secret or sadness. And here, in this new town, filling up with all kinds of folks, we can make a difference from the get-go. And I want you to be part of that difference, Macy. With your good heart and your quick mind."

In all her twenty-one years, Macy had never had anyone praise her like this. No one had ever wanted her for who she was, or what she could do. The thought that Hattie and Jean Ellen picked her— *her!!*— made her feel good and conflicted.

Did she deserve this second chance?

Hattie leaned down and smiled into her eyes. "You are a blessing, Macy. A gift from God above and I want your help in making other women, and maybe their children, know what a blessing God's love can be."

Her dream come true. A place where she could be herself and help others. A place where she was beloved, where people of faith meant every word of the Lord's Prayer. Could it really be like that?

Fear dogged her, but Hattie's words told her that fear wasn't of God. Not the God Hattie knew, the God Will represented. She reached up and placed her palm over Hattie's hand. "I will be honored to help."

"Good!" Hattie stood and breathed deep. "I don't know what the future holds, dearie, but I know the present! I'm happy and tired. We'll settle things day by day, but with God's help, Macy?" She turned as she opened the back door to go visit the necessary. "We'll make a difference."

We'll make a difference.

Macy went to bed that night, repeating those words in her head. Hattie believed in her. Jean Ellen had sent her on purpose, knowing full well about the baby she'd tried so hard to hide, and still Hattie wanted her help.

She fell asleep, ready to take on the world.

Chapter Nine

THE LAST THING ON WILL Barber's mind was sleep, despite the need to preach first thing.

He'd saved a man's life today. Well, as long as infection didn't set in and turn Buck's leg septic. He'd been called to do a priest's work, and ended up as a doctor. His hands shook, thinking of it. His breath caught, remembering the sight of his little son, gone too soon. He'd walked away from medicine for a reason, but facing Buck's family, he couldn't turn his back on the expected outcome. Instead of Last Rites, he'd done surgical suturing.

Maybe Buck would keep it quiet. He and Adeline were good folks. If he asked them to keep his secret, maybe they would. But would those children be able to stay silent? In a small outpost like Second Chance, all it took was rumor of medical help and doctors were bombarded. That's why snake oil and spirits salesmen made such a good living, because real medicine hadn't reached most of the prairie.

Thy kingdom come, thy will be done...

He wanted God's guidance, but he'd tried that before.

Did you?

He sat up, annoyed. Of course he had. He'd stood by his wife's side through all of her ups and downs. He'd pacified, placated and begged. What more could he have done?

Discern.

He stared into the darkness, seeing his vulnerability.

He'd never asked God's advice, or prayed for his own discernment. He'd married Elissa because she was beautiful, a trophy in every sense of the word. Being with her filled a shallow need inside him, a need he hadn't recognized until it was too late. Like Delilah in days of old, he put looks and flirtations above goodness and mercy. He was foolish then, and it cost a child his life. He couldn't afford to ever be stupid again.

He pulled himself out of the low-slung bed and walked to the back door. Frog song from the nearby lake greeted him. Chickie lay sleeping upstairs, and his little namesake was asleep for the moment, but that could change at any time. Still, he couldn't force himself to rest.

Folks would know about the doctoring soon. They'd wonder why he wasn't helping more, drawing folks into town with his skills. Didn't most folks want good land, good water and a good doctor? But that was it, he wasn't a good doctor, or he wouldn't have laid his tiny son in a small, square box five years before.

A noise emitted from the baby's box. Not a cry, not a sigh, something in-between, and the sound of the infant's breathing soothed him. Was Little Will put on his step as his atonement? Was this precious baby boy Will's second chance? He'd moved to the town because he wanted a new life for Chickie, one where children ran free, water ran abundant, and the crystal clear lakes called to him. A simple life, a preacher's life, perfect in its lack of finality until today.

Do unto others…

He believed that. He tried to live it. But if he wasn't doing all he could, was he living a lie?

A cry from the basket drew his attention. He waited, but when the baby's cries grew lustier, Will went and filled a bottle with the substitute mix he'd taken out of the chill bucket before he laid down. The milk felt cool but not cold any longer. He took the baby and the bottle to the old wooden rocker he bought from a homesteader last year. He sat, but he wasn't seeing himself in the rocker. He saw

Macy, bits of hair curling along her cheek, her neck, bent low over the baby as she fed him. She cooed to the child, laughed with Chickie, and brought her hand to whatever task came her way. Her quick smile made him want to smile more. Her bright eyes pushed him to be better. Stronger. More patient.

He'd messed up before. Could he trust his years and his faith to guide him this time? Was it love stirring his interest in Macy? Could that happen so soon? Or was it his old nemesis, lust?

No.

He knew better than that, he'd lived that choice once. This was different. Sweeter. Less intense. Except when he thought about kissing her, because those thoughts were about as intense as they could get.

He finished the baby's bottle, burped the little fellow, and laid him back down to sleep. Precious. So precious. He bent and kissed the baby's cheek, smooth and warm. He hadn't allowed himself to kiss a baby since burying Abraham. He'd barely allowed himself to be near babies since then, except in the realm of church and pastor. And then this little fellow appeared out of nowhere and he had no choice.

There's always a choice. This time you turned toward amends. Not away.

The baby sighed, brought his hand to his mouth and found his thumb. That meant Will might get a few straight hours of sleep. He smiled down at the boy, snuffed the single candle and found his way back to his bed by light of the three-quarter moon.

He'd lifted that crying baby so fast, rational thought hadn't entered into it. Crawling back into bed, he realized maybe that was for the best. Perhaps God put that child there in a moment of need so Will would have to make that leap of faith. Hattie had advised him to keep the baby with him for a while. Little did she know that the last thing he wanted to do was hand that little boy off to strangers. His presence here filled a gaping hole inside Will. Maybe it was selfish. Maybe it was foolish. He'd ask God's guidance on the boy and on Macy because he didn't dare make mistakes this time. He'd seen the cost first-hand, and he knew he couldn't pay that price ever again.

Sunday morning dawned with summer brilliance. The hot spell had broken through the night, and a lighter, easier air bathed the small town. Hattie had waited on the street while Macy gathered Little Will and Chickie, and when they entered the church a few minutes later, she moved halfway to the front. "Here, Chickie, you head on into that pew," Hattie directed. "This way we're close, but not too close if the baby kicks up a squall. Macy can follow you in and that way you can help keep Little Will amused, if you don't mind."

"I love helping!" Chickie slid to the far side of the small pew and beamed when Macy sat down next to her. "Isn't he just the sweetest thing, Miss Macy?"

How could Macy not agree? "He is," she answered, and when the boy reached out a hand and patted Chickie's cheek, Will's daughter giggled out loud. "But of course we must try to be our best and quietest in church, darling."

"I love it when you call me darling." Chickie hugged Macy's arm. "It makes me feel special."

Macy understood the desire to be special. She leaned her head against Chickie's curls and said, "You *are* special. In every way."

Chickie peeked up. "It's nice to hear."

Will stepped into the church sanctuary. He looked strong and affirming, tall and true. He wore a plain, dark vestment, perfect for a small town on a tight budget. He crossed to the lectern with his Bible, the image of gentle goodness.

Her heart tugged tight. She was drawn to him. His square jaw, his solid gaze, lightened by joy, shadowed by… something. Maybe that's what drew her. The sense that life wasn't always perfect, even in a preacher's world.

He mounted the steps, swept the congregation a look of welcome, and smiled when his gaze rested on them.

She smiled back, then wondered if that was brazen? But he smiled first, so it had to be all right. Wasn't it? She dipped her face toward the baby as heat stained her cheeks. Was she flirting with the pastor in church? Was she crossing some line of behavior? As he began reading from the book of Isaiah, she let the words comfort her. "Be not afraid… I am with you… I will uphold you…"

That was what she wished from faith. Not a pretense of goodness, doled out by others, but the sweet, bright light of a true heart for God. Did that exist? Did she deserve the blessing of that faith, the faith of a child?

Jesus made it clear he came to all, not the few. He made enemies by being kind and good and generous.

Were people power-hungry by nature? Self-serving by design? Could she choose goodness and mercy and live it?

Yes, she decided as Will's gentle words touched the congregation around her. God had given her a choice, same as any, and she could choose righteousness. But with that righteousness came honesty. She stared into her son's face, so perfect, so dear. A tear slipped out. Then another.

Should she confess to being his mother? If bad came from her admission, how could it be good? If folks condemned her for having a child out of wedlock, was she branding them both for life?

Isaiah's words spoke of blotting out sin. But did that mean she needed to bare her soul? Moses' mother did nothing of the kind, and her son was blessed. Would the same hold true today? She sat, listening to Will's gentle and sometimes humorous wisdom, and felt stupid for not having answers. As he drew the service to a close, her memories outweighed the grace of words. People could be mean, some downright cruel. No matter what befell her, she didn't want her son to bear the brunt of that cruelty, but she couldn't build a relationship with the pastor, based on half-truths. True love couldn't grow from sinful soil, but Little Will's parentage was no one's business. If that made her a liar, then she'd beg God's forgiveness. But if it saved the baby from scorn, she'd risk as needed, because that's what a good mother did. They sacrificed to protect their child, as Moses' mother did so long ago. And if that sacrifice meant staying away from a man of God like Will Barber, then that's what had to be done.

Will wasn't sure how a woman could hide in a small, prairie town, but Macy Evers managed to do it. She was out of sight when he stopped by the sewing shop, and it was Hattie who delivered Chickie's first dress. By the end of the week, he was fit to be tied. He stopped by Hattie's the first thing in the morning. "Mornin' Hattie." He glanced around her to see if he could glimpse Macy.

Nope.

"Pastor!" Hattie lit right up when she saw him and approached the front counter. "Nice to see you, and I see your team hitched out front. You off somewhere?"

"To visit Buck, see how he's doing. 'Liza's better and she's keeping Chickie and the baby. Is Macy here? I was going to have her go along with me."

"She's not at the moment, and we received four separate orders this week, Will, when the rail came through. I can't spare her a minute right now." He heard her words, but the expression in her tone said something quite different.

"It shouldn't take us long, and I might need an assistant."

Was that temptation he read in Hattie's eyes? If it was, she shut it right down. "Understandable, but if he's doing better, and I pray to God he is, I expect Adeline can help. She's a capable gal. Well." She dusted her hands against her apron and bustled back to her machine. "Back to it, I guess."

"Of course." He offered the shop one more glance as he went through the door. No Macy. "See you later, Hattie."

"Mm hmm." She nodded, her mouth full of pins as she stabbed a shirt cuff with more ardor than any cotton could possibly need. He climbed onto the wagon seat, clucked to the horses, and looped around the back of the Main Street shops.

She was avoiding him on purpose. And he figured Hattie might just be helping her. Why would they do that? He was smitten with Macy, he knew that. Now and again he thought the attraction went both ways, but maybe he was flat out wrong. He drove to Buck's, found everything to be well so far, issued a warning and was back on the road in no time. He guided the horses toward the small grazing ground behind his house, pulled up and set the brake.

"Pa! You're back already! Look who's come to visit!" Chickie danced with excitement, and in her new everyday dress, she looked like a little bird, hopping about the graze-shortened grass. "It's Miss Macy!"

"I see." He stood by the horses wishing he didn't want to drink in the sight of her, but he did. He wanted to smile and nod like she was any old neighbor, but she wasn't, and how did he know that?

Because his heart sped up every time he laid eyes on her. His palms grew damp and he wanted to breathe fast and slow at the same time. She made Chickie laugh. She handled that baby like it was her own, and she worked hard at Hattie's, learning the intricacies of seaming and sewing. *She seeketh wool and flax, and worketh willingly with her hands.*

When he tossed her fair looks into the mix, Will knew God had set her here, right here, for him. A woman of virtue and kindness, for all the days of his life. He moved forward as she stood, the baby tucked within her left arm. "I haven't seen you all week."

She looked anywhere but at him. "We're busy at the shop. Quite busy, actually."

So Hattie had said. He folded his arms and kept his gaze trained on her. "Hattie said as much, but she also said you were far too busy to ride out to Buck's with me this afternoon, and yet you're here, at that very time she said you would be working."

Eyes down, she hesitated, then slowly raised her chin and met his gaze. "Yes."

Her admission surprised him. She made no excuses, she simply bent, kissed Chickie's cheek and said, "I'll see you soon, okay? We have your second dress almost done, and next month we'll make your pink dress. I'm so eager to work on it, Chickie."

"I can't wait!" Chickie beamed up at her, unaware of the adult tension. "I'm going to run and put a bean in the pot for each day I have to wait. Pa told me to do that for Christmas and my birthday, and it works! When the pot is empty, the special day is here!"

"Oh, that's a fine idea." Macy smiled down at her, then turned back toward Will and handed off the baby. "I'll get back to seaming now."

"Macy, I—"

She stepped back and gave him a polite shake of her head, when what he wanted was a warm hug. The touch of her hand. A sweet, unending kiss. Did she really feel nothing for him?

"Goodbye, Will."

He watched her walk away, and he was almost ready to let her go but something pushed him forward. "Macy."

She kept walking, chin down.

"Macy." He hurried to catch up to her, and when he did, he dodged in front to slow her progress. "Talk to me. Tell me what's wrong."

A tear slipped down her cheek, then a parallel track formed on her other cheek. As a pastor, he'd soothed many a person's tears during hard times. He found his standard words impossible right now because his heart was directly involved, no matter how little time they'd had together. He said the lamest thing possible under the circumstances. "Don't cry. Please, don't cry."

Little Will squawked a protest. He juggled the baby until the infant belched. Between the crying woman and the burping baby, any thoughts of wooing seemed off the table, but he had to try because what other chance was there? Pretty much none if she continued to avoid him. When he did see her, they were surrounded by other adults, Chickie or the baby. "Macy." He stepped closer, wanting to reassure her. Somehow he had to make things all right for her. "Macy, my feelings for you are growing. I think about you. I dream about you," he admitted. "When you're here, everything seems more right than it's ever been. I know we just met. I understand the need for time, but can you look up at me and tell me there's hope? Because I won't hurry you, but I want you to know I'd like to court you, Macy Evers. And I've been scouring this small town all week trying to tell you just that, but you've dodged me at every turn. Can I court you, pretty lady?" He bent lower to see her face. "It would be my honor."

Long, drawn-out seconds later she shook her head. "No." She whispered the word as if unsure, but then repeated it with more certainty. "No, you can't court me, Will. You don't know me. You know what you see, not what I am. Who I am. You're a good man, a preacher, a man of God. And a doctor besides, so smart, so learned."

"Macy, none of that means a thing when two people grow to care about each other."

"You're wrong," she corrected him. She took a big step back. "Hattie needs my help at the shop. Will, I want to stay in Second Chance but I don't want to have to avoid you. So please, let's have no more talk of this between us." She raised her eyes to his. "You deserve a wonderful woman, Will. The kind of woman who matches you step for step, and that's not me." She ducked her head and walked away, not slow, but not fast, either. She moved as if weighted by all the wrongs of the world and Will's heart ached to see it.

"Did Miss Macy go?" Chickie came around from the back. "I wanted to say goodbye!"

"We'll see her regular," Will said, but would they? In a town this size, he'd have thought so but after the past few days he wasn't any too sure. He gave Chickie bread and jam for supper with a glass of fresh milk from Hornsby's cow, and when he tucked her into bed, Macy's words taunted him.

What made her feel unworthy? If she only knew him, knew his past, she'd understand the man he'd been, cocky and self-assured, and what his attitude cost. No one in Second Chance knew about Abraham. They knew he was a widower, and respected his privacy, but he'd kept the loss of his son to himself, a private penance. He stared out the window too long, and when he finally climbed into bed, sleep was slow in coming. And when it did, it was the worry-furrow of Macy's face he saw in his dreams. Her sad eyes. Her down-turned gaze. And when he reached out a hand to comfort her, she was gone. Just simply… gone.

Chapter Ten

WILL BARBER WOULDN'T STOP BEING nice and Macy was fit to be tied.

"There are worse things than a man courting a woman," Hattie supposed ten days later. Her tired sigh said Macy's behavior might border ridiculous.

"Hattie." Macy looked up from a buttonhole— a very nicely done buttonhole, something to take pride in— perturbed. "You of all people know why I can't consider such a thing. He's a man of God and I'm about as lost a soul as you can get."

"Are you lost now?"

"Well. No." She stabbed the shirt with too much vengeance and had to pause, take a breath and aim the next stitch with more care. "Not now."

"Then I don't see the problem. If you have feelings for him, that is."

Oh, she did, and he was only making it worse by stopping by with little gifts. Flowers he'd picked from the field abutting the lake. A hunk of fudge from the mercantile. A slim, paper booklet about making jams and jellies. It might seem silly, but she'd always wanted to be more domestic and the opportunity never arose. Had he really listened to her thoughts and wishes in casual conversation? The notion brought heat up from somewhere around her toes. "I do, but you understand the problem."

"The only problem I see is a stubborn nature," Hattie said as she re-threaded the machine. "Pigheadedness can be a downfall, for certain."

"I'm not pigheaded."

Hattie's silence had her re-thinking things. "Hattie, you know me better than most anyone, including whatever family I used to have. How do I tell him the truth? Do I just march right up to him and say I'm Will's mother and I abandoned him on your stoop?"

"All but the marching part, yes," Hattie replied. "The truth is always better than a lie, and if Will knows your reasons, I expect he'd understand."

Would he?

She'd love to believe that, because the man was wearing down her defenses with his kindness and attention. Did she dare confess?

"Pray on it, Macy. Prayer is the best equalizer, and God knows your heart, your soul. He saw you in Pittsburgh. He sees you now. Rest on Him."

It couldn't possibly be that easy. Could it? How would she know if she never tried? Determination claimed her. She would get Will alone and confess who she was. Would he forgive her? Would he understand?

She hoped so, but if he didn't, at least it would put an end to the one-sided courtship robbing her of sleep and rational thought. "I'll take Chickie's second dress over this afternoon. The underskirt is done and if I can work up my courage, perhaps we can talk."

"I'm not saying it'll be easy." Chin down, Hattie peered at her over her close-up glasses. "But it's better than tossing and turning night and day."

Macy wasn't so sure, but she spotted Will as she turned the corner from Second Street onto Main that afternoon. He was strolling down the street. Chickie skipped alongside, her face animated, her mouth moving. Will didn't seem to mind her non-stop chatter. He held Little Will snug in his left arm, and when he spotted her coming their way, he paused their progress. He smiled at her, for her, and the sight of this good man made her long to fly to him and take her place at his side.

Her heart leaped in her chest. Her breath caught. She wanted this image of father and children to be *her* family, *her* image. A longing so deep and wide she thought it might swallow her swelled within. A family... *her family*... forevermore. She took a breath, knowing the unlikeliness of her dream, and moved ahead with the dress in one hand. "I was just bringing this to the parsonage."

"And I was hoping I'd run into you, so it seems we had each other on the mind," Will's voice was casual but the look he sent her was anything but casual. "I'd say this is perfect."

He was right so she couldn't exactly deny it. "I can take this up to the house for you if you've got errands. I'll hang it right inside the door."

"Oh, Pa, can we walk back with Miss Macy?" Chickie grabbed her father's hand. "I'd love to see the dress all done, and then we can walk, okay? If you don't mind," she added.

"I'm glad you remembered your manners." Will palmed Chickie's curls with his free hand and turned around. "I've got time. Why not?" He fell into step beside Macy. He walked close, but not too close, and even with inches separating them, the scent of him filled her. A waft of soap, hay, dust and sweet baby robed him, a prairie mix. "Did you help with the dress, Macy?"

"The underskirt." She looked up at him. Big mistake. Bright blue eyes sparkled down at her, lake-water blue on a calm summer's day. "But my buttonholes are good now, and that's a relief." He laughed and she bristled. "Whip-stitching buttonholes is no easy task, Pastor."

"Call me Will, Macy. Please."

She wanted that openness with him, the closeness intimated by using his name, but until she'd been honest, she had no right to use it. As they passed the curving path to the metal smith's shop, a familiar voice hailed them.

"Hello!"

Macy turned, surprised. Dread filled her when she recognized the couple coming their way. They'd shared a rail car with her, but they'd gotten off hours before. They'd chatted back and forth as she rode the car west, not much, but enough to know they'd expected to stay in Iowa. And here they were, walking toward her and the baby they'd met on the train.

Her chest pounded. Fear grabbed her breath. She tried to right her features, but how could she when reckoning approached?

Will extended his free hand to the young couple. "I'm Pastor Barber. Nice to meet you folks. You're new here?"

"We are." The man shook Will's hand, then smiled at Macy. "And we had the pleasure of this woman's company partway out. I didn't realize you were settling here," he told Macy. "I thought you mentioned going on to Pierre."

"I did, too." His wife looked happy to see Macy. "I'm so glad we were wrong! It will be nice to have a familiar face hereabouts. Our plans were thwarted in Iowa and the claim manager told us about claims for sale by the lakes not far from De Smet, so here we are."

"Our harsh winter made for some rough decisions," Will told her. "Welcome to Second Chance."

"Thank you! And it's a pleasure to see this baby doing so well. Oh my, how he's grown, Macy." She beamed at Macy while blood beat against Macy's temples. "It must be so good to get home with him."

Will went rigid. As the couple bid them farewell and hurried on their way, Will's absolute stillness was worse than any rage she could imagine. And when she mustered the courage to look up, the quiet anger in his gaze said nothing would ever be all right again, and Macy knew that was exactly what she deserved.

"Chickie, head back to the house for a moment, please."

"But, Pa—"

"Now."

Chickie looked worried. She gulped, uncertain, then she did what he said with great reluctance, scuffing her feet along the dusty path. When she was far enough away, Will faced Macy and indicated the baby in his arms with his eyes. "Yours."

What could she say in her own defense? Nothing, so she breathed deep and nodded. "Yes."

"You left him."

Again she had no excuse. "Yes."

She thought it wasn't possible, but Will's expression went harder. Meaner. "You took your child and left him on a stranger's doorstep."

"On a pastor's doorstep," she whispered, wishing she could say more. "I was on my way to tell you, and then..." She indicated the retreating couple with a glance. "We met them."

"I'm supposed to believe that you were conveniently on your way to confess your abandonment while you just happened to be carrying my daughter's dress?" He shook his head and raised a hand to stop her when she tried to speak. "I don't need to know any more." He snugged the baby into his side as if protecting him, and that cut her to the quick. "Stay away from me. Stay away from my daughter. And don't even think to come anywhere near this baby. Do you understand me?"

Her heart didn't pound now. It broke into a million scattered pieces of nothingness, just as she deserved. She nodded, brought a hand to her mouth to choke back tears, turned and ran for the shelter of Second Avenue and Hattie's shop.

Why hadn't she told him sooner? Why had she risked him finding out? And what made her think her sins should be forgiven?

She was a foolish, foolish woman and as she let herself in through Hattie's back door, the tears she held back came forth. Hattie took one look at her, stood and crossed the room, arms open. And for the first time in her life, Macy Evers cried in the comforting arms of a loving person.

Will wanted to punch things.

He couldn't.

Two children depended on him to stay calm and cool, to be the loving example they so deserved.

How had this happened?

Oh, he understood the timeline, but that wasn't what he meant. How had he managed to fall in love with another scheming, selfish, self-absorbed woman who put herself above all others, including her child?

He couldn't believe it. Old doubts joined new. Memories swamped him, tweaking his past and poking fun at his future. What was wrong with him that he was drawn to women who took the lives of their children casually? Who had no sacrificial heart for the beauty of God's creation?

He stormed outside once Chickie was in bed and the baby lay sleeping. He picked up the ax and chopped wood until he couldn't stand, and still couldn't fall asleep. When the baby awoke before dawn, he stumbled to the little box, picked him up and fed him, wondering what he should do. No answer came. He fed the little guy, cleaned him up, and tucked him back into bed.

The baby had other ideas. He set up an instant protest. Will lifted him again and walked the floors as the baby fussed and fumed. And when the infant finally found his thumb and dozed off, it was past time for Will to be up.

He didn't remember getting through the day. By the time he hit the bed that night, he slept rock solid, but woke angry. His head hurt, his heart ached, and when he looked at his Bible, God seemed very far away. But had

God moved?

Or had he?

He wasn't sure but as he went through the coming days, the soreness of his soul waged war on his spirit. He blamed himself, he blamed Macy, he blamed his lost wife and in the end, he gave God a good scolding, too.

Nothing helped.

By the next week he'd pretty much decided to head into the mountains with his two kids and become a recluse. Maybe if he secluded himself into the outreaches of society, he could live the self-protected life he wanted right now. And when Hattie McGillicuddy came sailing up the walk to his door the following Wednesday, he wished he'd high-tailed it out of Second Chance the day before.

"Will, I believe it's time we had a talk."

Chickie had gone next door to 'Liza's to help squish berries for jam, a favorite job. Will held up his hand and attacked the cottonwood pile once again. "Nothing to say, Hattie. It's best left alone."

"Oh, really?"

Will sighed, because he knew that tone. Hattie had used it when dealing with the former saloon owner up the road. She'd used it when Ben Walker thought to dam up the creek that ran by his house, hogging water for his growing stand of cattle. And when Harriet talked in that tone, a body had no choice but to listen because she wasn't about to stop. "Say your piece if you must, but there's nothing you can say that changes the truth."

"I thought you were a man of God."

That stopped Will in his tracks. "I am." He set the ax down, faced her and spoke slowly. No way in the world was Hattie going to stand there and make this his fault.

"A man schooled in ways of God's word. A man who pledged to lead the faithful in good times and in bad."

He'd done exactly that when he gave up doctoring. "What's your point, Hattie?"

"You turned aside a perfect opportunity to be loving and forgiving and turned it into a condemnation, Will Barber. I thought better of you than that."

He pinched his fingers to the bridge of his nose, trying to thwart the headache that wouldn't go away. "Perhaps I see abandoning children as a crime. Not a choice."

"Oh, you self-righteous prig."

That got Will's attention. He stood taller and straighter. "Now, just a minute, Hattie."

"No, you just a minute, Will!" Hands on hips she faced him, and the scowl on her face was nothing compared to the fire in her eyes. "I came here to have my say and I'll do it, too. You cast out an absolutely lovely young woman because she made a choice you didn't like. Well, for your information, maybe you're not as smart as you think you are. Maybe you're not as good and kind and Godly as you'd have others believe, because if you think for one minute there's anything but kindness and goodness and righteousness in Macy Evers, then you're a stupid, narrow-minded man and you don't deserve her love. You didn't ask questions, you didn't wonder why she made the choice she did. But I expect when you read the story of Moses in Genesis, you smile and talk about a mother's sacrifice and a sister's dedication. Yet when the very same story is re-enacted before your eyes, you condemn and convict, a moralistic judge and jury."

Moses? Genesis?

Hattie's words cut deep, but the anger in her eyes cut sharper. "Shame on you," she continued. "You ran from doctoring when things went bad, and now you're thinking of running from the parsonage because there's a bump in the road. Shame on you, Will Barber, for not having the courage to find the truth of the situation because if you knew that, perhaps compassion would once again flow through your veins." She turned to flounce away, but not before she launched one perfectly aimed parting shot.

"Remember that woman in the streets of Jerusalem? The one sentenced to death by law? When that crowd of angry, self-righteous men approached Jesus about her punishment, do you recall what the Son of God said? He said the one without sin should cast the first stone. I don't know that a clearer picture can be painted than the example set by the Lord himself."

She strode away as if disgusted by him, as if *he* was the wrongdoer. He almost chased after her, wanting to have his say, but the truth behind her stance made him pause to re-evaluate.

Was he being judgmental?

Absolutely.

Did he have good reason?

He'd thought so, but a week of anger and a good tongue-lashing said he might be wrong. But he wasn't wrong. Was he?

Little Will squeaked from his netting-covered basket beneath the tree. He didn't cry, he peeped, and when Will crossed the yard, he stared down into the sweetest eyes he'd ever seen. Macy's eyes, peeking back up at him. And a smile so like Macy's he'd been a fool not to see it before. "You rolled over."

The baby laughed up at him, a gurgling sound, quite pleased with himself. He'd rolled over and laughed and his young mother had seen neither because he'd banished her from her child.

Realization sobered him. Guilt mounted within. He wasn't sure of the rights or wrongs of the whole situation, but gazing into the baby's happy countenance, he realized his wrongs finally. He lifted the boy, cleaned up his lower regions, and walked him over to Second Avenue. He turned and walked the short distance to Hattie's shop, unsure what to say or do, but knowing he had to do something. *Words would be good here, Lord. Guidance. Inspiration. Help me not to be stupid. Please.*

Chapter Eleven

H E WALKED THROUGH HATTIE'S DOOR. There were no customers at the moment. Hattie was at her machine, the treadle rocking the even rhythm of an experienced seamstress, and Macy sat on the other side of the shop, head bent over the hem of a pink dress.

She looked up, saw him, and paled. A woman standing before an executioner might look more relaxed than Little Will's mother did right now. The knowledge that he planted fear in a woman's heart shamed him. "Can we talk?"

Hattie let the machine go quiet. She stared at him, stared real hard as if deciding whether to let him stay or kick him out the door. Then she stood, nodded to Macy, and moved past Will to the door. She opened it, flipped the sign to say "CLOSED", and walked away.

"May I sit?"

Macy glanced at the chair in silent permission. He couldn't miss the way her eyes stayed on the baby, drinking him in. The baby Will had kept from her for over a week. He handed Will to her before he sat and when Macy smiled down at the boy…

The look on that baby's face set Will's heart to beating faster. He gooed and cooed up to his young mother, as if telling her what he'd done since they last saw one another. When tears of joy streamed from Macy's eyes, Will was pretty sure he was a low-down, no-good, presumptuous know-it-all who didn't deserve forgiveness. Still, he hoped she'd offer it. If nothing else, maybe she'd forgive him enough to eventually be friends. "I'm sorry, Macy."

She didn't look up.

Will splayed his hands as she whispered coos of love to her baby son. "I reacted badly when I found out about Will. I shouldn't have done that, and I hope you can forgive me. Please."

She sighed, and his heart went out to her when she did. He'd had plans, such plans, and it had all seemed so wonderfully good. Then he'd dashed them all without giving her a chance to explain because he'd decided no explanation was good enough. She'd walked away from her child while every day he wished he could have another chance to be with Abraham. Hold him. Cuddle him. Read him stories and take walks with the small boy perched on his daddy's strong shoulders. That would never happen because he'd turned a blind eye to the situation.

He'd judged unfairly, according to Hattie. Her talk of Moses made him realize that sometimes mothers had good reason for the harsh choices they made. "He looks like you."

Eyes down, she made a little face. "Do you think so?"

"I don't know why I didn't see it sooner," he admitted. "Once I knew, I looked at him and I saw you in every little blink and smile. I felt like life was carving another wound in my heart every time the little guy peeked up at me."

"Seems your sword goes both ways, Pastor."

Admitting she was right was the least he could do. "Yes, it does."

A hank of hair had tumbled over her shoulder. She pushed it back, away from the baby's face, then looked his way. "I was a bastard child."

The pain in her face hurt more than the words.

"My mother was not a nice woman. She had me for a price, and then when I was six years old, she married a man who fathered two other children. A brother and a sister. He hated me, what I stood for. When I was ten years old, he turned me out into the streets, they moved west and I never heard from any of them again."

Anger shoved sympathy aside. They tossed away a child as if she was trash? "They dumped you?"

"You sound so surprised, Will." Sad eyes studied him. "It's not an uncommon practice in the big cities. I wasn't alone on the streets, that's for sure, and lucky I was skilled at negotiating for food or nipping it as needed."

"Stealing."

She nodded. "Sometimes. Being a girl made shop-owners more sympathetic. Boys on the streets were common. When I was twelve, a woman pulled me in off the streets when the labor disputes got so out of hand. She wasn't mean, but she wasn't kind, either, and she prayed over me constantly because I was a child of sin. She had her friends in church pray, too, that I would be led away from the sin that formed me. They made life just as totally uncomfortable as they possibly could, with the exception of one lady in the church. Her little acts of kindness showed me more than all their spiteful praying ever did."

Spurned by the very ones who should have shown her Christ's gentle love. Will cringed inside, because he'd done the exact same thing.

"I landed a job at a factory. Long hours, horrible air to breathe, but I was able pay my way and put some by. Half went to Mrs. Ludvitz and half to me. The bosses at the factory liked to frequent the girls working there, as if we were there for their enjoyment. I kept my eyes down, and my production high, so my boss let me stay although I refused his advances. When times got rough with the steel factories last year, a bunch of folks lost their jobs. Everyone was angry. The whole city felt like it was burning with anger, and that's when my former boss found me. He was drunk, strong, angry and had his way with me." She bit her lower lip, pensive. "I didn't know what to do. Go to the police?

No one would listen to a street kid, even a grown one. Mrs. Ludvitz tossed me out the minute she realized I was with child, and there I was, back on the streets, pregnant, just like my mother before me."

God help her, Will prayed silently. *Help her to see that not all God-fearing people are like this. Help me to show her the love of the beatitudes… your love, lived on earth.*

"A police officer helped me. I will never forget his face, his name and his kindness. William MacDonald, a blessed man, with six children, he told me, and one on the way. His wife was Bonnie and she helped me get ready and introduced me to her friend Jean Ellen, the woman who sent me out here to Hattie." She stared at the baby, then the floor, as if too burdened to lift her head, but then she did lift it. She met his gaze and her eyes sparked with the strength and intelligence he'd noted from the beginning.

"You think what I did was terrible. I could have come here and pretended to be a widow. Many have done it before me."

Will knew that was true. He nodded.

"But I wanted God to love me for myself. For being the good person who believes in his Son, for loving Christ and how he sacrificed for us. How could I rationalize that if I was living a lie, deceiving everyone around me? And where does the lie stop?

"I read about Moses while I was with the MacDonalds." She lifted Little Will to her shoulder and rocked him when he fussed. "I thought it was a brilliant plan. She saved her son's life. She got to see him grow up and become a leader of men. She was able to do everything needed to care for her son, except claim him as her own, but that was a small sacrifice in exchange for his life. Nothing mattered more than her son's life, so I thought I'd do the same. I named him for Will MacDonald, one of the first people to ever treat me with kindness. And I came here, determined to give him up and watch from a distance because to go through life being called a child of sin and a bastard wasn't the life I chose for my beautiful baby. Not then. And not now, Will." She stood.

Will stood, too, confused.

She handed him the baby and moved to the back of the store. "You take him. Find a home for him, do as you will. I'll leave here and head further west and you needn't worry I'll come looking for him. All I want is for my son to have the chance I never had. To love and be loved, to be cherished by a family. He deserves that, Will. And whether or not you approve, that's how it has to be."

Approve?

Of her leaving?

How could he possibly approve that when all the man wanted was to beg her forgiveness and claim her as his own? Yes, he'd been foolish, short-sighted and judgmental. And rude. And mean-spirited. He cringed as the list grew, but what he wanted now was for Macy to stay right here in Second Chance and give him exactly that. A second chance to love her. He moved forward.

She stepped back, both hands up, palms out. "This is hard enough, Will. Just go. Please. I'll gather my things and take the next train back to Tracy. I can go in several directions from there, so I won't be a problem here."

"You're not a problem, Macy."

Her pained smile said otherwise.

"You're a solution." Will took another step forward. "You're a blessing."

"Will—"

"I'll have my say now. You had yours."

She huffed, then acquiesced but didn't look happy about it. "Go ahead."

"I've made big mistakes, Macy." He mulled the baby in his arms as if pained. "I married Chickie's mother when I was a young doctor. I was doing pretty well in Baltimore. She was a beautiful woman and I was a tempted young man who didn't look beyond tomorrow. We married, and when we had Chickie I thought I was the luckiest man in the world.

"But Elissa didn't like being a mother. She didn't like that Chickie took attention away from her. I hired a nanny to look after the baby, and we could barely afford such an expense, but I did it because Chickie needed someone to mind her. When Chickie turned three we realized Elissa was expecting again and she was angry. So angry." He paused. In retrospect, he understood the gravity of her anger and depression. Too little, too late.

"We had a son, a little boy named Abraham. So beautiful, so strong, such a sturdy little fellow." He gazed down at her son, but it was his son he saw, a blonde-haired, brown-eyed little fellow with a quick smile. So sweet. So dear. He took a breath. "I was teaching by then, as well as doctoring, so that helped our income. Household help for two wasn't any more than for one, so that was all right, but one day the nanny was sick. It was a cold, fog-filled day, so gray and wet it was hard to navigate streets much less fields. We didn't have room for the nanny to live with us, so she lived up the road a piece, in a walk-up. She couldn't come that day and I was at work. It took me a while to get home through the fog, and when I got home Mercy…" He caught her frown of confusion, and corrected himself, "I mean Chickie. Mercy is her real name."

"A beautiful name, Will."

He acknowledged that by nodding slowly. "It fits her nature, doesn't it? Such a kind, good child. Anyway, she was upstairs in her room, all alone. She said Mommy told her to go there and stay there because Mommy didn't feel good and there was too much noise. I couldn't find Elissa. I couldn't find the baby. I looked all over that little house and they were gone. I raced outside, looking everywhere, but I couldn't see anything, the fog was just so thick. A foghorn blew, long, slow and deep. And I knew, somehow.

I stood there, unable to see, unable to find them, unable to save my little boy." He clenched the baby in his arms a little tighter, a little closer. "And when they found them two days later, they assumed they fell into the water."

"It could have been like that, couldn't it?" she asked softly. "With the fog and all?"

He looked right at her. "I wish it was, but I knew Elissa. There was no reason for her to take an infant out walking the shore in a dense fog. No sane person would do it. I'd been too busy and too stubborn to see what was before my eyes, that Elissa wasn't mentally stable. I made excuses for her, I provided help for her, and I went on working as if it would all be okay. It wasn't okay, Macy. I put my children in grave danger by ignoring what I saw in their mother and I lost my son because of it. She may have been the one to walk into that water, clutching our baby boy, but my negligence walked right alongside her."

Sorrow and self-recrimination filled Will's eyes. He reached out a hand to Little Will's face with a touch so tender and kind that Macy's eyes went moist with the wonder of it. "Maybe that loss is what makes you so good with children and folks, Will."

"Not so good at the moment," he replied, and when he raised his gaze to hers, she saw the warmth she'd dreamed of since she first arrived in Second Chance. "I hurt you, Macy, not because of what you did, but because of what lay in my past. If I could take back my words, I would. I don't have that power, none of us do, but here's what I want, Macy Evers." He moved a step closer again, so close she could see the tiny points of ivory in his sky-blue eyes. "I want us to leave the past behind. I want us to be like that woman in the streets of Jerusalem, to go forward and sin no more. To accept God's forgiveness for anything we've done, and give ourselves a second chance."

"Will, I—"

"Shh." He put two big, broad fingers against her lips, and then his gaze strayed to those same lips and stayed there. When he leaned forward to claim a sweet, long kiss, he claimed Macy's heart right along with her mouth. "Let's begin anew, Macy Evers." He whispered the words when he finally broke the kiss, and it wasn't any too quick. "Together. You, me, Chickie and my little namesake. We're in a town that celebrates new beginnings. Why not you? Why not us?" He feathered the words against her cheek, her ear, and then kissed her again, and he kept right on kissing her until the baby protested. "Oops."

Macy laughed and took him from Will. "I think he needs tending, Will."

"I didn't bring anything with me, I was in such a hurry to see you."

"Well." She moved to the door. "We'd best get up to the parsonage in that case."

"Will you let me court you, Macy?" Will pulled the door open, but paused her before she went down the steps. "Will you give me the chance to prove my feelings for you? To treat you like the precious woman you are?"

His words touched her. The earnestness of his expression did, too. She faced him straight on and locked eyes with his. "We're in a tough country out here, Will."

He nodded. The past winter had shown that, sure enough.

"And none of us knows how much time we have to do good on this earth."

That was also true, but what was her point?

"So I'd like to propose a compromise."

A compromise? He didn't want a compromise, he wanted a marriage, straight and true. He wanted a wife, and not just any wife. He wanted *her*, Macy Evers, and he would make it his personal goal to help erase all those early sorrows of her life as they raised these two beautiful children the way God intended. With two parents who loved them and cherished them.

"Why don't we forego the whole courtship idea—"

Her eyes twinkled up at him. Will looked down at her as realization dawned. "And just get married?" he asked as he dropped to one knee. Her happy face said he was on the right track. "Macy Evers, will you do me the honor of becoming my wife and the mother to my wonderful little daughter?"

She leaned down and planted the sweetest of kisses to his mouth, a kiss that put him in mind of finding a judge, right quick. "I would be delighted to be your wife, Will."

He stood back up. "I don't have a ring."

"We've got two kids, Will. I think that's even better than a ring. Don't you?"

Oh, he did. He clasped her against his chest gently, mindful of the baby, enfolding her in his arms and near his heart, exactly where he wanted her forevermore. Little Will started squawking louder and longer. He took the baby, re-settled him in one arm, and offered his future wife the other arm. "Let's head home and take care of our little guy. And Macy if you decide you want to keep working for Hattie once we're married, we can juggle who's watching the children, day to day. My job's flexible."

"Your job is flexible until more folks figure out you saved Buck's life," she replied. "I expect things will get busier then, but I'd like to help Hattie in the shop when I can. I like learning new things and putting my hand to fine work. It makes me feel good inside."

Will understood the importance of feeling good inside. He'd lived the lack of it for too many years. "I think it's a fine idea. And we'll make do as the days go on. Together."

She sent him a smile so bright and fine, Will decided right then God had sent her here, to Second Chance, South Dakota, with him in mind. His blessing… and as he planted a kiss to the baby's cheek, he realized it was more than a blessing. It was his atonement at long last.

And it felt wonderful.

Epilogue

"MACY."
Macy heard the note in Will's voice late November, the one that said "trouble" and she hurried to the back door. "What's wrong? What's happened?"

"It seems my reputation for strays is alive and well." He lifted a small, brown-haired little girl into his arms.

The child shrieked in fear, old enough to know she didn't belong in the parsonage. Will crooned, cooing soft words of comfort as he brought her inside.

"It's another child." Chickie whispered the words with reverence as she came down from upstairs, as if taking in stray children was something special. After the past summer, Macy knew it was. "What's her name?"

"I don't know." Macy looked the wailing girl over as best she could, then said, "Aha!" She removed a scrap of paper tucked up the child's sleeve. "I've taken sick, bad sick. Please look after Jessie. She needs a good home." She peeked around Will's arm to face the still bawling child. "Come here, Jessie, girl. Come see your new mama, darling."

"Her new what?" Will sounded surprised which was just plain silly. Didn't he preach about God providing for this, that and the other thing? Macy was newly faithful enough to believe it wholeheartedly.

"Her mama of course." Macy shushed the little girl by whispering her name as she sank into the rocking chair. "A sweet thing likes this needs to be looked after. She needs a place that loves children and makes them feel special no matter what their circumstances."

Will gazed down at the sad child, then knelt beside her. "Then you're right, this is just the place, I expect. What do you think, Chickie? A little sister?"

"Oh to have a brother and a sister is the best ever!" Chickie proclaimed. She hugged her father, then knelt by Macy's other side. "We'll have three children in the family! I'm so happy!"

"I can't disagree," said Will, as his eyes twinkled up at Macy.

"Well…" Macy reached out a hand to Chickie's curls, so soft and full. "I think we're going to have to figure on four, Chickie Barber. And I can't tell you if the next one is a boy or a girl, but I can tell you it will be born in softer weather than we've got today."

"Ma, are you going to have a baby? For real?" Chickie's eyes went wide. She stared up at Macy, then clapped her hands together. "I can't believe this! Three babies and a pink dress! This is the best year I've ever had!"

"Chickie and I are in full agreement," declared Will, grinning. "And I expect that with our change of circumstances here, you might not be available to help Hattie as much as you thought." He filled a small tin cup half full of water for Jessie. The child peeked up at him, grabbed the cup and nearly swallowed it whole before sighing.

Macy cuddled her as Will drew up another ladle of water. "Then it's most fortunate that Hattie has sent for another helper from Pittsburgh. A very accomplished dressmaker should be arriving on Tuesday. Her name is Nellie and I hear she's got a fine hand with tucks and gathers, Chickie."

"No one's better than you, Ma." Sincerity deepened Chickie's declaration. "You're the best sewer and the best mother anyone ever had!"

Macy gave her oldest daughter a half-hug, delighted. She might not be the best sewer or the best mother yet, but

Macy hadn't shirked from taking challenges as a child and she wasn't afraid to do it now. "I don't have to be the best, darling." She smiled at Will over Chickie's head. "I just have to be good enough."

The baby stirred upstairs. Will stood. "Looks like I'll be writing my sermon tomorrow. Or by lamplight," he decided. "I'll get the baby."

"Did you save any of Chickie's clothes, Will?" Macy asked as Jessie tucked her chin further into her chest and yawned widely.

He shook his head as he settled Little Will in the middle of the rag-rug floor covering. "I'm sorry to say I didn't, but I bet the Hardy's have an outfit or two around. How would that be, Chickie? A trip to Sadie's house? You can see the girls and Ma can mind the little ones."

"I'd love to go visit! If it's okay with Ma of course." Chickie had stood quickly, but now she turned back to Macy. "Do you need me here? To help with Little Will and Jessie?"

Macy shook her head. "You go with your Pa and see if you two can scare up some clothes for our new girl. Chickie, you've got a good eye for color, so I'm depending on you."

Will's daughter drew herself up taller, pleased with the new responsibility. "We'll get it all set!"

She grabbed her wrap and raced straight to the barn while Will watched. "You've been good for her, Macy. She's growing up faster than I want, but so well that I can't complain." He bent down and gave her a kiss, a good long kiss, and when he went to kiss her again, Macy nudged him away. "Get on with you, Will. I'm going to lay this child on a cot and snuggle that one." She indicated Little Will, pushing his body up onto all fours, nearly able to crawl. "By the time you get back, the stew should be ready and we'll see who sleeps tonight and who doesn't."

Will moved toward the door with a confidence he'd never had before. Macy didn't fuss over the added responsibility.

She welcomed it.

She didn't fret over loss of sleep.

She shrugged it off as if it wasn't any old thing, though Will knew there were days she was bone-tired. Being with child sapped a woman's strength, but that made sense to Will. Growing a body, sheltering a new life had to require its share of energy, but Macy never complained. That gave him just one more thing to love about her.

He followed Chickie outside, hitched up the wagon, and headed for Buck and Adeline's claim, a different man from the one who traveled there months before. A man with purpose, a man of decision, a man with a family. Now he understood the joy in Buck Hardy's eyes when he was going to be okay, and the grief he'd read in Adeline's when she feared for Buck's life. The price of a fine wife was as the good Lord said, far above rubies.

He had Macy. Sweet, hard-working, beautiful, loving Macy, a gift from God. Will clucked to the horses, fiercely content, pretty sure he was the luckiest man in the world.

By far.

FROM THE DIARY OF

Harriet Beth McGillicuddy,

FOR POSTERITY:

IT WAS SURELY A BEAUTIFUL wedding, simple and true. There were a few local women who tucked aside hopes and dreams of marrying our good pastor when Macy walked down that little church aisle, but Jean Ellen and I think God intended Macy for Will all the while. And didn't Chickie look fine in her new pink dress, scattering wildflower blossoms along the rough wood floor? Not one person minded the board floor or the need for new paint inside, such was the radiance of the bride and groom.

The gifts were small but useful! Jars of this and sides of that, sacks of flour, beans, sugar and salt. A fine bounty!

The nip in the night air tells me we'll be pulling pumpkins before long, squashes, too, but Jean Ellen is sending a likely young woman my way by name of Nellie. Maybe she'll lend me a hand putting things by when she comes to start her new life here in Second Chance.

Hattie's Rosemary Shortbread Cookies

1 cup butter, softened
1 1/2 cup confectioners' sugar
2 ¼ cups all-purpose flour
1 egg
2 tablespoons minced fresh rosemary
1/2 teaspoon salt

Directions

In a large bowl, cream butter and confectioners' sugar until light and fluffy. Add egg. Mix well. Combine the flour, rosemary and salt; gradually add to creamed mixture and mix well.

Shape into two 8-1/4-in. rolls; wrap each in plastic. Refrigerate overnight. Cut into 1/4-in. slices. Place 2 in. apart on ungreased baking sheets.

Bake at 350° for 11-13 minutes or until edges begin to brown. Cool for 1 minute before removing from pans to wire racks. Store in an airtight container.

DEAR READER,
   I hope you loved this sweet story of faith, hope and love set in my newest historic town "Second Chance", South Dakota.

I love stories of good overcoming evil, of good people reaching out a helping hand to others, of that pioneer spirit that meant so much to the growth of our nation!

And don't you love Hattie McGillicuddy? She's not just smart, she's a woman of action, and I love take-charge women. And I'm anxious to see if her plan of bringing women west will work for their betterment and the betterment of our little town of "Second Chance". My guess is: Yes! ☺

Thank you for reading "The Pastor Takes a Wife". May God bless you in all you do, and may you always see the second chances coming your way!

Second Chance Christmas

A Sewing Sisters Society Story

Ruth Logan Herne

Dedication

This sweet story is dedicated to my beloved aunt, Myrtle Isabelle Herne Roth, whose example of hard work and honesty showed me the many options available for women. Thank you, "Sis" for taking the time to be nice to a little kid!

"...She seeketh wool and flax and worketh willingly with her hands..."

~ Proverbs 31: 13

Chapter One

S HE'D ESCAPED WITH THE MONEY sewn into the hem of her petticoat, the clothes on her back, and the one simple frock she'd snatched from the clothes line before the Allegheny City police came to arrest her.

Nellie Bausch glared out the window of the west-bound train, half-wishing she'd stayed in Pittsburgh, just to show up the troop of interfering old biddies. Common sense took hold, though.

Money would have ruled the day as it generally did along Ridgewood Avenue, and she would have spent the next two years languishing in prison. She'd been riding high the past three years, her beautiful clothing in demand by all of the wealthiest ladies of Pittsburgh. Blessedly, she'd lived well beneath her means and she'd been smart enough to squirrel money aside.

Money she'd earned by the work of her hands, despite the well-staged story cooked up by several of her wealthy clientele. As a plain, dusty, brown town came into view up ahead, she stared out the window, stared hard, and in her mind she didn't see the drab, dust-strewn buildings rising before her.

Nellie saw potential.

God had given her a lace-making mother and a clever eye for making things pretty and from what she saw right now, Second Chance, South Dakota could use all the help it could get in the 'making things pretty' department. The train groaned to a stop and Nellie lifted her satchel and one small bag. She didn't have to wait while others disembarked, because she seemed to be the only person making this sleepy, prairie town a final destination.

Well, good for her.

No need to fish out the note in her pocket, she knew just where she was going. Hattie McGillicuddy's Shirt Shop, Fine Goods Available by Order. Now if she could only find someone to show her the way. The temperature was dropping quickly as the chilled November day met the colder night while the sun stretched thin on the western horizon.

She turned on the narrow platform and spotted movement at the wagon and metal shop across the way. Human life. *Perfect.* After the constant hustle and bustle back east, the lack of activity here was already making her palms itch. Heat from the smithy forge warmed her chilled face as she approached. "Sir?"

Focused on the job at hand, the man stayed forward-facing, bent over a curve of metal.

"Sir?"

His hammer tapped repeatedly, and a strong, firm profile matched the task at hand.

Should she walk away? Clearly he wasn't hearing her, unless he was just rudely ignoring her…

He turned just then.

Soot marked his left cheek, but Nellie didn't pay one lick of attention to that because a pair of the most gorgeous blue eyes, framed by long, thick lashes above a dangerous-looking five-o'clock shadow left her speechless, and Nellie was never speechless.

But then awareness rose in his face.

Not the good kind. The kind that looked downright annoyed by something, and since she was the only thing around, Nellie was pretty sure she'd inspired the aggravation.

As his eyes moved from the tips of her toes to her hand-stitched and very regal hat, his mouth dropped open. He set the tools down, scowled and faced her head on. "What?"

Rude by half, and that was a preposterous thing after she'd just spent all that time coming to this desolate spot of nut-chafed brown on brown. "I could use directions, if you would be so kind. To Hattie McGillicuddy's sewing shop."

His look of disdain deepened, and she hadn't thought that possible. "We only have six roads in town, Miss."

"But it is getting late," she told him, determined to keep cheerful, although she was sorely tempted to give him a good kick in the shins for disparaging her outfit like that. Back east, this kind of dress would have cost dearly, and people would have paid willingly.

You're not back east, Nellie. Simple is more normal on the prairie.

Well, forgive her for not having time to whip up a few more simple dresses before being tried and convicted for a crime she didn't commit.

He sighed, frowned, turned and pointed. "Turn left on Second Avenue after the lumber mill sign. The mill's set back from the road to make use of the creek and the rails, but if you turn there, Hattie's shop is just down a piece, on the right. If you get to Cutter Road, you've gone too far."

She curtseyed, and when his brows shot up higher, she realized an old-fashioned curtsey was probably another bit of overdone propriety out here.

Good, because she hated curtseying, she wasn't a big proponent of anything that made women or workers feel less than others, and that wasn't about to change. She'd toss the curtsey overboard gladly, but looking good and dressing nicely?

There was nothing wrong with that and this, this… *smithy*, with dirt on his face, could like it or not. One could be humble and still look good, the Bible was full of examples, although as she started to move away, she realized the extra bows at each tuck of her layered skirt might be considered a bit much. She wasn't here to impress the local metalworker, though, even if he did have the most amazingly gorgeous blue eyes she'd ever seen.

She bobbed her head in pretend thanks, and turned with an intentional flounce.

Most of her skirt turned with her. The part that danced along the edge of the smithy's poker started smoking, instantly.

"You're on fire!" Slow? Hard of hearing? Focused?

Oh, the metal worker was focused now, all right, as he hoisted a bucket of soiled water and doused the smoking, smoldering skirt and her with filthy, ice-cold water.

She shrieked softly, for two reasons. One, it was wretchedly cold weather for bathing in frigid water and she felt the chill to the core of her being. And two, he'd just ruined her only dress other than the plain cotton calico in her bag. And two petticoats, and a chemise and…

Propriety said she should stop there, but the gaping burn hole that went straight through three layers showed that her stockings weren't burnt… just gray with smithy-water.

She stared down, distraught.

"Did it burn you? Do you need a doc? We have one. He's a preacher, too, so if you need a preacher, he can do both."

She pulled her cape around her more tightly. If she'd done that in the first place, the swoosh of her skirts wouldn't have fluffed so near the red-hot poker, and replacing a wool panel would have been much easier than ruining an entire skirt and its array of underpinnings. "I'm not burnt, just ruined, but that seems to be my current lot in life, Mr.?"

"Eichas." He stepped back and moved toward the shed opening. "I'll walk you down to Hattie's, you've had a good scare."

"And then some," she muttered. He started to reach out a hand to help her over a rough, rutted spot in the road, but then he glanced at his dirty hand and her arm and must have decided against it. Good thing, too, because she didn't need to replace anything else at the moment. He strode quick, in hard, long steps, as if walking her to the seamstress's shop was possibly the worst punishment ever, and when they got there, he stepped back.

"I'll pay for any repairs to your dress." He looked angry, as if paying for a dress was wrong beyond words. But beyond the anger, he looked almost... vulnerable. For a brief moment he appeared to have the weight of the world on his shoulders. Sending her up in flames seemed to add to an already lengthy list of regrets.

Well, join the club.

She turned away from the sorrow in his gaze, climbed the steps and forced her shoulders back. She didn't know Hattie McGillicuddy, and the impression she was about to make wasn't the way she envisioned their first meeting. Wet to the skin in a half-burnt dress, showing off her undergarments, and covered in smithy dirt and dust. But if Jean Ellen's friend didn't take one look and throw her straight out the door, then maybe she'd come to the right place after all.

If ever a woman was in the wrong place, this was her and Second Chance was it, Levi decided as he retraced his steps back to the smithy.

Gussied up dresses. Fancy ribbons and bows. Layers and fluff and ruffly things.

You caught her on fire.

Levi's heart had stopped. Luckily his hands had no such option, and the look on her face when he doused the burning gown with soot-water indicated she wanted to kill him.

She might yet, after she got warm, but that look— as if she couldn't have gotten any lower on the ladder of life, and then did— cut him to the core.

He'd seen that look before. His stepmother had been a fancy dress-wearing woman, and she'd tried her best to talk his father out of coming west, but they'd come because everyone did what Henry Eichas said.

And then she'd left him, his three younger sisters and her tough-as-nails husband, as if being there, being their mother and Henry's wife, wasn't good enough.

"Levi." His sister Rachel hailed him from the opposite side of the road. "I brought the wagon in to pick up that lumber. We can ride back home together."

"I can't go, yet. I've got stuff to finish."

She crossed the rutted road. "This late? You said you'd be done by sunset."

"Gotta work when we've got work and I got interrupted."

"Interrupted? So you have to feed the fire again?"

"Pump it up, leastways. Either that or start cold tomorrow, and that would be a sorry waste of fuel."

"It would, I'll wait," she decided. "I can go visit the mercantile for a little bit or stop by Hattie's and chat."

"The mercantile would be best, I expect Hattie's got her hands full with her new apprentice right now."

"She's here?"

Rachel had the nerve to sound excited by the prospect, although Levi couldn't begin to imagine why. The deepening shadows hid his wince from his sister. "Yes."

"Macy told me she's got a fine way with tucks and smocking, old and new all at once. Hattie's friend back east called her a wonder with a needle, and won't that be a treat?"

A treat?

Sweet, sensible Rachel waxing enthusiastic over the prospect of fancy dresses? "Not much need for fancy on the frontier, Rachel. Out here, things need a use, a purpose. Use it up, wear it out. I don't see extra buttons and bows being cut up into dish rags, do you?"

"Of course you don't see it, Levi. But you could, if you tried."

He couldn't see her face. He didn't have to. The grim acceptance in her voice said she'd go along, of course. But not because she wanted to. Because she was half-afraid not to.

"Rachel, I—"

"I'll be back in thirty minutes. Does that give you enough time?"

It should. He nodded, mad at himself, mad at their parents, mad at life. "Yes."

She walked off in her simple gray dress, unadorned. His sisters made their own dresses and aprons with the patterns their father had purchased as they came of age. Watching Rachel, he realized their dresses didn't look like the other girls in town. They were plainer. Squarer. Not fitted the way that little seamstress's gown fit, in any case, with all the right curves in all the right places.

Funny, he'd never noticed such a thing before, but for the last four years they'd all been working from morning until bed, trying to eke a living out of thick-grassed prairie by using the money he earned at the shop. The shop had a rough start, then did well once the flood of Irish came out Yankton way. But they'd had a sorrow-filled winter. Lots of folks had given up their claims and headed back east where things were still tough, but in a different way. It had been a lean summer. Fewer people making money meant fewer people spending money. But now they'd been declared a state of the union, and the very word held promise.

They'd proved up their claims nearly five years before, so he owned the land and the shop, free and clear. And he had a pouch of money put by, from his father. Enough for each girl to have a small wedding gift and to add stock annually. But then it occurred to him that the girls rarely saw anyone. They only came to town for occasional church services and supply runs for the claims.

If no one ever saw them, how would they get married? And weren't those his father's final instructions, when he handed over that drawstring pouch? "Keep the stock growing, don't skimp when you buy good breeders, and give your sisters their share of this for wedding money when the time comes. I've held it back from them, to raise 'em up proper, and not wanting frippery to spoil their minds or their hands to hard work. Hard work will build this country. The weak won't last out here. And the farm and the business are yours, Levi. My only son."

Levi stoked the fire, reheated the metal, and when things were just right, he applied the metal band to the wagon wheel, punching the nails into place as the metal cooled in a water bath.

The weak won't last out here.

His father's mantra, part truth, part dictator.

Henry hadn't been a nice person. He'd married a woman who wanted finer things in life, and then didn't give them to her, deliberately.

That was cruel.

Not like beating people, cruel. Henry Eichas was too subtle for that. But cruel, nonetheless, and here was Levi, a wainwright and wheelwright, working wood and metal the way his father had done before him, knowing how to add bone dust to strengthen, and how to forge tools and metal strapping.

Given a choice, he could live on the carpentry side of the shop. He loved the smell and feel of wood, but to design the wagons he loved so well, he needed both skills. Since his father's death, Levi had run both sides of the shop, all day, every day, save Sunday when he turned his hand to farm work with the girls.

He loved creating wagons, but what would he do when

his sisters left the farm? What then?

He didn't know. Will Barber would advise letting God work things out, but then the kind-hearted pastor didn't have three marriageable sisters in his care.

He finished up and carted the coals over to the inn. "Thelma, I've got coals here."

"Levi!" She smiled as he unloaded the cart of hot coals into her stove with the heavy-duty metal bucket. In turn, she handed him two loaves of bread and a cake. "This is a perfect barter, Levi Eichas!"

He laughed because Mrs. Thornton always made him laugh. "Well, you get old coals, half burnt and we get good food, fresh from the bakery. I expect I'm getting the better end of this deal."

"And I see it the other way, so we're both happy." She smiled at him. "There's Rachel heading our way, you go on now. But I'm hoping you'll all be coming into town for the Thanksgiving feast next week, Levi. We're joining the country as a new state, celebrating that which we still have. Our freedom to make our own way." She indicated the bread with a glance. "And we'll pray for those lost in last year's harsh weather."

"Eating together? The whole town?" He must have looked as surprised as he felt, because there'd been little time for town get-togethers since the Eichas family moved to Second Chance fourteen years before.

"Exactly that, at the church and it's high time, too," she declared. "Evening, Rachel. Did you happen to see my Thomas over at the mercantile?"

"Buying molasses, I did."

"Then I expect he'll be right along," Mrs. Thornton added. "A safe ride home, you two."

"Thank you." Rachel turned as Levi pushed the cart back toward the shop. "Was Mrs. Thornton telling you about the Thanksgiving Day celebration?"

"She was."

"Ginny mentioned it at the mercantile, and I put us down to bring potatoes and a roast of beef."

"Without asking?" The words came out before Levi thought fully, and Rachel's expression showed her displeasure.

"You're my brother, not my father, Levi." She climbed into the wagon with a firm clip to the movement and her voice.

"I know this, Rachel."

"Do you?" She turned to face him when he climbed onto the wagon seat. "Do you see the things you do to make me— us," she corrected herself, meaning her, Esther and Miriam, "toe the line? While your work in town is important, our work on the farm is equally so."

It was, but wasn't he supposed to be in charge, being the oldest? "Of course it is."

"Don't placate me, Levi." Her voice toughened. "Our father left directives, and I respected all of his hard work, but Levi," She paused for a moment. "He was a man riddled with faults. Can't we work to be our own people, now? Now that he's gone?"

He'd been thinking the same thing, but it sounded riskier coming from his sister. "We can, but it's hard, Rachel. With so much to be done, and so little time to do it."

"Then perhaps the fault lies in our attempts, for the good Lord has made the days as they are for thousands of years."

She was right. He knew that. And hearing her discontent made him see his own more clearly. But what were their options, for real? So many had left the prairie after years of struggle. His trade, passed down from his father, allowed them finances to weather storms and bugs and drought. Divided, they would all fall, and despite his longing for happiness, the sensibilities of hard work and a communal spirit had gotten them this far. "Isn't it better to be comfortable and industrious, than impoverished, with time on our hands?"

"You twist my meaning, because you know we can do both."

"Rachel." He directed the horses along the single trail southwest, out of town at an easy, steady pace. "If I knew how to accomplish that, we'd already be doing it."

Chapter Two

"WHAT IN THE NAME OF all that's right and holy has happened to you, child?" A largish woman hopped up with more alacrity than Nellie would have supposed when Nellie walked through the door of the sewing shop. "Merciful heavens, you're tattered, torn and soaked to the skin."

"Don't forget burned." Nellie pulled her cloak wide and lifted the left side of her once-beautiful skirt. "Through three layers. Who knew that forge equipment would get that hot?"

"This happened at Levi's place?"

Nellie peeled her cape off and Hattie hung it on a hook a good distance from the Franklin stove. "Is Levi the fairly young blacksmith?"

"With old eyes, that's him. Oh, my dear." Hattie clucked and fussed over the dress as if it was a mortal wound. "Let's get you out of all that, wrap you up and tuck you into something else. I'm so very sorry this happened, what a dreadful first impression you now have of Second Chance. Give me your satchel, I'll grab you another gown and I'll have someone run to the platform for your trunk. You must be plumb wore out, Nellie."

It was now or never. She looked straight at Hattie and blurted out the truth. "There is no trunk, I was lucky to get out of Allegheny City with the clothes I was wearing. There's one dress, no night clothes, and there was nowhere to stop on the train to re-group and buy things. I'm afraid you've got me," she made a face because she was pretty disreputable at the moment, "and one work dress."

"Oh, there's a story to be heard for sure!" Hattie pulled out the single work dress and a length of toweling from a back shelf and handed both to Nellie. "You run on back there and get yourself cozy while I make tea. We've got fresh bread and I made a bean soup that sticks to the ribs and once we have you fed and warm, we'll figure out a sewing party to set your clothing to rights. Leaving in a hurry like that had to be vexing."

"Being wrongly accused of thievery and over-charging was worse," Nellie told her when she slipped out from behind the curtain. "I've never cheated, never stolen, and as for over-charging, only those with a great deal of money tend to quibble about paying proper coin for a well-done job."

"There's truth in what you say, more's the pity, but come here, sit down and have a bite. I'm so sorry to hear about your troubles. Jean Ellen sent word that you stirred up a bit of a beehive on Ridgewood Avenue."

"It wasn't even my beehive," Nellie told her. "But when a rich woman's son takes a shine to a working girl, you'd think society as a whole was threatened with extinction."

"You speak well."

"St. Mary's Academy in Pittsburgh, a marvelous school. I couldn't go on to finish high school once my father was killed in the labor uprising, but they gave me strong basics. I like to read." She shrugged. "And study things. How they work, how they go together, what works well."

"That's a fine talent and a solid base." Hattie lifted the steaming teakettle and filled the cosy-covered pot. "We'll let that steep, but don't let me forget it. I've been known to do that when the conversation is right, and I expect that's the case tonight."

"There's not much more to say, in truth." Nellie savored another spoon of delicious broth. "Things were set up to make it look like I took an expensive brooch from Mrs. Goldblum's collection. Of course I didn't, but the brooch *was* in my sewing bag and when I found it there, I panicked."

"What did you do?"

"I put it back, of course. I never thought about folks really believing I'd take anything. I was making money, paying my bills, and working hard." She met Hattie's gaze across the small table. "I was respected, and that felt wonderful. So when a certain steel mogul's son started paying mind to me, I was flattered but not the least bit interested."

Hattie didn't try to hide a look of doubt. "The steel families have done quite well, and to marry into one of them is a rare fortune for a woman."

"From my observations, men of great fortune rarely wish to *marry* working class girls," Nellie replied. "Flirt with them, yes. Enjoy a dalliance? Yes, again. But I wasn't interested in any of that, and when he pushed the matter, I may have blackened his eye."

"No."

"Yes. To his mother's chagrin, and it wasn't enough to cast me out of their house and not use my services and bad talk me to everyone who'd listen. Mrs. Cumberbie wanted me out of Pittsburgh, and she wasn't afraid to use whatever means at her disposal to make sure it happened. Hence the brooch in my bag, and the police coming to search my little walk-up not far from where Jean Ellen lives."

"You didn't take the brooch."

"No, ma'am, I did not, nor would I have. An immortal soul is a precious possession, and mine means a great deal to me. Staining it with an act of thievery when I had plenty of money and goods in my possession would have been foolish, and I haven't entertained the option to be foolish in nearly a decade."

"Where did you learn your sewing techniques?" Hattie asked. "Jean Ellen says they're quite advanced."

"Two things, actually." She sipped broth again and sighed happily. "This is quite delicious. I would love to learn better cooking skills while we work together, because that is a part of my education that went by the wayside. Now, back to the question. My mama was a German lace maker."

"How delightful!"

"It was," Nellie agreed. "She had a clever hand at design. With needles or bobbins, it didn't much matter, her creations were beauty and strength, woven seamlessly together."

"And the other part?"

"Well, this will sound odd, but I love puzzles."

Hattie frowned, clearly puzzled herself.

Nellie laughed at the face she made, then sat back. "Deciding the subtleties of a gown is like a mystery, isn't it? If I pull here," she pointed a finger in the air to her left. "What effect does it have there?" Her other hand indicated a lower section of imaginary material. "If I nip and tuck, then gather, will the flow be just right, or will it make the wearer look big? And if stays are tucked just so, is the wearer comfortable or gouged? So many little thoughts go into making the simplest of gowns look their best."

"I've never heard it put better, and I can't wait to see your work, but I will wait," Hattie decided as she stood. "Because I think we could both use a night's rest. We'll get busy first thing tomorrow, and help plan the food for next Thursday's Thanksgiving celebration, a way to celebrate our new statehood."

"A town Thanksgiving?" The thought of a whole town celebrating together seemed odd. "With everyone in the town gathering together?"

"Like a New England pot luck dinner, only planned. There won't be turkey, but we've got meat promised from a few folks, including Levi's family, so we'll work hard between now and then, and we women will cook up a storm. You'll have multiple lessons at once."

"God has blessed me as a quick learner, but I don't want to be the possible ruination of the very first Thanksgiving dinner for a brand new state."

Hattie laughed and shrugged an arm around her shoulders. "I'll keep your tasks simple. And your skirts away from fire."

"Wise words." Nellie noted the hot stove with a glance. "Rooms in the big houses are broader and stoves are caged."

"And when you're busy carving towns out of prairie dust, that action alone takes the majority of effort. Bigger rooms come with future generations."

"So simplicity isn't just advised, it's truly a necessity."

"Pretty much."

Nellie turned to Hattie and gave her an impetuous hug. "Well, there's my challenge. One of many I've noted since arriving. How to make simple look pretty, and places more inviting."

Hattie's smile went wide. "I knew you'd do all right here, although I expect a few toes will be stepped on in the way of it. But in the end, I think you're just what Second Chance needs, Nellie Bausch."

Nellie thought so, too. But if all the town took Levi Eichas's viewpoint, Nellie had her work cut out for her.

Chapter Three

"WHAT IF IT SNOWS? HEAVEN knows we've gotten early blizzards before." The young woman named Samantha wrinkled her brow the next morning as her mother penciled a list beside her. Hattie had introduced them both, Ginny Beltry and her daughter Samantha. Ginny and her husband Hi ran the general store on Main Street.

"Blizzards?" Nellie looked around the room full of women. "Full-fledged blizzards hit this far west?"

"With common regularity, so we prepare in advance," Hattie reassured her. "But in this case, we need to be ready and hope for clear weather. There's no changing the skies or a man's love of good cooking, so as long as we abide by that, we'll be fine. I've warmed up many a meal in my time. If we get snowed out, we can agree to gather the following Sunday, all that are able. Which reminds me, Ginny." She turned toward the shopkeeper's plump, pretty wife. "In case of bad weather and no train, can you get in enough shirting cotton to get me through a few months of orders?"

"Gladly. And while I have deep regard for a variety of fabrics, I have to say the rich, regal tones that just arrived are some of the nicest looks I've ever seen come west."

The group of women moved to see the new display. A young woman wearing a squared-off, sack-like gray dress caressed the bolt of deep blue. "Miriam, this is the exact color of your eyes."

"And Levi's." The slightly smaller woman grazed a finger over the cloth. She was wearing a similar dress, austere in its plain, squared lines. "So well-made, it's like a pleasure to touch."

"And it wears well," Nellie told them easily, because talking about fabrics and notions was dear to her heart. "There are so many threads per inch and the dye inlaid, just so, that using a material like this, or any on this table, in fact, gives great value. Although I'd not advise it for a work dress, but for something special or going to church, this is beautiful and quite a bargain at Ginny's prices."

"Ginny and Hi mind folk's pockets as well as their coffers," Hattie remarked and the whole group nodded.

"What about you, Rachel?" Miriam pointed toward the end of the table. "I think that rich brown and gold would go well with your coloring."

"You've got a wonderful eye." Nellie met Miriam's gaze. "With ivory lace accenting a ruched outer skirt, double-tucked, but not too wide." She winced, remembering yesterday's catastrophe.

"Oh, I can imagine it with ivory lace." Rachel turned toward Nellie. "You do have a knack for these things. I'd have never imagined such a dress, but your words make me see it."

"And Samantha, this softer blue with sprigs of yellow is perfect for a blue-eyed blonde, but you can wear the deeper pinks, too."

"What would you pick for Esther, Rachel?" Miriam studied the new fabric. "Esther's at home, tending things so we can be here. She's built like Rachel, only smaller, but looks more like Levi."

"But not as grumpy," Rachel noted.

"Ahem." The surprising sound of Levi clearing his throat just inside the door changed the room's atmosphere.

Rachel's face went flat. Miriam's did the same. Samantha looked worried, and Nellie was pretty sure no one man should have the power to change a fun gathering with one throat-clearing sound. She moved his way. "A sunny nature is a wonderful thing in a woman, and industry is hugely important in a good man. It is nice to see you again, Mr. Eichas."

He studied her as if trying to figure her out, as if she was a mystery, but then he did something quite surprising.

He smiled.

Her heart lurched. Her breath caught. Blood ceased to simply flow in her turncoat veins. It raced, from stem to stern, driving her color up, no doubt.

"Pounding metal is stern work for sure, but I will try to be less grumpy."

"Levi, I'm sorry." Worry darkened Rachel's face as she moved away from the beautiful fabric. "I should never have spoken like that."

"I was being too light-hearted as well." Miriam moved to his side. "You've worked hard to keep things going and we all appreciate that effort."

"And now that we've made decisions on food, Miri and I must get back and help Esther with afternoon chores. Ladies, it was a pleasure to work with you." Rachel pulled on her cloak and tied a scarf around her head. Miriam did the same, then turned toward Nellie and grasped her hands. "Thank you for sharing your wisdom with us. Now I can look at fabric and see things more clearly."

"Like a picture puzzle."

"Yes, exactly!" Miriam squeezed her hands and let go. "Levi, we'll see you later."

"Yes."

Ginny bustled over. "Now, Levi, what can I get for you?"

"A short list, a few things I'm low on at the shop."

Ginny accepted the list and she and Samantha gathered the items quickly. Hattie moved back to the fabric side of the shop, leaving Nellie facing Levi.

He swept her plain dress a look and frowned. "I'd still

like to pay for your ruined gown, Miss."

"Not if it makes you grumpy."

To her surprise, he smiled softly. "Well, there's that." He lifted his shoulders. "I should try and do better, there's no joy in grouchiness. Whereas in our brief meetings, you seem well-equipped to turn things around as needed."

"I cannot fret about what can't be changed, but in my head I see ways to change so much, and that's reason enough to be happy."

"A simplistic reasoning for a complicated woman."

His words struck her, and then she followed his gaze to her plain dress and understood the comparison. "Liking pretty clothing doesn't make me complicated. It makes me feel good about being me. And when your work is with fabric and trim and lace, the best advertising is to wear something that looks good. Something I made."

"You don't see that as showing off?"

She laughed and pointed out the door. "You have a spit-polished buckboard in the bay of your shop. Does it do you well to make it plainer than it needs to be, or does it speak well of your work for it to gleam in the sunlight? For the leather seat to be soft, and cushioned?"

"I almost don't like that you make sense." He glanced down the street, then back to her. "Of course a wagon must deal with a great deal of stress."

"As does every woman I know."

His brows knit tight, but then he smiled again, and this time he smiled right into her eyes and about near sent her heart into apoplexy. "You've won this round, Miss?" He left the question open-ended.

"Nellie. Nellie Bausch. Note that I'm not curtseying, and I thank you for your advice on that, Mr. Eichas."

"Levi."

"Levi."

The softness of his name coming off her lips put him in mind of things he hadn't given consideration to before.

He considered them now, seeing her smile, hearing her voice, and yet, wasn't this the exact kind of woman who'd left their family high and dry years before? Why would he even entertain such an idea? On this he could agree with his father. A woman not meant for the prairie, shouldn't be on the prairie.

And yet your father brought your stepmother here purposely.

The twinge of conscience bothered Levi. His father had never done anything on chance. His deliberateness was good in wood crafting and metallurgy, but might be called cunning in life.

"Nellie, come pick some fabric so we can make a new skirt."

Levi winced. "A narrower one. Please."

"I've learned my lesson, for certain. But it was my carelessness that caught the heat, Levi. The fault was never yours."

Gracious and kind. Why did that surprise him?

"And now I must pick some quick material and get back to the shop. Have you ever considered window curtains for your business, Levi Eichas?"

"Why on earth would I?"

She paused, and in her eyes he could almost see what she was seeing. "Not the forging side, but the carpentry side where you display the wagons. You have two fine windows there, common enough back east, but a dear thing here in the west. If you were to frame those windows in calico or a bright check, it makes the entire wagon display side look more inviting. And inviting windows bring folks in off the street."

"Well, in case you hadn't noticed, our streets are a little scant of late."

"But that won't always be the case, will it?" She frowned slightly. "Sure, you've had a bad year out here, the news of storms and loss made the eastern papers, but if that was the norm, we'd have never heard of it. The exceptions don't chart our course, Levi. They offer change and opportunity, but it's how we handle those exceptional moments that helps guide our way." She fluttered a hand as Ginny set down a small number of things on the counter. "Good day, Levi."

It hadn't been all that good a day. He'd been grumbly, then called out on being grumbly and that was one mirror he didn't care to look into. Surliness had been his father's nature. He remembered some of his natural mother, her smile, her scent, and sometimes her voice. Just glimpses, really, but those memories made him feel good. Maybe if he tried harder, he could embrace her softer nature. Take more for his mother than his father. He paid for his goods, and when he turned to go, Nellie and Hattie were in deep discussion about some bit of fancy. With her head bowed over the bolts, he could see she took the subject seriously.

No one should be that concerned about their style of dress, especially out here where nature and circumstance could wipe out a holding with little notice. Life took on a serious note when mortality and survival ruled the day.

He left the store, faintly disappointed that she didn't look up because he wanted her to glance his way.

She didn't and he found that even more disturbing than if she did.

"I've never seen a body get through a shirt that quickly." Joy deepened Hattie's praise. "And well done, too. That's a pleasure because we've got this stack of orders here, and Thelma was hoping we'd have time to make fourteen square tablecovers for the dining room at the inn."

"They have fourteen tables?" The thought of the small

inn with that many tables surprised Nellie.

"No, they've got seven, so a cloth for each, and a back-up for washing."

"That's a sight of laundry." Nellie pursed her lips. "Does she have a preference for color or material?"

"She said whatever I thought would look right, but if you want to head over there and give the room a look, maybe you'll come up with an idea."

"Do you mind?"

Hattie shook her head. "Not a bit, I'm going to make some biscuit dough to go with that gravy and there are two slices of meat, just perfect for the two of us. And baked pumpkin to go with it."

"Now there's a treat. Hot pumpkin with salt and pepper is a favorite."

"Well, good! I'll see you in a piece, then. Do you need to make notes?"

Nellie slipped a measuring tape into her pocket with a small pad of paper and a pencil. "Yes, so I'm all set. Do I need a note of introduction?"

"Oh, you dear sweet Easterner." Hattie's grin indicated no such thing was necessary. "Working Ridgewood Avenue and that whole North Side, I expect you needed your share of introductory notes, but not here. Here we're fine with a good hello and an honest handshake."

"Then I'm off." Nellie pulled on her cape, fastened her scarf securely, and slipped out the door. She shut it firmly. A stiff north wind had risen the past few hours. It tunneled down the narrow street, rattling signs along the way. She walked south, then turned left at the corner. Chin down, she cut diagonally across the rutted road, deep in thought.

"Whoa!"

The sharp command jerked her head up.

Twin horses pounded her way from out of nowhere.

Her heart leaped, but her feet refused to move. She stood, frozen in place, unable to scream, jump or do most anything a normal person would do to save their skins.

"Nell!" Strong arms whisked her to the right as the horses suddenly veered to her left. A whoosh of air splashed her face, showing just how close she'd come to being trampled. She hauled in a deep breath that seemed to go nowhere near her lungs.

Panic grabbed hold of her. She couldn't breathe, she couldn't think, and all she could see was the manic eyes of twin horses as they tossed their heads and reared back.

"I've got you. I've got you." Levi's deep, low voice cut through the fear. "Don't try to breathe so hard, just loosen your shoulders. Bending low can help, too, Nell."

His tone soothed. His voice brought comfort, and when he encouraged her to bend over, she did.

Her chest loosened. Air bathed her lungs, sweet air, and while that felt good, the entire incident stoked her in fear. "I never heard them coming." She straightened some, took a slow, deep breath, and sighed. "How can that be? One minute I was walking along, the next I was under attack."

"The wind whistles bad along this stretch." Levi helped her straighten and when she lifted her eyes to his, his worried expression seemed to make things better. "The wind and the noise of sign chains rattling must have covered the horse's approach."

A middle-aged man hurried across the road. "Are you all right, miss? Tom Bailey's overhead sign came crashing down in a good gust. Meadow spooked, and Willow took right off with her, as if they hadn't been teaming together for seven years now."

"I'm shaken, but fine, and that's mostly my own fault for not diving to the side. I froze." She exchanged looks with both men and hated to admit her own foolishness. "I don't know how that happened."

"You had sidewalks back east, I expect."

"Well, yes, but horses too. And wagons. And the occasional runaway."

"A boardwalk makes a difference, though," the older man suggested. "A horse ain't likely to go every which way, climbing and butting their heads on overhangs. They'll go straight or take a side road, most likely."

"You're graciousness is most kind," she told him, "but I have to learn not to daydream on the streets of Second Chance. I can see that now."

"Well, don't give up all your dreams, miss." The older man tipped his cowboy hat lightly. "Most of us come west with dreams. It's a land that can wreck those dreams or shore 'em up, one way or the other. Best to keep yours intact, but pay attention to the road while you're moseying."

"Advice well taken," she told him. "Are the horses all right?"

"Spooked by their own foolishness, but they'll be fine, and thank you for askin'. It was you I worried most for, and I'm might glad Levi took quick action, and didn't spill a coal in the process."

She hadn't noticed the barrow carrying two metal buckets of coals until that moment. She looked up at him and raised a brow in question.

"I take my late coals to the inn for the bakery ovens," he explained. "Waste not, want not. I just happened to be at the right place."

"You saved my life."

He brushed that off as Jed Forrest hurried after his horses, but Nellie took his hand in both of hers. "I was dumbstruck, Levi, and that's not a common occurrence for me, but I couldn't move for anything. Thank you for being there."

Chapter Four

GREEN/GOLD EYES, WARM AND COOL at once, framed in pretty lashes under not-too-thick brows. And her hair, a mix of raw and burnt umber, twin colors of the prairie. The fracas had loosened some locks from beneath the scarf, and when the wind teased and danced through the waving tresses, he wondered what it would be like for his hands to do the same thing. He held her gaze, and if decorum didn't dictate otherwise, he was tempted to lean down and kiss her, just to see what that was like. He was pretty sure it would be well beyond nice by any man's standards.

"Levi, is everything all right?" Reverend Barber called from behind him, and Levi was forced to break the connection and push thoughts of kissing aside. He turned as the reverend drew near.

"Fine, but a good scare for Hattie's new apprentice."

"You must be Nellie." The reverend extended his hand and offered Nellie a firm handshake. "My wife worked for Hattie and was quite pleased to hear you'd be coming west to take her place. Something about pin-tucks and gathers got her all wound up."

Nellie laughed, and Levi was pleased to hear it sounded like her normal laugh. Sweet and inviting. "Well, tucks and gathers will do that, for certain. It is a pleasure to meet you, Reverend, and I'll be pleased to join Hattie at service on Sunday."

"Our pleasure to have you, and then we're doing an

additional service of thanksgiving on Thursday, before the food festivities begin. Levi." Will Barber turned more fully his way. "Rachel told Macy you'd all be there, and Macy's excited at the prospect of working with your sisters."

"They're much the same," Levi admitted. "It got me thinking they need to get off the farm more often. Now that the weather's turning and food's put up, I'm hoping to get into town for services. Barring blizzards, that is."

"Not being able to predict when they'll hit makes travel a caution, for sure," answered the reverend, "but we'd love to share services with you and your sisters, Levi." He faced Nellie directly and tipped his cap. "Glad you're not hurt, miss. I'll let you get on." He headed back the way he came, head bent against the strong wind.

Levi lifted the handles of the barrow. "I'll see you where you're going."

"In case any more wild horses go on the attack?" She tipped her gaze up to him. She couldn't possibly know what effect she was having on him, could she? He hoped not. Fancy had gotten their family into trouble once, and he had enough on his plate with three sisters in need of husbands.

"A rare occurrence here, but you had a scare. That's never fun."

"No, but then I had a rescue, and that's something to ponder, isn't it?" She flashed him an almost mischievous smile and he had to smile back.

"It could make a good tale, I expect. Told right, of course, with the proper amount of embellishment."

"You've listened to women speak before." She laughed, and when she led him toward the back door of the inn, he paused.

"I was going to see you to your destination."

"And so you have, because I'm going exactly where you're going, it seems."

"Does it seem that way, Nell? For real?"

His question stopped her with one hand paused in mid-air, just shy of knocking.

He wasn't bold by nature. He knew that, but being with Nellie made him feel strong, protective *and* bold. "I wouldn't have thought it likely we'd be going in the same direction, and yet it's been the only thing on my mind since meeting you yesterday afternoon."

Uh, uh.

Romance had almost cost her freedom in Allegheny City, and it *had* cost all her personal belongings. She'd come west to make a place for herself, on her own and independent. She wasn't about to be sweet-talked by a grumpy wainwright who ran a tight ship with knot-tied purse strings. "I expect that's because we both have business with the innkeeper."

She flashed him an easy look, as if not understanding his meaning.

Oh, she understood, all right, and it didn't matter that he had the nicest blue eyes she'd ever seen, like a calm, clean lake on a bright summer's day. Or that his hair curled around his collar, just so, as if at least part of him had a sense of mischief. Or the way his broad, sturdy hands had grabbed her up, out of the horses' path, and set her gently aside.

After knocking the wind right out of her, of course.

The door swung open. "Nellie, come in. And Levi, how perfect that you arrived together."

"Well, the work was done, and coals don't do for saving," Levi told her. He came up the back steps with the first bucket and poured them into the open stove chamber.

"Thelma, this kitchen is so well put." Nellie untied her scarf, before she realized her hair had tumbled down on one side. "Oh, bother." She grappled for pins, then frowned. "I must have lost pins in the street. Well, this is not how I usually stop by to do business, Thelma." She reached around, took a pencil from her pocket, and quickly twisted her hair up, off her shoulders. "Now I must borrow a pencil to make notes, but at least I'm presentable."

"I thought you looked quite fetching as you were," Thelma replied. She took a pencil from the countertop and offered it to Nellie as Levi approached with the second bucket of hot coals. "What say you, Levi? Didn't Nellie look fine with her hair down?"

"Having three sisters has taught me to keep many opinions to myself." He held the now-empty bucket with one hand and accepted a small box of baked goods with the other. "Although the sight of these custard tarts will make all three of them quite content."

"Well, good!" Thelma patted his shoulder. "You have a blessed night, Levi, and a safe trip home. That wind is high."

"It is." He turned away and Nellie waited, sure he'd turn back and say goodbye. Bid her farewell.

He didn't. He went down the stairs and out the door. A moment later she saw his silhouette pass the window as he trundled the wheelbarrow back to his shop.

"Such a good man, and he's grown up with the weight of the world on those shoulders, but solid shoulders they are! I'm glad folks flock to him for good, quality work, because having a fine-tooled wainwright and wheelwright in town is a blessing, for sure.

"Now, here, dear." She reached her hand out for Nellie's wrap and hung it from a hook alongside the back entry. "Let me take you into the dining room. We've only a few overnight guests today, and if we're quiet we won't be disturbing their evening meal." She took Nellie into a quaint, squared area flanked by a wide, turning staircase on one side and a lovely stone hearth with a stove on the other.

"What a beautiful room." Nellie kept her voice soft so

she wouldn't annoy the two occupied tables. "I'll measure here." She withdrew her tape, but when she went to procure her pad of paper, it wasn't there. "Bother. I must have dropped the pad with my pins. Do you have a piece of notepaper, Thelma?"

"I do, right in the desk." Thelma pulled out a piece of paper and handed it over. Nell jotted the table size down, then did a quick sketch of the room. When Thelma gave her a curious look, she tapped the paper lightly. "I was thinking that if you were to shift the tables slightly, so they're facing the stove rather than the kitchen door and the desk, we could do bright gingham coverings with the bigger, broader check. Then if you did white curtains at the front windows, we could trim them with gingham and you've instantly changed the whole look and feel of the room."

Thelma studied the room, then her. "And I have a hooked rug in the upstairs hall that would be just the right color if we used the red gingham."

"Red or blue would be lovely, but I think the red would be more cheerful and go with summer flowers best. Then you blend the outside with the inside."

"You've sold me!" Thelma led the way back to the kitchen. "I hadn't thought of going with something like that, I was thinking plain-old, same-old. Using the checkered material would brighten everything, Nellie. Would you like to get the material or should I?"

"I think you know yourself best," Nellie replied. "If you pick out the material from the mercantile, I'll have you order twenty-four yards of the gingham and three yards of white. That allows me seamage and gathering space."

"I'll run right over tomorrow. If Ginny's got enough in stock, I'll get it right down to you and Hattie. If not, I'll have her order it in."

"Perfect!" Nellie finished her notes, tucked the paper into her pocket and returned the pencil to Thelma. "I'll get on, then. Hattie and I are going over the schedule tonight and with both of us working, we should soon make progress on her orders."

"You tell her I'm delighted by her new apprentice!"

Honest approval. That was something lacking along the wealthy streets of Alleghany City. Cool disparagement ruled the day at most homes, hoping to push prices down. Nellie liked this way much better. Thelma's honest smile made her feel good about advising the innkeeper to order almost thirty yards of material, but Nellie could picture what the room would look like when all was complete. A proper inn, set in Western fashion with hometown comfort.

She walked back to Hattie's without mishap. The wind still blew free, and the signs still made their racket, but no horses careened down the pitted road. Lamplight shone from upstairs windows here and there, with darkened shops below.

A new town, a new beginning.

There were no neighborhoods yet, to speak of. A house here or there, abutting a shop or the lumber yard.

But the thought of being part of this newness appealed to her. She hadn't thought it would, but it did, or maybe that was because she was passing the edge of Levi Eichas's work place.

He'd flirted with her.

She'd liked it.

But she could ill afford to have this new opportunity fall apart around her, and there was precious little hiding in a prairie town like Second Chance. If things went bad, how did one avoid discomfort? Her experience back east had taught her a valuable lesson. She was a new arrival in Second Chance. Levi was an established businessman and farmer, a man others depended on. She'd seen how quickly people turned against her on Ridgewood Avenue. She didn't dare risk a changing tide in this new town. She'd keep her focus on work and fellowship, following Hattie's example of keeping life sweet and simple.

Chapter Five

LIFE STOPPED BEING SIMPLE ABOUT the time Nellie Bausch sashayed into his shop, Levi decided.

The fact that she hadn't been burned to a crisp was of good note, but after her cool send-off at the inn tonight, Levi determined he'd be smart to go his own way.

That lasted about an hour.

Rachel couldn't get over how amazing Nellie was.

Miriam was brim full of ideas for how to make things prettier and brighter, starting with… oh, just about everything in the place that had seemed just fine to him the previous morning. That was no longer the case among his sisters, and Esther was agog about the idea of meeting Nellie in person.

They were out of control with excitement, and because that had never happened before, Levi didn't have a clear thought on how to handle it.

"I must go into town, it's decided," Esther told them at dinner. "You've all gotten to meet her, and I haven't, so tomorrow—"

"There's a need for you to come into town tomorrow?" Levi was pretty sure there wasn't.

"To meet Nellie, of course. When I was in town two weeks past, Macy said that Hattie said that her friend said never had she seen such a hand with layers. And a new skill learned is a blessing, isn't it, Levi?"

It was, but he wasn't one bit fooled by Esther's skill-building talk. "We need to learn layering now when we've gotten along without it so far?"

"I do believe you promised to limit your grouchiness." Rachel passed a dish of freshly warmed carrots around the table.

He had said exactly that. Which seemed the right thing to say at the time. In retrospect, he probably should have just stayed grumpy. "That was because I stumbled in on ill-conceived conversation."

"Well, any conversation is a nice change," Esther declared. Being the youngest, she was more inclined to go toe-to-toe with him. "And while I love working outside and tending the animals, I do not intend to be the only spinster on the prairie. When our mother was my age, you were already three years old, Levi."

"And I do believe Thomas Thornton has cast an eye on Rachel," Miriam added.

"Miri!"

"Well, there's no use denying it, and not much good admitting it, because we're not off this farm often enough to catch anyone's eye."

Levi stood. "You'll be in town for church on Sunday and Thanksgiving four days after."

"And of course, that will be a lovely change." Rachel scolded her sisters with a firm look. "We've done well as a family, Levi, and you've held us together. None of us find fault in that."

He hadn't really thought they did, until Rachel mentioned they didn't. So if they didn't find fault with that, what was bothering them?

"I'm going to focus on having all washing and ironing done on Monday if the sun cooperates," declared Miriam. "We'll all want to look fresh and nice for the holiday celebration."

"It will be marvelous," Rachel added softly, but when Levi went outside to have a look around, their tones niggled.

They were happy to be going into town, but dissatisfied. With him? With the farm? They'd had their best year ever, due to their fighting spirits and combined efforts, and that was something to be proud of after the previous winter's wrath.

His horse came up lame on Saturday. He sent the girls into church on Sunday while he tended the gelding. He used the mare to go back and forth the first days of the week, and each day he hoped to glimpse Nellie going this way or that.

He didn't see her once, but that might have been his fault because never had Levi enjoyed a busier week. Phillip Dickinson drove south to place an order for a new wagon box and ordered a new buckboard, right after the reverend stopped by to request new metal for his wheels. John Michael O'Connor drove up from his double claim north of Yankton and put a down payment on a wagon. Terrence Shaw brought his wife and girls into town for supplies, and laid down money to have Levi fancy up a courting buggy. By the end of the day on Wednesday, Levi stared at the once-empty board, now covered with orders, and swallowed hard.

Even with a long winter ahead, how could one man get all this done?

He'd no more had the thought, when a man came through the smithy shed. "Are you Levi Eichas?"

"Who's asking?"

The man removed his hat, came forward, and stuck out a hand. "Sol Eichas, your uncle's son from Minnesota. I've purchased a claim on the north side of town, not far from the lake, but I've worked the family trade," he swept the shop a quick look, "since I was a boy. If you need help here, I'd be obliged of a job."

His father had talked about his brother Oscar, and his family back in Minnesota. They'd parted ways less than agreeably, but knowing his father, Levi figured plenty of blame fell on Henry's stubborn shoulders. "You work wood or metal?"

"Both, but I prefer metal. There's something about forging and shaping that draws me. But I can work both sides of the shop, my father schooled me well."

"As did mine. He passed away nearly four years back and we've been working night and day to make up the difference here and at the farm." To have a cousin show up out of the blue tweaked Levi's curiosity, though. "Why didn't you just stay there, in your father's shop?"

"Do you have brothers?"

Levi shook his head. "Sisters, though. Three."

"Well, I have two older brothers. They'll inherit Pa's shop, that's the way of it. And I couldn't see spending the rest of my years taking orders from them, two good men who hurry their corners."

Levi understood exactly what he meant. The fine line between good and exceptional was important to him, too. "We'll give it a try because I could use the help over the winter, and then we'll see."

"A chance is all I need." Sol put out his hand. "I take direction well, and work a full day."

Levi had tried a young apprentice the previous year. He hadn't taken direction at all, and loafed more than he worked. "All a man can ask. And if you're as good as you claim, we'll have a busy winter and strong spring." He named a wage that Sol agreed to, then invited him out to the farm for supper.

"I'll say no tonight, because I hear the town's in a tizzy for the holiday tomorrow. I expect your sisters are preparing as well."

Levi hadn't even considered how busy the women folk were, getting things ready for Thanksgiving, which meant he was an insensitive lout. "You're right, of course."

"I'm staying at the inn tonight, then I'll be wintering here in town. I've leased a room over the mercantile."

Living close meant blizzards and cold wouldn't keep Sol Eichas away from work. "A wise choice after last winter. Sol, it's good to meet you. I'll see you tomorrow."

"At church, then at dinner." Sol put his hat back in place and headed up the road as Levi closed things up.

He hadn't seen Nellie, not once, but he'd see her tomorrow for certain. The sudden urge to clean himself up and put on fresh clothes surprised him, but it was a holiday with a service. He wasn't cleaning up for the knowledgeable seamstress whose dress he ruined. He was doing it because the occasion warranted. And that was all.

"You fixed your gown?"

The note of happiness in Levi's voice made Nellie's heart jig, but she composed her face before she turned. "You sound surprised."

"I am astounded." Levi stared at the skirt, then her, and the appreciation in his beautiful blue eyes might not have been just for the skirt repair, and that made her heart flutter faster. "How did you do it, because there's no patch visible."

She shuddered on purpose. "Patching is an unholy science, Levi, and I'd thank you to never use the word in my presence again." She was half-afraid he wouldn't get the joke, but he did, and laughed out loud. "How would you fix a dry-rotted slat on a wagon?"

"I'd remove it and replace it. Oh." He nodded. "You removed the skirt panel and put a new one in its place."

"I had to replace two, actually, so they'd match but it worked out fine, don't you think? And I narrowed the planes of the skirt to avoid tragic results and I actually owe you a debt of gratitude, Levi."

"For scorching your clothing? I can't believe that's true,

Nell."

Nell.

He was the only one who shortened her name like that. She loved the sound of it, with his hinted accent, a blend of growing up with a German immigrant father in America, land of many tongues. "I do owe you, though, for showing me the importance and hazards of clothing out here compared to back east. I've reduced several patterns to accommodate the difference, and I might not have realized the importance if it hadn't been for our notable meeting. It taught me a valuable lesson."

"I'm glad you weren't hurt, Nell."

He said the words softly, and oh… how nice it was to hear such words. And his gaze, so straightforward, so deep. "Thank you, Levi. And now I must get back, I'm working with Miriam and Esther on setting the desserts. They'll think I've abandoned them."

She waved and hurried away to the far side of the church where the women were organizing the day.

And then he saw it, plain as could be. His sisters' unadorned dresses stood out in the crowd. Everyone had donned an apron, but where the other women had patterned, fitted gowns, his sisters were dressed in the same simple straight-cut dresses they always wore.

It struck him then, struck him hard.

His father had never allowed the girls to go to Hattie or have a say in their clothing. And he'd brought the bolts of plain gray and brown home as needed, never allowing a word of discord.

Why hadn't he noticed before?

It wasn't that their dresses were wretched, and they weren't soiled, stained or torn. They were just plain, and his sisters were not plain women. They were good, kind, hard-working beautiful women. Why was he just realizing that?

A soft laugh from the pie table drew him. Nellie had

laid a bright, plaid cloth across the planked surface. With Esther's help, she was arranging pies and cakes with sprigs of dried flowers here and there. And then she took her place behind the table, shoulder to shoulder with his youngest sister, ready to serve others with a smile.

He wanted that for his sisters. It sparked a memory, not of his stepmother, but way back, of his mother, making things nice and happy. And then it was gone. All gone.

But the contrast of the moment struck him deep, and when the day was winding down, he made his way over to Nellie and asked for a moment.

She blushed, and it made him smile to see it.

He affected her. Well, she affected him, and there was no use denying it, but on the other hand, a woman like Nell could never fit in on the prairie. Could she? Would she even want to with her wide skirts and puffed sleeves?

Most likely not, that would be like putting a sun-loving flower in a cool mess of shade.

Looking into her gold/green eyes, he had to work to pull his thoughts back to the matter at hand. "I'd like to commission your help on a project."

The light in her eyes faded slightly. Was she hoping he'd approached her on a more personal topic? Like holding hands, and taking a walk in the cold, crisp November night? "I don't know that it's right to conduct business on a holiday, Levi, but I'm listening."

She sounded a little disappointed, and it spiked hope, but first things first. "I'd like to order a gown for each of my sisters."

Her eyes went wide. She glanced at the three young women across the room, and looked surprised. "They appear to have a fine knack for sewing, Levi."

"They do, but they've never had the chance to have a pretty frock. Like other women are wearing." Now *he* was about to blush because he'd never in his life thought he'd be talking about women's clothing. "Our father thought plain suited all, but I think he was wrong about that."

"You've suddenly come to this conclusion?" She faced him frankly. "Rachel is in her twenties."

He frowned. "You think I'm being foolish."

"No." She put her hand on his arm, and her expression said the exact opposite. "I think you're being absolutely marvelous. Do you want the girls to pick their fabrics?"

"I'd like to surprise them, something pretty for Christmas. Like your dress, here." Talk about awkward. He kind of waved to her gown, but tried to make it not look like he was noticing her gown.

"Something pretty, but not too fancy, suitable for church and gatherings."

"Yes. That. Exactly that."

"I'd be honored to accept this job, Levi."

"And is it too quick to have them done by Christmas?"

She shook her head. "I've a love for sewing and creativity, so working on these will be my reward for plowing through men's shirts." When he lifted a brow, she added, "We have a stock order with railroad men, and it's plain sewing, straight and true, so I'll be delighted to have something more imaginative to work on."

"Ah. Well. Good. Do you need a deposit, Nell?"

"If you would stop by the shop and give one to Hattie tomorrow morning, that would be perfect."

"I'll be sure to."

"And, Levi?" She aimed a look up at him, a look that said more than words, a look that made him feel special, like he'd never felt before. "I think you're simply wonderful to do this."

He felt wonderful when he talked to her. He felt strong and able and courageous when he talked to her.

He liked it.

He whistled all the way home, and when his sisters exchanged glances, he kept right on whistling, thinking of how things could turn around so quick. Was that of God?

Or just circumstance? Or good, old-fashioned waiting for the wheel to come 'round?

God, he decided, as he directed the wagon to the door. "I'll tend the horses. That was a real nice time today, wasn't it?"

"It was." Rachel smiled as she gathered an arm full of pans and handed them over to Esther. "Such a special thing, to give thanks as a big group."

"And to be a state, now." Esther accepted the stack from Rachel while Miri opened the door. "And Hattie said we'd soon have the vote for women, long overdue."

"Nellie said women back east have been marching, demanding change."

"Well, back east is different, I expect."

"But shouldn't be, of course." Esther wasn't one to be talked down. "I'd like to see women given all the rights of men, owning property, sharing the vote, and I hope to live to see it come to pass, but if I don't, I pray my daughters will. And then their children and beyond."

"Fine words for someone who's never even gone walking," laughed Miri.

"Well, that's a sad bit of truth there." But Esther actually smiled when she said it, which made Levi wonder which young man might have caught her fancy today. "But you never know when the right person and the right time might come along."

He left them to put things in order while he took care of the horses.

Change was in the air, like the dark line of slate gray clouds snugging the northern horizon, but just the thought of changing things up felt downright good.

Nellie's gaze. Her expression. The soft, merry tone of her voice. Talented, honest and true, she sparkled wherever she went.

His thoughts gave him reason to pause.

Beauty would ebb and fade. The depth of a good woman's worth was chronicled in the Bible, how she set her home and heart, a beautiful Proverb. And he saw how quickly his stepmother stepped right out of the picture. Testing a woman too far was wrong, he'd witnessed that with his father. And he was pretty sure Henry had done it on purpose, a rather crude way of pushing a wife out.

He didn't want to be that man. He wanted a home where kindness and caring ruled the day, but every now and again his bit of temper reminded him of his father. Was he too much like him to take a chance on a spritely woman like Nell? Would it be selfish to risk quenching the bright light within her?

Then don't quench it. Enjoy it. Take part in the joys of life.

He wanted to, and that was funny because he'd never wanted to before, but seeing Nell, hearing her laugh and her talk, and the vibrant expressions on her face made him wonder what a lifetime of that vibrancy would be like.

But there was the farm to consider, finally enjoying a solid year. Stock to care for, his sisters to oversee, and the balance of a busy, full-time job in town with a growing agricultural operation on the prairie.

A bird flitted by, one of those little birds that liked to skip up and down trees and brush. The flash of its white belly reminded him that God promised care for the least of his creatures. Still, Levi decided practically, little birds came with limited choices.

His were many, but as he ducked his head against the increasing north wind, there was only one image, one choice on his mind.

Nell Bausch and her warm, easy smile.

Chapter Six

PICKING OUT MATERIAL WAS EASY, Nellie decided, because the girls had hinted their choices before Thanksgiving, but setting the proper sizes without a point of measure was more risky. But Levi wanted to surprise his sisters, and even in their square-shouldered sack dresses, Nell could get an idea of size.

"We'll alter as needed when you're done," Hattie supposed when Nellie hesitated to make the first broad cut of the brown and gold floral she'd purchased for Rachel's gown. "Miriam is almost exactly your size, Rachel is taller and built narrow, like a reed, and Esther's much the same but inches shorter."

Hattie's words helped Nellie envision the sizing. She took a deep breath, then cut the cloth. If she could accomplish one dress per week, on top of her other commitments for Hattie, then all three gowns would be complete before Christmas. And when she finished Rachel's gown on the following Saturday afternoon, she couldn't hide her excitement as she grabbed her wrap and scarf. "I must show Levi, and make sure this meets with his approval since he's the one commissioning the work." She didn't say she'd been chomping at the bit all week, hoping he'd stop by.

"Of course, dear." Hattie barely looked up, but she smiled, eyes down. "A satisfied customer is a wonderful thing."

"Indeed."

She thought he'd walk around the corner and check up on her work.

He hadn't.

She'd been tempted to stop into his wagon shop.

She didn't.

She'd survived being scorched by romance, but just barely, and not that long ago, so why would she risk her standing in a new and very small town by paying mind to a grumpy carpenter?

She wouldn't risk it, she decided firmly as she stepped into the carpentry side of the shop, nowhere near that pesky fire. She'd put a lot of hard work and hours into Rachel's gown. She wasn't stepping one foot closer to the forge than she needed to.

"Can I help you?"

She paused, surprised, when a stranger came through the metal working side of the wrap-around corner store. "Is Levi here?"

"He'll be back shortly, he ran an errand." She must have looked as disappointed as she felt, because the man motioned to a chair near the wall. "He should be back soon. Why don't you sit and wait?"

Sit and wait? How would that look to the town at large, that the single new seamstress was hanging out at the wagon shop, waiting for Levi Eichas to show her the time of day?

She clutched the wrapped up dress a little more closely. "It's not necessary. I wanted him to see the work he commissioned, but we can do it another time."

"Are you sure?" The man moved forward. "I'm his cousin Sol, and I do believe I saw you at the Thanksgiving celebration, didn't I?"

"I was there, and I believe I served you two slices of pie."

He laughed out loud. "You did, and it was the best pie I've had since leaving Minnesota. Listen, I—" He paused and waved a hammer toward the door. "Here's Levi now."

She turned.

Levi strode through the doorway, saw her, and there was

no minimizing his happiness as he smiled in appreciation. "Nell."

Oh be still her heart every time he said her name. "I brought the first dress for you to see. Rachel's."

"You have it done already?" His smile deepened, and the blue of his eyes made forget-me-nots pale by comparison. "You're amazing."

"A good machine and a great pattern are a seamstress's best friends," she told him. She moved to the back bench, and carefully undid the ties binding the muslin around the gown. Then she lifted it out, and held it up for him to see. "What do you think? Will Rachel like it?"

"Nell." One word, one single word of respect and admiration, as if her work left him speechless.

Her heart tripped faster. Stronger.

"Rachel will love it. The colors are perfect for her, all kind of brown and gold like her eyes and hair."

"Miriam had suggested this material before the holiday dinner, and I agreed. And the ivory lace simply offsets the deeper tones, don't you think?"

He laughed, but not at her. No, his laugh sounded joyous, and she realized she'd never heard him laugh before. "Well, as long as you think so, that's what matters. All I know is that it's beautiful and Rachel will love it. Thank you, Nell."

He smiled down at her, then reached out and touched her hand.

Her tell-tale heart ramped up again. Her breath caught somewhere in the vicinity of her chest and wouldn't let go. And her eyes…

Oh, her eyes locked with his, and Nell was pretty sure she would be all right just standing there, gazing up at Levi Eichas, all of her days.

"It's a beautiful dress, Miss."

"Sol." Levi turned as if he'd just recalled Sol's presence. "Sol, this is our new seamstress in town, our resident expert on tucks and gathers, I'm told. Nellie Bausch, my cousin,

Sol Eichas."

"It is a pleasure, sir."

"Mine, too, ma'am." Sol smiled at her, then nodded toward the gown. "Do you make things for children, as well?"

"I do, and gladly."

"I see." Sol motioned back to the metal-working side of the shop. "I'll get back to pounding out that strapping. Nice to meet you, Nellie."

"You too, Sol."

She turned back toward Levi. "I must get back, I want to spend the evening cutting panels for Miriam's dress, but I'm so very glad you like this, Levi."

He raised his hand slowly, hardly enough to be noticed, but Nellie noticed it all right when he touched her cheek so softly. "It's beautiful, Nell."

Emotion swelled within her, because Levi's gaze hinted he wasn't talking about the dress alone. "Thank you, Levi." She bundled the dress back inside the muslin for safety's sake, and wasn't a bit sure how she got back to Hattie's place, because Nellie Bausch was pretty sure her feet never touched the ground.

She couldn't be attracted to Levi, but she was. She shouldn't risk her new job, her new status, her freedom to work as she chose, because once a woman married, she pretty much gave over any thought of independence she once had.

Nell liked her independence. She treasured her skills, the God-given talent that worked so well for herself and others. But truth to tell, standing there in the wagon shop, with the scents of wood and metal and linseed oil all around her... she liked Levi Eichas even more. And that might be a pickle.

"You're taken with her." Sol set his latest wheel on the wooden rod suspended at the front of the work space.

Levi leveled him a look that said he'd rather not discuss it.

"I might be a country boy from the deep woods, but generally when a man is taken with a woman, he does something about it," Sol supposed mildly.

Obviously Sol either didn't understand his look or ignored it, and having worked with his cousin for over a week, Levi was pretty sure it was the latter. "Like you know so much about women? A single guy, working metal?"

"I was married for five years."

Levi stopped hand-planing the curve of a sleigh runner and faced Sol.

"I lost Greta nearly two years back."

"Sol." Levi didn't know what to say. "I'm sorry. Real sorry."

"Yup." Sol grimaced as he worked the metal for the next wheel in line. "Us, too." When Levi raised a brow, Sol continued, "I've got two little kids back home. A boy and a girl. Ethan's four, Sarah's two. My ma's looking after them while I get settled here. I figured to bring them out next spring, but the thought of coming up on Christmas alone, well." He stared out the window, his gaze following the path Nell had taken. "It's just smart to seize up on happiness when you've got the chance. That's all I'm saying."

The truth in Sol's words made pure sense to Levi.

He was a cautious man. He'd lived life trying to please his father and care for his sisters, not because he was noble. He'd laugh at the notion.

But because it was the right thing to do, and doing the right thing had always meant something to him. Something good and solid and true. "You make sense for a country boy."

Sol smiled softly. "Well, life has a way of making us sensible, doesn't it?"

"And you won't be alone for Christmas, the girls would have my head if you didn't come spend it with us." Levi wasn't about to take 'no' for an answer, so he continued on. "And no bother with gifts, the gift of your company is the best one of all. They'd love to hear stories about family. Esther will pester you with questions and she'll write everything down."

"The family scribe."

"Yes." That was Esther, all right.

"She gets that from Aunt Myrt, the oldest Eichas sister. She's got a story for everything, and it all makes sense. She's got a hand with writing, too. Maybe she'll come visit. Or Esther could go there and meet family."

"That's a thought." He'd never considered having the girls go back to Minnesota to meet their aunts, uncles and cousins. His father had never said a nice thing about any of them. Hearing Sol's stories made Levi realize his father had skewed his opinions with his negative talk. Sol's words brought a family alive in Levi's mind, a family he'd wrongly shrugged off. Esther would love it, for certain. He looked left, through the first wide window, toward Hattie's. The idea of courting a woman in sight of the whole town held little appeal. There were no secrets in Second Chance. But there didn't seem to be a whole lot of choice, so he set his work down, grabbed his coat back up, and strode out. "I'll be back."

"All right."

He heard approval in Sol's tone, but that might be because he wanted approval. He walked straight down to the mercantile he'd just left and ordered a sack of candy drops. When Samantha folded the top of the bag just so, he handed over money, pocketed his change, and retraced his steps, only this time he didn't go back to his workplace. He walked right on by as he turned right, walked up Hattie's steps, and through the door.

"Levi!" Hattie stood. She looked delighted and not all

that surprised to see him. "Come in, come in! We were just going to take a break for tea, will you have some with us?"

He shouldn't, there was work waiting, but one look into Nell's eyes and he changed his answer. "I'd like that, Hattie. Nell?"

She took a half-step toward him in the smallish area.

"A little present for you." He held out the bag. "I figured it might be nice to have something sweet while you ladies work."

"Oh, Levi." She took the bag and lifted her gaze to his.

Instantly he knew he didn't deserve the admiration he read in her eyes. He was sour sometimes, a little grumpy and grouchy, all habits he needed to break, but looking down, gazing into Nell's eyes, he realized she didn't see the grumpy, overworked business owner.

She saw him.

His heart beat faster and stronger as he realized something fresh and new. Nell didn't nail him for his father's indiscretions or temperament. She didn't see Henry's edicts and choices. She saw him as he was, a man, striving to make his way.

He felt free for the first time in a long time, and all because of the look in Nell's eyes.

"These will be such a treat, Levi. I thank you." She bobbed a little curtsey then, not the formal kind he eschewed, but the endearing kind, a nod of gratitude.

"The pot's all set, and Nell made some rosemary shortbread cookies just yesterday, perfect to go with our tea."

"You baked these?" Levi sat at the tiny table and felt like a story-book giant who couldn't find a place to plant his big feet.

"Burnt them, more like," Nell admitted with a smile. "We gave a few to Mr. Branson for his sow pig. I had no idea it took such a knack to operate a stove, get the temperature just right, and bake things evenly."

"It's all in timing, but if you don't have time for it, it's tough," he agreed. "That's why we contracted with Thelma for the baking in exchange for the coals. Rachel's got a hand with it, but she's got a hand with everything and it's not fair to stick her with extra work just because she works hard. Miri and Esther would rather do farm work. They love being outdoors, but that sticks Rachel with too much in the house again. It's a puzzle."

"As are so many things in life, and that's why I find so much of it amazing." Nell accepted the cup of bracing tea from Hattie and sat back. "The puzzle of people, places and things, and how it all comes together. It's fascinating, don't you think?"

He didn't think that at all, he found it all kind of regular, but he nodded. "Sure. I guess."

Hattie laughed. "You know, I was always a people watcher, too. Wondering why this and how that and it's a sure bit different out here where there aren't so many things to question."

"The up side is there aren't so many folks asking the questions, either." Nell puffed cooling air over her teacup, then sipped carefully. "And there's some promise in that, let me tell you. Although I do find the progressiveness of women more defined back east. Some women, anyway."

"Progressiveness?" Levi lifted one brow. "You mean those suffragists?"

"Them and others, wanting rights for women."

"Such as?"

"A husband taking over property owned by the wife once married. The inability to enter into contracts once married. The government has offered civil rights to people of color, and well-deserved. How I wish they'd do the same to married women."

"And the two shall become one." The edicts of marriage were Bible-based. Surely she didn't find fault in that? "Isn't that an act of faith and trust?"

Hattie made a noise somewhere between a sigh and a

snort.

"Faith, hope and love, and the greatest of these is love." Nell made the statement softly. "But the fairness of the law takes away the right to make one's own decisions, and that's wrong, Levi. I'm a smart woman. I was educated through eighth grade, as are many women these days. That education shouldn't be discounted as if we were or are lesser beings. Take your sisters, for instance."

"Yes?" He said the word with caution, not too sure what he was getting himself into.

"Do they own your farm?"

He shook his head. "No, the farm is mine, but I have a small inheritance in keeping for each one, left by my father."

"And the shop is yours."

Why did it feel like his big feet were now treading deep water? "Well, sure. It was my father's, he taught me the trade, and now it's mine."

"And you need both?"

Hattie got up, moved away and started busying herself doing something as far from the small table as she could get without going outside in the cold.

"Well, need is a funny word, isn't it?"

"How so?"

Levi set his cup down and leaned forward. "Well, there's this. We've had a few rough years. We lost my father, so the whole shop fell to me. Trying to find help that worked hard and well before Sol showed up wasn't working, so my time was here, in town, making money."

"While your sisters put their hands to running the farm."

"Yes, and they did well, but we'd have lost the farm without the business in town. And there were two years when just the opposite was true. When there was little money in the territory to spend on metal and wood, the crops and cattle got us through."

"So you see it as a cooperative."

"Because it is," Levi insisted. "A balance of one against the other."

"And yet Rachel and Miriam and Esther own nothing of that cooperative. Not even a paycheck."

He'd come down the street to talk with her, to get to know her better, but her words lodged in his chest.

He didn't make the laws. He didn't break the laws. He was a simple man, working hard, in a family of industrious people. They were a group with one goal: To make do, get by and build financial security.

"I've angered you." At least she had the decency to look sorry about that as he stood. "Levi, I'm sorry, I shouldn't have picked at you like that. I see that ways are different out here. Or maybe more the same than I thought, knowing that single women can stake claims as long as they meet the demands."

"Single women running a claim?" He scoffed. "It's been tried. Few have succeeded." He reached for his coat and shrugged into it. "A person alone out here is in for a very big surprise because this is a harsh land. Family working together can be a blessed thing, Nell, but maybe you don't have any experience with that."

"I don't," she admitted. "And I apologize again that my speaking out hurt you. You and your sisters have an agreement that works for you, and that's good."

"But it could never work for someone like you, could it, Nell?"

She stared at him, as if realizing the import of his question, but then her gaze dimmed. "No." The single soft word came out with regret. "I watched my mother's lot as a widow. I saw how our lives were turned upside down by property laws, and I would never wish that on another woman or her children. Fair is fair in my book, Levi. And equitable finances should be part of a strong—" She hesitated, and finished with the word, "union."

Which meant marriage in his book. A husband, a wife,

bound as one, just like God decreed. He turned toward the door, vexed. "I've got work."

"Of course." She eyed the candy bag with a hesitant expression, as if wondering if she should hand it right back to him, but he left before she could be even more insulting.

Chapter Seven

WOMEN'S RIGHTS.
He didn't trudge back up the street, mulling her words.

He strode, hard and fast, wondering what in the name of all that was good and holy she was talking about. When two people joined in marriage, wasn't it the husband's job to take the lead? He pushed through the door with more force than necessary, surprising Sol.

"You're back quick."

Levi peeled off his coat, slung it on the hook, and moved back to the plane with quick, decisive movements. There was work to be done, and he aimed to do it. He'd no more than lifted the curved board into his hands, when he stopped and faced Sol. "You were married. Did Greta prattle on about women's rights? About fairness and equity?"

"It was a topic of conversation, I admit. I take it Miss Nell has feelings on the subject."

"And little fear voicing them."

Sol shrugged that off. "Would you prefer her to be afraid to have an opinion? I can't see that being a good thing. I look at my little Sarah, and I want the world and men to treat her well. Or they'll have me to answer to, let me tell you. But what if I'm not here? What if God calls me home too soon to shelter these children until they're full grown?

"Should Ethan inherit everything because he's a boy?" he went on. "And should Sarah's inheritance go to a husband because she'll be a woman? That's plain foolish."

Sol meant business, Levi read it in his direct gaze. "So you think all this rights stuff is good? Even though it goes against the Bible?"

"My Bible doesn't say women can't hold property. Does yours?"

"It speaks of a man heading a house, and women submitting everything to their husbands." Levi blustered, just a little, because wasn't that the same thing? Mostly?

"And it speaks of loving your wife like Christ loved the church. As honest, intelligent men, do we show love by seizing someone's property and the proceeds of their hands and hard work?"

Levi swallowed hard, because that was exactly what his father had done, and wanted him to do.

"And while Timothy speaks of women being silent in church, Paul sends letters of introduction so that women disciples are welcomed." Sol stood and straightened his shoulders. "Levi, losing my wife was the greatest pain a man can feel. And if I'd been the one to die first, I'd already made sure that everything I needed to do to make Greta my sole inheritor was done. I told you I'm a man who doesn't cut corners. Not in my work. And not in my life. I wasn't able to save her, and God took her home, but I was smart enough to realize that preparing the way for her security and that of my children, was not just a smart thing to do. It was my God-given duty to love her like Jesus loved the church. He died for us. Giving over the name of our property seemed little enough to do in comparison."

Sol agreed with Nell.

Sol had actually signed his property to his wife.

Levi couldn't pretend that Sol's words didn't surprise him, and when Sol asked his next question, Levi knew exactly why he asked.

"How often do you get to church, cousin?"

Sol was calling him out, and Levi couldn't lie. "Not as often as I could, I suppose. There's always something to be done."

"Well, if you're going to pull out the Bible only when it suits, it's sparse quoting. Taking Sunday as the Lord's day, giving yourself and your family time to simply be is pretty plain, I think." Sol reached out and plucked his hat off the wall peg. "You're blessed to have family, and you gain from their hard work, but don't be foolish about time, Levi. Because none of us know the day or the hour and regrets can last too long. I'll see you Monday. Or tomorrow, in church."

Sol departed quietly, but his absence left a hole filled with questions. Questions with no answers.

Levi carted the coals over to the inn, then closed up shop and headed home. Miriam was in the big shed, minding a cow giving birth at a rugged time of year. With winter fast upon them, would the little one make it through?

"I'll go help Miri," he told Rachel as he dropped off a single loaf of Thelma's bread. "Travels down, so Thelma's not baking quite so much, but I told her this was fine. Where's Esther?"

"Working at the Barnes' claim. Fred wanted to hire help and Esther signed on with our work caught up here."

"She signed on? What does that mean, exactly?"

Rachel raised a calm expression to meet his less calm version. "To work, Levi. To make money. There's nothing she can't handle, and Fred's an honest man. He'll pay accordingly."

His sister, out to work, like a common laborer. He opened his mouth, then shut it, quick.

Would Esther feel the need to work if she owned a quarter share of their claims? Or would she feel secure enough to stop and breathe now and again?

"Do you have something to say, Levi?"

Oh, he had stuff to say, but suddenly he wasn't sure it was the right stuff. Could Nell be right? Was he an old stick in the mud who held people to standards that kept them indentured?

He went back outside.

Night fell quickly in December, and he held a lantern high as he moved toward the shed. The plaintive bawl of a fresh calf pushed him to move faster, but when he got there, all was calm.

"A fine, well-boned heifer, Levi." Miriam stood back, letting the cow nudge the baby up. "She breathed quick and loud when I tickled her nose, and look, she's rising already, looking for milk."

Miri hadn't needed his help. Esther was off doing a man's job. And Rachel could run this place on both sides of the house door, without blinking an eye. She wasn't as quick at barn chores, but she never sat down, so twice as much got done.

He lifted the lantern high and studied the calf. She stood, wobbled, then stood firmer, a miracle every time he saw it. She crossed the few feet to her mother's side and pushed against Dolly's flank.

The cow mooed softly, encouraging her, and the calf bumped her head around, then ducked lower. When she finally latched on, mother and baby seemed absolutely, perfectly content.

And that got Levi thinking that maybe things were way messed up. Maybe it was men who weren't all that necessary. He'd watched many a woman on the prairie do men's work, but if put to the test, he didn't see widowers putting their hand to sewing, knitting or needlepoint. Nor much in the way of cooking or putting food by for a long winter.

No, they either hired someone in, brought a mother or an aunt or spinster sister on board or remarried.

Shame hit him low. He'd been brought up by a strict taskmaster who kept women down on purpose, but Levi had been an adult for years. Why hadn't he seen this sooner? Why—

"She's right sweet, isn't she, Levi?" Miriam came closer

and hugged his arm. "Aren't we so very blessed to have them? To have a growing herd, and a warm house at least most of the time? Good, solid, sensible clothing and work orders coming in?"

"You don't hate me, Miri?"

She turned, astounded. "What's gotten into you, Levi Eichas?"

"For working you so hard, for all the days and nights of struggle?"

She stepped back and held her lantern high, studying his face. "You're fevered."

He almost laughed. "I'm not."

"Overtired, then."

"Well, there's that, but that's commonplace enough on the prairie."

She shook her head. "I don't understand."

"Me, either. But maybe. Just maybe, I'm starting to." He stepped back and allowed her to go through the door first, her lantern held high. He swung the half-door closed and latched it snug against the prairie wolves that roamed in the dead of night. And when they got back to the house, Esther was walking her horse into the paddock.

"Esther."

She finished closing the gate and turned, stubborn and resigned. "Yes, Levi?"

Her expression indicated she expected a scolding for going to work, and Levi kind of enjoyed seeing her face light up when he said, "Finding work is a noble thing. We all understand the work of our hands is good and true, but picking your way home on a rutted road in the dark is dangerous and I love my sisters too much to have them tempt fate. Leave Barnes' place earlier from now on, you hear?"

She stared at him, then threw her arms around his neck in a big hug. "You're right, of course, and I rued that decision all the way home."

"I expect you did." He pulled the house door open and allowed the girls— *women*, he corrected himself— to go first. "Rachel, that smell is a wonderful thing to come home to."

"Well, thank you." She exchanged a puzzled look with Miri, a look Levi wasn't supposed to see, then nodded toward the table. "Thelma's bread is the perfect addition to supper, and everything is ready once you've all cleaned up."

"I'm going to fill the pots with bath water and get it warming," Levi announced. "That way we're set for services in the morning."

"So we'll repair that fencing when we get home?" Esther wondered.

"We'll do it because it needs to get done," Levi told her as he moved toward the door to go fill buckets. "But I came to realize today that I pick and choose when I want to mind God's word, and that's an unwholesome thing."

Rachel moved closer. "Are you feeling all right?"

"I asked the same thing," Miri told her. "I suspect a fever."

Levi laughed, facing them, and his reaction only seemed to confuse them more. "I'm fine. I just feel convicted to be less grumpy and more reasonable. And maybe listen better."

"I'll make a poultice."

"And I'll cut the onions."

"I have no need of mustard, onions or anything else. I just need to find my way right with God. So we'll start with church."

They all three stared at him. Rachel recovered first. "Well, that seems like the very best place to start, doesn't it?"

"Agreed." He strode out the door, filled buckets at the well, and lugged them in and out of the small house several times. And by the time the night was through, he was rugged tired, but convinced that at last, he might be going in the right direction.

Chapter Eight

"A SEASON OF PREPARATION AND ANTICIPA-TION, much like a mother's womb."

Reverend Barber's words didn't just touch Nellie's heart the next morning.

They touched her soul. The thought of a future, a husband, a family…

Who would want an independent, outspoken woman? No one, of course. Outspoken women were barely tolerated in the busy city. Here in the outlying of the Western prairie, saying too much most likely got one into trouble, and she'd had her share of that lately. She faced the small altar, asked God's blessing on spinster women, then turned.

Levi Eichas was standing right behind her, waiting.

Her heart leapt, then settled. She'd spent the whole night, well, other than dozing here or there, wishing she could snatch back her hastily offered opinions of the day before. "Levi, I'm glad you're here. I need to apologize for my quick tongue yesterday." She made a little face of regret. "I have strong beliefs, but I know such thoughts aren't always welcome, and I meant no harm to you. Forgive me. Please."

She didn't bow her head in contrition. She faced him head on, knowing she was wrong and willing to hear his piece.

He put out his arm.

Nellie frowned.

People moved by them, heading out of church, or crosswise to have a word. And still Levi stood in front of her, with his arm crooked, just so. "May I escort you home, Nell?"

Heat moved from somewhere close to her toes straight to her cheeks. "You still want to?" Oh, it was a silly thing to say, and it came out as more of a squeak than a question, but when Levi reached out and tucked her arm into his, his action said more than words ever could.

"I do still want to, and I've given more than a little measure to your words."

She winced. He noticed that right off and inclined his head with the tiniest smile.

"There was a sting, I admit, but it was well-deserved, and I can't say anyone's ever stood up to me and made me think things over."

"Well, they should have."

He did laugh this time, and more than one person glanced their way. "True enough, and I have the feeling you're unafraid to call someone out as needed, Nell Bausch."

"Levi, I should have bitten my tongue." She paused and faced him. "Heaven knows I have plenty of faults, not the least of which is being a wanted woman."

"You're what?" He pushed the church door open and a blast of wind pushed right back. "What do you mean?" He held her arm snug as they proceeded down the steps, making sure she didn't slip and fall, and the feel of him, keeping her safe, made her long to be kept safe forever, which was a crazy thing for a spinster to wish for.

Unless she didn't remain a spinster.

She pushed that thought aside as she confessed her manufactured, sordid past. "I mean I'm being hunted by the law, a woman scorned, accused of being a common thief."

Poor Levi. He stopped dead in the street, staring at her, and if they hadn't been noticed before, they were surely being noticed now. "Are you a criminal, Nell?"

"I am no such thing, nor have I ever been, but that's the

way of the world sometimes, Levi. Being a single woman can leave one targeted by so many, when one would hope that simple Christianity would lead them to be kind and good. Sunday's lessons are not always carried out in Monday's reality, truth to tell."

"I can't deny being guilty of that myself," Levi admitted thoughtfully. "But why would someone do this? Who targeted you, Nell?"

She pulled a breath and spoke softly because the entire town did not need to hear about Ridgewood Avenue. But Levi did, because a man shouldn't escort a woman home without being privy to possible imminent arrest. "A rich man's son showed interest in me."

Levi's steady gaze met hers. He reached up and tucked a wind-whipped strand of hair behind her ear. "I don't find that hard to believe."

"Well, thank you. He seemed sincere enough, but when I showed no interest, he may have pushed his advances more stridently than was prudent and got a good sock in the eye for his troubles. When his mother realized what was going on, she did not leap to my defense, let me tell you. She and her friends set me up as a common thief, although I had money in the bank and in my purse. The lack of reason should have been my ticket to freedom, but in Allegheny City, steel families rule the day and would have ruled the courtroom. I'd been invited out here to work with Hattie, so I fled."

"You didn't stand your ground to clear your name? Why?"

He looked genuinely puzzled, and they were creating a stir by standing there, talking, so she moved forward, toward Hattie's. "No one would have believed me, Levi. There was nothing taken, I put the jewelry back when I found it in my bag, and there was no evidence of need, but when a single woman is accused by a group of rich matriarchs, who do you think the judge will believe?"

"They'd see you jailed for defending yourself against unwanted advances?" Levi looked confounded, as if the thought of injustice had never occurred to him.

"There are many people jailed unjustly in the city, especially when the city is ruled by money and prominence." She waved a hand to the tiny town surrounding them. "Here, everyone knows everyone and they see the character within. When there are so many people underfoot, some with means and many with barely a hunk of bread to put on the nightly table, it's mighty easy to get lost in the crowd." She gently pulled her hand away from his arm. "Knowing such things about me, I understand if your invitation to see me home is withdrawn."

He tucked her arm right back through his. "I withdraw nothing."

"But—"

He kept walking and if anything, held her arm firmer, but still gentle, as if caring for her. "You're a vexing woman, Nell."

She nodded quickly. "I know."

"And now to hear you're running afoul of the law. Well, I can't say it's not a troubling conversation."

"I understand completely, Levi, hence my offer to withdraw."

"But most troubling is the fact that you only gave that bugger one black eye. I'd have preferred it was two, because a man who thinks it fine to take liberties with a woman should be flogged."

"Well, it *was* only one black eye," she admitted, "but very obvious, and his mother was not pleased to have him shown up like that."

"Then she should have raised a better son."

She paused as they drew near Hattie's steps. "You don't think ill of me? Again?"

He tugged her arm— and her— closer, then turned to block the wind whistling through the narrow street. "I think your honesty is refreshing. Now that I've gotten over the insult, of course."

Heat rushed her cheeks.

"And I think while I was busy picking this and that in the Bible to live by, I was forgetting to be my own self. To see things through my eyes, not the eyes of my father, who wasn't a gentle or thoughtful man."

"I'm sorry to hear that, Levi." She laid her gloved hand over his. "It would be so good for children to grow up loved by two parents. It is a blessing denied to too many."

It was.

Levi thought of Sol and his quiet belief and resolve. He was a single father, but he longed for equity and fairness for his children. "Would you like to take a buggy ride today, Nell?"

"You'd leave your work to go riding?"

A fair question from a fair woman. "Depending on the company, yes. I've come to realize that picking and choosing when I want to listen to God's word means I'm not really listening at all. It's a habit I'd like to break."

"Then, yes, Levi. I would like that very much. But you know it will do you no good to try and talk me out of my beliefs about women and equality, don't you? In all honesty, it would never do for us to be unclear on that."

"Oh, you made it plenty clear, believe me." He grinned down at her. "But that made me realize I've got other changes to make before I move forward. I would like my sisters to have the best Christmas they've ever enjoyed, and to feel like they're special women, no matter what their future holds."

"Well, the dresses will be a nice part of that. What time shall I be ready to ride?"

He thought for a minute. "Let's say one o'clock. That ridge north of us says we could get snow later. We won't go so far that we have to worry about a storm and that will get us back in time for supper. Will you have supper with me, Nell? At the inn?"

She looked surprised, intrigued and excited, all at once. "Like a courting dinner?"

"Yes."

"Levi—"

He silenced her with a kiss, a very good kiss at that, because he was beginning to realize a woman like Nell might just talk a thing to death, given the chance, and Levi was pretty sure kissing beat talking. Within short seconds he was absolutely convinced he was correct. Kissing outranked talk by a hefty margin. And just when he was thinking about maybe a lifetime of kissing Nell, and how good that would be, a voice— a man's voice— broke in.

"So it's only my advances you greet with a punch in the face, Nellie."

Nell jerked back.

Levi turned around, but he stood right there, in front of her, protective and kind.

"Samuel."

"I've come for you, Nellie Bausch. It's time to quit this nonsense and see things the way they are. The way they should be. You and me, together." Samuel Cumberbie made a move to go around Levi.

Levi blocked his way.

Samuel's expression soured. He looked at Levi like eyeing a bug under a monocle, and Nell knew what he was seeing. Plain clothes. A plain shirt. Suspenders, a coat, a plain scarf and hat.

His expression said he found Levi lacking.

He was wrong, so wrong, but what was he doing here? Why had he come? Surely he hadn't really come west to fetch her back, had he?

"We need to talk, Nellie. It's important that we do."

"We have nothing to say, Samuel. I believe I made that clear."

"I've come a long way." He stepped forward, but Levi stood firm, between them. "I know what the ladies did was wrong. My mother's passion for appearances taints her judgment at times."

"You call setting a young woman up as a thief, and setting the law on her a lapse of judgment?" Levi faced Samuel straight on, and his voice—

Strong, rigorous and defined—

Made her heart sing.

"We don't look kindly on people being unjustly accused in South Dakota."

Levi's stance appeared to have little effect on Samuel. "Nellie doesn't belong in South Dakota. She'll never fit in here. She's brought herself up, out of the lower class, by her industry and dignity. What kind of person would stand in her way? Going back to Allegheny City as my wife will ensure her and our children a place in society like no other." He shifted to the right, and met Nellie's gaze. "My mother was wrong in her accusations, and you in your thoughts because my interest in you was most honorable and sincere." He went down on one knee, right there in the cold, gray street. "I'm asking your hand, Nellie. I can give you anything you want. Anything you crave. Anything your hard-working heart desires. We'll want for nothing and there will be no woman of Pittsburgh or Allegheny City who looks on you with anything other than the utmost respect. I pledge my word on it."

Marriage?

Samuel had come all this way, clear to the deep west,

offering marriage against his mother's wishes?

She stared, amazed.

How did this happen? Was it a ploy to get her back to Pennsylvania and pop her straight into jail for a crime she didn't commit?

"And there's this." Samuel stood back up and handed over a sheet of paper. "It's official word that there is no reason for your incarceration and that the warrant for your arrest has been set aside."

So he wasn't here to trick her into coming back. He was here as he said. To propose marriage. She swallowed hard around a lump of disbelief. "Samuel…"

"Nell." Levi turned her way, and there they stood before her, two men showing interest where none had stood just days before.

She took a deep breath. "Levi, it seems we won't be able to go riding after all."

He stared at her, straight and hard, but for the life of her she couldn't turn her head and meet his gaze. Not and keep her composure to do what must be done.

"I see." He stepped back, then waited for long, slow beats of time, but in the end he dipped his chin, turned and walked off.

Her heart walked off with him, but a woman could only handle so much at a time. She turned back to Samuel as Hattie hurried along the street in their direction. "Let's get in, that wind is blowing free and there's a hint of snow on the air. It wouldn't surprise me one bit if we don't have an old-fashioned squall coming up." She pushed open the door, waited while Nellie and Samuel stepped in, then faced him as she unwound her scarf. "Samuel Cumberbie, I believe. My friends in Pittsburgh send me the Post Gazette pretty regular, and your family's connections are mentioned in great detail."

"Ma'am." Samuel dipped his head.

"I'm Hattie McGillicuddy, formerly of Massachusetts, at

present a resident of Second Chance, South Dakota. What has brought you all this way so close to Christmas, young man?"

"That would be the urge to follow my heart, Mrs. McGillicuddy."

"Hmm." She folded her arms and faced him once she'd hung her coat on a wall hook. "Well, the heart's an interesting thing, that's for certain. It can be given, but rarely taken. You two look as if you have things to talk about, so I'll keep myself busy back here." She moved to the living side of the building. "And you can have some privacy in the shop area."

"There's no need for privacy," Nell assured her. "In fact, in light of our past, I'd prefer a chaperone, Hattie."

"Then you shall have one." Hattie picked up a quilt square and began working away. "Pay me no mind."

Nellie took a seat, relieved. Samuel took the chair opposite her. The steel baron's son might talk of honorable intentions, but Nellie knew the ways of the wealthy more intimately than most. Taking what they wanted when not freely given wasn't a rarity among the gilded, and her reputation had been besmirched enough. "Is this paper sincere, Samuel?"

"It is, with my mother's apologies."

"Those would be unwritten, I wager."

"She is not a woman prone to admitting her faults and flaws in public."

His words struck a nerve with Nell. She'd spoken frankly to Levi the previous day, needing honesty and integrity. He'd walked away, but he'd come back on his own, openly acknowledging his mistake.

That was an admirable trait.

He'd promised to make things more equitable with his family.

Samuel promised to make her a rich man's wife, bowed to and curried.

Levi disliked curtsies and flouncy, flammable skirts.

On Ridgewood Avenue, she'd be curtsied to by hard-working women like herself, as if marriage boosted her to a new level of elitism.

"I have no interest in marrying you, Samuel."

Surprise wiped the calm from his face. "You can't mean that, Nellie."

"Oh, I mean it, all right." She carefully handed the reneged arrest warrant back to Hattie, who immediately folded it and secured it into the bosom of her dress.

"I appreciate the offer, and you've complimented me greatly, but I have no wish to go back east, nor a wish to be part of the affluent. I'm a simple woman, Samuel. You know that."

"Simple doesn't have to mean stupid, Nellie."

Hattie sucked a quick, sharp breath, but she held her tongue, a struggle, no doubt.

"And that shows our incompatibility, Samuel. If I disagree with you, it's simply because I'm beneath you. And stupid. That's not the kind of life I wish for myself. It's not the kind of life any intelligent woman should wish for herself." She stood and extended her hand. "Let us part easily, not as enemies."

"You can't mean this." He stood, gripping his hat. "I've come all this way, Nellie. I won't take no for an answer."

"Oh, you will." Hattie stood as well, quick and firm. "I've got a fine Ithaca filled with buckshot that adds convincing argument. I'd prefer not to use it. And with snow coming, I'd suggest you grab the next train going wherever, and find a connection because once the snow means business, travel gets mighty lean out here."

"Nellie."

Even the way he said her name was wrong. All wrong, compared to Levi's quiet, firm "Nell".

"You need to leave, Samuel. I've moved on, I've no interest in going back east, and as you can see." She waved her arm to the bolt of gingham for the inn, a pile of shirt parts, and the pieces of Miriam Eichas's dress, "I've got plenty to keep me busy."

He stood still and silent, disbelieving, but when Hattie moved even closer to Nellie's side, he took the hint. "You'll regret this, of course." He leaned closer, his gaze dark. "You could have had everything, Nellie. All the glitz and glamour of being a steel baron's wife. It appears my mother was correct in her take that you are a foolish, foolish woman."

She didn't waver because his opinion— and his words— meant little. "I do have it all, Samuel. Right here, in Second Chance."

Hattie strode forward, swung the door wide and waved him out, and when he left, she shut and locked the door behind him. Then she turned to face Nellie. "Well, that was an unexpected turn to the day, wasn't it, dear?"

"On my word." Nellie grabbed a chair, sat down hard, and fanned herself. "One man offering a buggy ride, then one offering marriage and all the fancy trappings to go with it. And so soon after Reverend Barber's sweet sermon about anticipation. I promise you, Hattie, I never anticipated any of that!"

"And that cloud ridge appears to be moving south, which means snow by supper."

"My first South Dakota snow."

"First proposal, first snow."

"But I'm that sorry to miss a buggy ride with Levi." She stood and moved to the window. "He stood up for me to Samuel."

"Levi's a man of courage and valor."

"And he calls me Nell."

Hattie smiled broader.

"And he doesn't necessarily like my ideas, but he likes that I have ideas and thinks about them."

"A rare and wonderful trait in any man," Hattie declared.

"I don't suppose I could ride out there and go for that

buggy ride, do you?"

"No, absolutely not. First, we have no horse, the livery is closed and a woman, even a progressive woman, is not going out to beg a ride she just refused. Sometimes we have to let go and let God's timing work things out. It's not as if Levi won't be back tomorrow, working in his shop up the road, same as ever. And then you can explain about Samuel."

"You're right, of course." Nellie moved to the window and looked right, then left. "Although tomorrow does seem like a far sight of time away."

"When you're that smitten, minutes can seem like that," Hattie agreed. "And with your love of sewing, I don't think it's breaking the Sabbath to sit and work on Miriam's dress together. There's something sacred and sweet in helping create a gift for another."

"There is. And we can have tea as we stitch, and I'll try to be patient while I wait to speak with Levi tomorrow."

"Perfect."

Chapter Nine

NELL WAS LEAVING.
  She was leaving with a dark-gazed, fancy-dressed rich man, to go back east and be catered to.

Levi put his hand to every task he could think of on Sunday, to push the thought of Nell's leaving aside, but it didn't work. And when the dark ridge of clouds brought snow and wind, he realized he'd misjudged the weather. He often slept in town over the winter, when the possibility of bad roads and drifts meant rough travel, but he'd been too taken with the idea of courting Nell to make a proper assessment, and now he was stuck on the prairie. By Wednesday the storm had blown itself out, and a bright, thin sun melted a share of the snow, leaving just enough for the horse and sleigh to make it to town.

He'd have to go see Hattie about the dresses. He didn't want to, but with Nell gone, he needed to make sure his surprise wouldn't be thwarted. Would Hattie have time? And would she be able to make them that little bit fancy, the way Nell would?

He didn't want to think of her. The way she smiled, the way she stood her ground, the way she admitted her flaws and faults so freely, with a humble gaze and a stalwart heart. Being with her, even those few weeks, made him dream things he'd never thought to dream before.

He pulled into town, directed the horse toward the shop, and saw Sol inside, working. He put the horse up at the livery, dipped his chin and shoved his hands into his pockets.

He could do this. He would do this. He had little choice.

He entered through Sol's work area and stopped, dead.

Red-checked curtains framed the two big, front windows. Short across the top, longer panels came down and were pulled back along the sides. The whole look made the gleaming buckboard appear more complete.

He looked at Sol, then back to the curtains, then back at Sol. "Where did these come from?" But even before Sol answered, he knew. Oh, he knew, all right, and the sizable knot constricting his heart came loose.

"Miss Nellie came by on Tuesday, waltzing in here like she owned the place—"

Levi had to grin, because that was Nell, all right.

"She stuck those up there, talking nonsense about framing how we see the world and how the world sees us, then left as quick as she came with a box full of table covers for the inn."

Nell was here. She hadn't left with Cumberbie. She was here, in Second Chance, so what was he doing, wasting time in the shop? "I'll be right back, Sol."

Sol's laugh followed him out the door. "And I'll be here, working."

He strode down the short street to Hattie's shop, then up the steps and through the door, his heart racing, his pulse thrumming, but it wasn't until she looked up…

Until her eyes met his. Until she stood and smiled as she moved forward, that he believed.

He hugged her. Oh, he shouldn't, most likely, propriety being what it was, but right now the thought of holding Nell— *his Nell*— in his arms took precedence. "You're here."

"And where on earth did you expect me to be, Levi Eichas?"

He pulled back and gazed into hazel eyes with an impish spark. "Clearly, I was foolish."

"If you thought for one moment that I was getting on

a train," she waved toward the depot as if he didn't know where the trains came through. "And head back east." This time she hooked her thumb back, over her shoulder. "With the likes of Samuel Cumberbie, then I cannot argue your status. I came here to Second Chance for just that. A second chance. And a new beginning, a new town, and new friends. And here's where I intend to stay."

Should he tell her how his heart ached the past few days, thinking she'd gone? Should he tell her how much she meant to him, even after such a short period of time? Was this normal or was he rushing things?

She reached up her hand just then, her right hand, and soothed a bit of hair from his forehead. "And if life holds more surprises for me here in Second Chance, surprises I'd never even thought to imagine, I'll be the happiest woman in the world, my beloved Levi."

Beloved?

One look into her eyes said her words held true.

He kissed her. He kissed her hard and long, a kiss intensified by the thought that she was gone from him forever, and yet here she was, waiting. "I love the curtains, Nell. You were right, they make everything look nicer. From the inside and the outside. I thank you."

"I had just enough yardage from the inn's table covers, and it helped me pass the time while I was thinking of you out on that prairie, thinking who knows what about Samuel and me." She reached up and kissed him again, and he liked that she kissed him just as much as he liked when he kissed her, for all the convoluted sense that made. "Because all the while I was thinking how wonderful it would be to make a life with a good, strong, honest, not-grumpy prairie man, right here in Second Chance."

"I hear married men are less grumpy," he admitted with a smile, and Nell didn't miss a beat.

"I expect that's because they've got a wife who's handy with a rolling pin as need arises."

"I shall take that as a warning." He smiled down, into her eyes, and when Hattie walked into the shop from the back quarters, Levi looked up. "I've got a notion to marry your new assistant, Hattie."

"So it seems, which means it's mighty tough to get long-term help these days." She gave them a hearty smile as she said it, though, and approval brightened her eyes.

"Except that this woman intends to be a working wife, and someday maybe a working mother." When Levi lifted his brows, she motioned up the road. "We have a perfectly fine shop right there where we can spend the winters as needed, and I can work either there, or here. In fact, if we add on a room to the back of that shop, with an upstairs, we could have a kitchen, a sewing corner, a bedroom and a nursery. At some point in time," she finished quickly.

He shouldn't be amazed, but he was. While he'd spent a good three days brooding, she'd been finishing orders, trimming his shop, and planning their future. Now the question was, did he have enough energy to keep up with a fast-talking, fast-walking woman like Nell?

One look at her bright pink lips and sparkling eyes said he'd find a way to keep up, because life with a woman like Nell would keep him on his toes, happily.

"And we've completed Miri's dress and I'll start on Esther's tomorrow, so that all three will be ready before Christmas service. With Hattie's help, of course. Setting that many tucks and gathers isn't a quick job."

Women throughout the town had been caught up in Nell's gift for style. Levi didn't care overmuch about that, but he was caught up in the woman herself, and that was even better. "I'll be excited to give them the dresses. Per-haps Sunday, after church? Can you and Hattie come out to the house as long as there's no storm? We'll have Sol come too, it's tough for him to be alone here on Sundays, missing his kids and all."

"Sol has children?" A look of interest lifted Hattie's

brows.

"He was widowed two years past, and he's got a pair of youngsters, ages two and four. They'll join him here in spring. Right now he's on his own, working to make money to improve his claim."

"I see." She smiled, picked up a stack of shirt parts, and moved to her machine. "We'd love to come to dinner on Sunday, Levi, to surprise the girls, and that way if there needs to be a pinch here or a tuck there, we can take care of it right away. But, now, the work of the day awaits."

She was right. He didn't want to leave, but when Nell squeezed his hands, and smiled into his eyes, he knew the leaving was a temporary parting. And when he walked back up the road, he spotted those red-checked curtains from halfway down the street and smiled.

She'd made a difference already, and he wasn't talking about the windows, though they were nice.

She'd made a difference to him. And to his sisters. And to the town, no doubt, given the chance. He walked back into the carpentry side of the shop, whistling softly, ready to work.

And ready to dream.

Epilogue

"I CAN'T BELIEVE WE'RE HAVING COMPANY to dinner." Esther tucked her hair more firmly beneath her bonnet and smiled at Nellie. "It's like those stories I've read, where folks put the daily by and take Sunday for its own measure."

"God's time and rest time," added Miriam. "Nellie, you should have sat up front here with Levi, he's surely vexed by having you so far away."

"Miriam." Levi sent her a glance that didn't look at all perturbed, but pretended to be bothered.

"Well, aren't you?" She laughed and poked him in the side, and he laughed too.

"My hope is to spend many Sundays with Nell at my side, so no, I'm not vexed at all." He shot a quick look into the back of the wagon. "I prefer to describe myself as hopeful."

Esther's eyebrows shot up, and she put her hands to her mouth to cover the laugh, but Nell answered gently. "It is a hope I share, Levi, and I hope your sisters don't find my nature too tiresome, troublesome, or bothersome."

"Well, if Hattie can stand you, I guess we all can." Common sense and warmth marked Rachel's words. "And I just look at that fine featherstitch along that bodice, and I'm hoping you can take time to show me how it's done. I've tried it from paper instructions, but it comes out bunched or botched. Most un-feathery."

"It's not you," Nell assured her. "The size of the needle

and a fine, fine thread make it work. The same stitch with a regular sewing needle doesn't look right."

"I never thought of a finer needle and thread."

"That's the only difference, Rachel, I assure you. And practice, of course."

Levi pulled the first wagon up to the house and swung it around in a gentle half-circle. "Sol and I will take care of the horses. And I do believe Nell and Hattie brought some of those rosemary shortbread cookies she's learning not to burn."

Nell winced. "I'll tame that oven yet."

"Or another, perhaps."

She looked up.

Levi's eyes twinkled down at her, and his smile. She could grow old loving that smile, and die a happy woman. She held his gaze and didn't mince words. "Learning the traits of another oven would be fine as well."

She and Hattie carried their bundles into the house, and if Levi's sisters were curious about them, they held their tongues out of politeness. But more than once, Nell saw Esther glance at the muslin-wrapped packages, as if wondering. And maybe even hoping.

"We've got just enough plates," Miriam said as she settled them onto the table. "And forks a-plenty."

"And with a tender chicken pie, we've no need of knives," Esther added.

Sweet and simple. After life among the rich, and the insincerity surrounding her there, the humble grace of these beautiful women placed them far above rubies. "And here are the cookies, with not a one burnt this time, although your brother does like to tease me."

"Having Levi tease and smile is possibly the best Christmas gift we've ever received." Rachel smiled softly as Sol and Levi tromped through the far door. "It is a present of no cost and highest value, Nellie. Which makes us so very glad you came."

"Well, I'm glad she came, for certain," Levi announced as he and Sol hooked their coats. "And while dinner smells good, and those pine shavings make the stove smell fancy—"

"The smell of Christmas when one has no tree. Nell's idea," Esther told him.

He smiled at her across the room. "I'm not surprised. Nell and Hattie, I think dinner can wait a moment or two, don't you?" He indicated the packages with a shift of his eyes.

"The seasonings in a fine meat pie only grow better with waiting," Hattie declared. She picked up the first bundle and peeked at the twine. "Rachel."

"What?" Rachel's eyes went wide as Nell handed her the package.

Hattie inspected the next bound package. "Esther."

"For me?" Esther bounced their way, clearly excited.

"And Miriam."

"Gifts from you?" Miriam looked at Hattie, then Nellie. "Oh, but you shouldn't have."

"From Levi," Nellie corrected her, as he came closer. "You must open them and see what you think."

A scramble of twine and muslin followed. And then...

"Oh, my word."

"I've never..."

"Levi, how did you know?"

Rachel's eyes filled with tears.

Esther's went round as she lifted the soft folds to her cheek.

Miriam sat right down and cried.

"Well, now, you're supposed to be happy." Levi shot Nellie a worried look. "Not upset."

"Happy tears are the best kind," she told him, and broke decorum by hugging his arm. "Women of kind heart often cry when happy. Or angry," she added cheerfully.

"May we try them on?" asked Esther.

"And have dinner in them." Miriam's expression went from tears to joy at the thought of dining in her new dress.

"They're yours, you may do as you wish."

"And how beautiful to have you all dressed up for a special dinner," added Sol. He gave Levi a *thwack!* on the back. "You did all right for a somber fellow."

"I followed the advice of trusted advisors."

Hattie fussed with coffee while the sisters changed into their new gowns, and when they returned to the main room, Hattie clapped her hands together while Nellie sighed. "So very beautiful, every one of you."

"And the fits look good." Hattie bustled forward, all business for a moment. "I do think we can take Miriam's in a touch at the waist, but other than that, we did well."

"Oh, you did. You both did." Rachel's gratitude shone through her eyes and voice.

"Your brother commissioned us." Nell directed her gaze and attention to the kind, gentle, not-so-grumpy man at the end of the table. "He gets the credit on this."

"Levi." Rachel crossed the room and hugged him tight. "It's beyond precious. Thank you."

"I love it so much." Miriam followed her sister's lead and hugged her brother. "It's exactly what I would have picked out if I'd had a choice."

"And mine looks like it was made for me, because it was," Esther added when she hugged him. "You have made hearts happy this day, big brother."

"Good. It is something I should have thought of or done long before now, but having finally thought new thoughts and survived, there's one more thing you need to know."

"If it concerns a certain seamstress, I think we have that figured out, brother."

His smile agreed. He circled the planked table and clasped Nell's hand, but shook his head. "I think that's an understanding not in need of words, at least that's what Sol keeps telling me."

"A happy man is a visible presence," Sol observed, and he smiled when he said it.

"No, this is about us. Our claims and our family." Levi pulled Nell a little closer, but kept his gaze on his sisters. "I'm going to have our land written in all four names. Each of us will be one-quarter owner, so that if you marry, or don't marry, you are now and always will be either women of property, or women who can sell property."

"Levi." Rachel stepped forward, amazed. "You surprise me, brother."

"It's the right thing to do," he told her softly. "And again, one that should have been done by our father, before he passed, and I apologize for not seeing the need to respect your stations and your well-being. We've been partners in this endeavor from the beginning. We'll stay shared partners from this point on. The only thing I'd ask is that if you marry and decide to sell your share, you sell it back to us, first."

"As if we would do anything other, but yes. Oh, Levi, yes!" Esther began another round of hugs, and when the matter was getting quite out of hand, Hattie took a fork to a tin cup and made a great rattle until they all looked back at her.

"I do believe we've got supper waiting, and with the reverend rather long-winded this morning, I'd like nothing better than to sit and pray and rejoice with all of you. Over food," she added with a broad smile.

"Dinner sounds wonderful."

"And smells better!"

They took their seats like a family, united, and when Levi bowed his head and said a prayer, a circle of happy, thankful hearts joined in a sweet "Amen".

The five-room claim house was far removed from the glamorous life Samuel Cumberbie had dangled as bait. Nell didn't care a whit. The faith, hope and love surrounding the flickering Advent stove gave a brightness deeper than any jewel she'd ever seen back east. It was the glow of hope and home, everlasting.

And it was good.

FROM THE WRITINGS OF
Harriet McGillicuddy,
SECOND CHANCE, SOUTH DAKOTA, FOR POSTERITY:

WELL, IT CERTAINLY WAS A busy fall here! Having Nellie come with all her tricks and techniques for putting gowns just so was quite a change for the women hereabouts. It is such a pleasure to have a seamstress of that caliber in this small town, and what a perfect pairing, her and Levi Eichas. She brightens him like she brightens everything around her, and if ever a man could use a good-hearted, strong-minded, go-getter like Nellie, it's our Levi. And married life must agree with him, because he certainly seems less grumpy than he was before!

When spring comes, Levi's adding a wing onto his shop, a spot to live in when he and Nellie over-winter in town, but spring will bring problems, too. Sol Eichas has moved here to work a claim and build with his cousin Levi, and while all that's well and good, leave it to a man to not have a clue about the reality of a situation. Sol's children are coming west in the spring. His sister is seeing them out here, and then what's a man to do with a claim that needs tending, while working in town with Levi and managing two youngsters, racing about, tempting fate at every turn?

Well, that got me to thinking, and I've contacted Jean Ellen, and it is possible that she's got just the person to send west to do a bit of hem work, and child care. Jean Ellen says Ann's a delicate one, for sure, so maybe we're wrong to press, but I always found a tree learns to stand in the wind by standing in the wind. Adversity builds strength.

I'll take that wisdom to the grave, but not for a while, Lord be praised! For there is still work to be done in Second Chance, South Dakota. A strong-hearted town doesn't just appear, you know.

It gets formed, a stitch here, a tuck there, and in my time, I've noticed it gets formed a whole lot better and nicer if the women take their stand and have their say.

My opinions on that and possibly on a few other things didn't set well with the elders back in Massachusetts, but here in the west, a woman is a most important thing, and I'm not afraid to say so!

Second Chance Inn Old-fashioned Custard Tarts

Preheat oven to 375 degrees, then reduce oven temperature to 350 after ten minutes of baking.

FOR THE PASTRY

2 cups flour
1 Tablespoon sugar
6 Tablespoons ground walnuts
1 teaspoon salt
¾ cup soft butter
1/3 cup water
1 egg

Mix flour, walnuts, salt and sugar. Cut in the soft butter using two knives, criss-crossing them or a pastry blender until mixture resembles a soft "meal". Or use a Cuisinart food processor, but they didn't have one of these at the inn, I tell you! ☺

With fork, blend water and the egg. When thoroughly mixed, add to flour/nut mixture.

Mix until pastry cleans side of the bowl. If dry, sprinkle a bit more water onto pastry. Form into one large patty and then roll out, cutting rounds to fit into muffin or tart pans. Using additional flour to dust the table top eases the pastry rolling.

FOR THE CUSTARD FILLING

2 ½ cups whole milk
7 egg yolks
2/3 cup sugar
Nutmeg

Heat the milk until quite warm. Don't boil. Mix eggs and sugar thoroughly, using mixer or whisk, until pale, then add milk in a thin stream to keep eggs from curdling. Mix thoroughly. Pour custard filling into small pitcher or large measuring cup with a spout. Fill tart pans about ¾ full. Sprinkle with nutmeg. Bake at 375 degrees for the first ten minutes, then reduce oven temperature to 350 degrees. Bake until set, about fifteen to twenty minutes more. A convection oven tends to "pull up" the top layer of custard, so the gals from Second Chance advise using the regular bake setting for these tarts.

And you can add coconut to the tarts when almost done…. Making them coconut custard tarts. The crust is more cookie-like than a typical pie crust.

DEAR READERS,
Thank you so much for reading "Second Chance Christmas" the second story in my "Sewing Sisters Society" series!

You've probably guessed by now that I'm a God-loving, women-empowering kind of gal, and when I have the honor of writing stories, I want to see women overcome as needed, forge their success, grab hold of faith with both hands, and realize a full and blessed partnership in love, home and family. And I want my heroes to be flawed but fixable, the kind of men who see the value in a strong woman.

The Western frontier was not an easy place. It was rugged, dirty, hot, dry, wet, cold, windy, brutal and don't even get me started about the grasshoppers! But brave, bold folks made their way through all of that, so we can enjoy what we have today.

If you loved this story, there are links to my books after the third novella "Second Chance at Love." I hope you enjoy them, and I welcome your comments, e-mails, reviews, etc.

You can reach me at *loganherne@gmail.com* OR *www.ruthloganherne.com* or friend me on facebook or follow me on Twitter!

And may every Christmas you have be filled with the grace, faith, hope, love and joy God intended with the birth of his only begotten Son.

Merry Christmas!

Ruthy

Second Chance At Love

A Sewing Sisters Society Story

Ruth Logan Herne

Dedication

This one is dedicated to the courageous people who chanced the voyages from other nations to become the melting pot we know as "America" today. Your courage and conviction have built a nation. May your offspring and their offspring never fail in that same courage.

My flesh and my heart fail, but God is the strength of my heart and my portion forever.

~ Psalm 73:26

Chapter One

ANN SHOULD HAVE STAYED RIGHT where she was in Pennsylvania.

Guilt, fear and sorrow made for somber seatmates as the dark train chugged west across desolate land. Beiges and browns mixed with hints of gray, and the three stretched wide in every direction, occasionally broken by claim shacks looking no bigger than the muskrat lodges in Crawford Pond.

Quick tears stung her eyes.

She couldn't think of water. Of her home. Her old home, she corrected herself. Or her life there.

The Lord is my shepherd. I shall not want…

Well, He wasn't her shepherd. He wasn't any such thing, He wasn't Lord, God or any other lofty name men of the cloth spewed.

He was nothing. Nothing at all.

Ann squared her shoulders and lifted her chin in anger because anger was so much better than all those other feelings combined. Anger was manageable, most times.

The rest?

She clung to her satchel and the anger, sure of both. She'd boarded this train at Aunt Jean Ellen's insistence. Her maiden aunt meant well, but if it wasn't for Jean Ellen's friend needing immediate help, Ann would have stayed tucked in the valley, waiting for the sun to rise and then fall each day, an acceptable monotony. She'd go back to that soon enough, once she got her aunt's friend Hattie on the mend.

The whistle blew, sharp and long. She peered ahead. A puff of gray-black smoke obscured the view as the whistle repeated to announce their arrival.

"Second Chance! Second Chance, South Dakota, coming up! For all who've purchased tickets to this most particular destination, the train will be pulling into the station in three minutes." The clean-shaven conductor called out the current destination as he moved through the half-empty car, then he slipped through the door to the car in front of theirs.

Four people moved. Ann, from her seat on the front left, and a woman with two small children from the rear.

Ann didn't look back. She refused to look back. Hearing the chirps of their voices was difficult enough. No, she stood rock solid, eyes forward, ignoring the plaintive words of the children.

"I don't bemember." A swish of a skirt said they'd drawn close behind her, but the wee girl's voice was scarcely more than a whisper.

"Our pa will remember me!" bragged the boy. "'Cept I'm bigger now, 'course. And I can almost tie my boots tight, like real tight. He might remember you, Sarah. And he might not."

"Ethan." Haughtiness chilled the older woman's tone. "Your father will remember both of his children. What an awful thing to say."

"Not awful if it's the truth," the boy reasoned. "Aunt Ivy, I've *got* to use the necessary." Dancing feet indicated the boy's desperation. "Really bad."

"We're almost there, Ethan."

"Really, really bad!"

The brakes screeched. The train slowed. As it chugged to a stop, the boy pushed ahead.

"Ethan!"

"I gotta go!" The conductor was coming from the car

ahead of theirs. As he opened the door, the boy dashed through the connecting door looking left, then right before running down the short flight of stairs.

"Ethan!"The woman— Aunt Ivy— screeched his name as she pushed past Ann. She half-flew through the door, clutching the hand of the little girl. "Ethan, where are you?"

"Aunt Iby?"The tiny voice pulled Ann's eyes down.

Ann didn't want it to. She didn't want to look into a child's eyes, but the hint of childish worry left her no choice. She dropped her gaze.

Big brown eyes rounded in fright as a crush of people moved back and forth across the platform.

They might have been the only passengers from that car to disembark, but it seemed the spring rush was on, although there was no sign of spring to be seen under the thick, gray sky. Single men streamed from various train cars, and several small families moved their way from the far end of the train.

"Ethan!" Fear turned the older woman's call to a shriek. A couple of people turned, but then went on their way. "Ethan, where are you?"

"I want Eaffen."The girl's chin quivered. Her lower lip pudged out. And as the small throng of people obliterated the view, big tears slipped down her cheeks, one after another. "I want Eaffen. I want to go home. Pwease, Aunt Iby? Can you dust take me home?"

"Not now, Sarah! I must find your brother, I'm half beside myself with worry and I cannot deal with your tears again! Ethan!" She spun left, looking hard, then right.

No Ethan.

"Take charge of her." The sparrow-like woman thrust the little girl in Ann's direction. "I must find her brother, what if he's in front of this train when it starts up again? Or lost?"

Take her?

Watch her?

Ann's throat seized. Her heart did, too. She stared at the woman and shook her head. "I can't."

"Please!" The older woman left her no choice. She took the girl's hand and thrust it into Ann's. "Just for a moment, I must find her brother!" She dashed forward then, shouting the boy's name while the little girl sobbed.

"I want to go home, pwease." The child didn't screech the words like some would. She cried them in a tiny, soft voice, as if she'd been praying those words for way too long. "I dust want to go home."

A normal woman would stoop to the girl's level. A normal woman would croon words of comfort, and maybe even gather the child into her arms.

Ann stopped being normal a lifetime ago, and the last thing she wanted to do was take a child into her arms. "Here." She thrust a hanky into the tot's hands.

The wee girl ignored the gesture and cried harder.

Ann scoured the depot for Aunt Ivy or Ethan, for anyone who might be able to step in and offer this child hope.

Neither was in sight.

Her heart went hard, then soft, then hard again.

This wasn't her fight, this wasn't her job, this wasn't right by anyone's standards. She'd come here to get away from reminders of what had been and could never be again, and here she was, barely off the train, already mired in a past she didn't want to remember and was scared to death she'd forget.

"Sarah? Sarah! What on earth?" A tall, broad-shouldered man hurried their way. He stared at Ann, then the child, before lifting his eyes back to Ann. "What are you doing with my daughter? Who are you and where are Aunt Ivy and Ethan?"

His daughter.

The worry in his face made her words stumble, but the reality helped ease her voice because he was about to take this child off her hands. And then— maybe, then— she could breathe again. Act normal. "Ethan dashed off to the necessary, Aunt Ivy followed and Sarah was most unhappily left in my charge."

"Ivy left her with a complete stranger?" The man's expression darkened as he bent. "Perhaps you became acquainted on the train?"

"I assure you, sir, no such thing happened. I was minding my own business, and they minded theirs. Until we disembarked and then, well." Ann shrugged as he scooped up the wailing child. "Here we are."

"Sarah, Sarah, darling. Pa's got you, honey, I've got you. Aunt Ivy brought you out here to me, and we'll never be apart from each other again, darling. I promise. I promise."

He cradled the girl against him as if she was the most precious thing in the world, and Ann's chest seized tight, seeing it.

Had Jonah ever held their children like that? Oh, he'd cared for them in his own manner, but not with this outpouring of love, the strength of tone. No, all this seemed new, and for a brief moment she wondered if this father took foolish, careless chances with his children's lives.

She squelched the thought, but it refused to leave completely, lingering on the outskirts of her mind as a group of people headed their way.

"Solomon, never have I been so happy to see someone in my life!" Like a brown bird, Aunt Ivy sprang up the steps with moves belying her age, half-dragging the boy alongside. "If ever there was a child in need of a good thrashing, this is it!" She thrust the boy forward. Distress heightened her voice and anger tightened already taut cheeks. The boy's face paled at the onslaught. "I near to suffered my death just trying to keep him alive on the journey, and had I known Violet was going to take ill, I'd have canceled our tickets and waited. But here we are, alive and unscathed, no thanks to this wretched imp!"

Ann wanted to look away. She needed to look away, she needed to run away because the thought of this man hitting this boy, a boy not even school age, just for being a boy?

Oh, her heart couldn't take it and her brain wouldn't allow it, therefore she should turn and go, even though she had no idea where she was going in this new town.

"Sol, are these your children?" A bright-stepping woman hurried their way, and Ann's first thought was 'sunshine'. The woman seemed light, and it wasn't just her blond hair and pale skin, but the way she carried the blue and yellow dress. She moved with quick, delighted steps, as though happy with life. A part of Ann hated her on sight.

Another part thought how nice it would be to walk in this woman's path for a while because Ann was that sick and tired of her own.

"Oh, aren't they so absolutely beautiful?" The woman drew close, smiling. "You must be Sarah, and your Pa wasn't wrong when he said you were about the prettiest, sweetest little thing in all of Minnesota. And you." She re-directed her smile down to the worried boy, and stuck out her hand. "Ethan, I'm your cousin Nellie, I've just recently married your cousin Levi and your dad and Levi work together."

Ethan darted a troubled look from her to his father and back.

"You're an Eichas?" Ivy didn't ask the question. She demanded it.

The blonde straightened and turned her way. "By marriage, and happily, and don't tell me you're Aunt Ivy?"

The narrow woman glowered. "I'm Ivy Eleanor Eichas Gruber."

"Oh, you don't look anything like what I pictured," Nellie told her. "You're so much younger than what 'great-aunt' implies, and I have no great-anythings of my own, you see, being second generation immigrants. This is a true delight!" As the older woman's face relaxed, Nellie turned toward Ann. "Are you Ann?"

Ann nodded slowly because she couldn't think of anything else to do.

"Well, I suppose I shouldn't see this as a huge coincidence, that you all traveled the same train together. This isn't like Pittsburgh, where trains roll in and out throughout the day, going every which way. Ann." She paused for breath and grasped Ann's right hand in two of her own. "How happy we are to have you here. Hattie gave us quite a scare with her fall, and she's doing better now, but as you can see." She waved a hand around the nearly empty station. "We've got our share of people moving in and out, and Hattie's sewing shop is the only one for some distance. The amount of sewing when you have a land filled with single men is of an amazing quantity. I'm so happy to make your acquaintance." She dipped a quick, friendly curtsy. "I'm Nellie Eichas, and I work for Hattie, too. I was just on my way down here to meet you when I came across Sol's boy, in a moment of delicate necessitation."

"Nellie, thank you for helping him." The man smiled at the sunny woman as he stooped and opened his free arm to the boy. "Ethan, come here, come to your Pa. I can't believe how much I've missed you two. I've been fairly bursting, waiting for this moment for months. And now it's here."

Nellie turned her attention back to the prim-lipped older woman. "Aunt Ivy, I know it was Sol that brought you out here, but I'd love to drive you out to the farm and see Levi's sisters. Unless Sol has plans?" She looked up at the children's father and he shook his head.

"No plans of note, Nellie. Just to get these two settled and fed."

"Are there children out there?" Ivy asked. A firm sniff said there better not be.

"None as yet, but we're hopeful that will change at some point."

"I'll be gone in forty-eight hours, if it doesn't change until after that, I'd be glad enough." She glowered at the children, and they shrank back in unison. "In my day, children minded the first time, every time."

Ann was pretty sure that day had never existed, but she kept her mouth closed.

Nellie faced the man. "Sol, if I take Aunt Ivy out to the farm, can you see Ann to Hattie's shop for me and explain my change of plans?"

"I'd be glad to, Nellie."

"Good! Ann." She turned back toward Ann and if she noticed Ann's silence, she made no note of it. "I'll be back in town tomorrow and I'll have a chance to work with you then. For today, I'll leave it to Hattie to settle you in while I take Aunt Ivy on a little excursion."

Ann had little choice, it seemed. She nodded, and as Nellie bustled Aunt Ivy in one direction, Sol snugged Sarah in one arm and took Ethan's hand, but then he paused, eyeing her suitcase. "Well, this won't work, will it?" He spoke softly, as if mulling the possible answers, and when the boy saw the direction of Sol's gaze, he jumped up and down.

"You need a free hand to haul that suitcase, Pa." When Sol smiled and nodded, the boy puffed up his chest just so. "When I'm bigger, I can haul maybe three suitcases that size, all at the same time!"

"I expect that will be so," Sol agreed, and he let the boy's hand go in order to pick up her larger bag. "We're going to go down the steps and into the street, Ethan. Mind you watch for horses and wagons and such. I didn't bring you all this way to have something happen to you."

"I'll mind, Pa."

The man said the words casually enough, but they swiped daggers at Ann's pretense. Small children in peril, everywhere she went.

She couldn't deal with it again. She wouldn't deal with it again, the thought of facing less than happy fates repugnant. She stretched out a hand. "I can manage my own bag, sir."

"I've got it just fine." Sol picked up the heavy bag as if it was nothing, then indicated the boy with a thrust of his chin. "You hang onto him, keep him from harm. I'll tote this on down the road."

Keep him from harm.

Her throat swelled. Her knees shook. She wanted to reply, but no words choked out, and when the boy reached right up and clasped her hand, Ann Hazel was pretty sure she'd fall right down and die on the spot.

She didn't. But she wanted to, and it had been that way for a long, long time.

Chapter Two

S OL COULDN'T WAIT TO GET his children out of there, away from two embittered women, and settle his precious youngsters into their new lives in the west. He'd never in his life expected Aunt Ivy to accompany the children, and he had to hope they weren't scarred for life, because Ivy Gruber wasn't an easy person to be near in the best of circumstances.

Hopefully the children would have short memories of the trip, replaced by good ones of their new home.

And this woman— *Ann*— a new helper at Hattie's place. He chanced a glance her way.

Hooded brown eyes, jaw set, eyes forward, she walked down the street somberly. Not sullen, exactly. More like sober and silent, as if nothing in God's world brightened her days.

Ethan spotted the smithy shop and whooped. "Pa! Is that where you work? Can I help? I think I can be a big help now, I turned five!"

"You need a few more years under your belt before you help in the shop," Sol told him, and when the boy frowned, Sol added, "But there's plenty to do on the farm."

"Miss Tillie said you were a darn fool to leave a family business behind," Ethan told him. He looked around. "And Joe said she was wrong and you needed to find your way. Did you find it, Pa?"

A loaded question if ever there was one and shame on Tillie for speaking loose in front of youngsters. Sol met the little guy's earnest gaze. "I found a place to find it, son, and that's the first step, isn't it?"

"I 'spect it is," Ethan agreed. He started to dash ahead when he spotted the sign over the new board sidewalk. "E-I-C-H-A-S! That's us, Pa!"

"Cousin Levi just had those signs made so folks could find the smithy and the wagon shop. And look at you, able to spell so soon! Who taught you that?"

"Miss Lizzie and Uncle Joe. She comes out to visit and she likes sitting with me and teaching me things."

"Lizzie and Joe, is it?" Sol nodded. "She's a fine match for him. We need to turn here, ma'am." Sol jutted his chin left and turned. Met Ann's gaze.

His heart slowed. His breath did, too, to see such utter sadness in her face, her eyes, her very steps. He knew that look. He'd seen that look, day after day, in the silvered glass back home. He'd buried his wife, and he'd hit the ground running, caring for a toddler and a newborn and a job and—

Oh, he knew that look, all right.

Grief, painted in shades of gray to match the leaden sky.

Hattie had put up a new sign too, to celebrate the town boardwalks. The woman looked up, read the sign, and kept moving forward. Not like she wanted to, but like she had no other choice.

He recognized that, too, and while he felt sorry for her, his children had faced enough hardship in their short years. Sol aimed to see they were raised up proper, surrounded by joy and hope. He motioned the woman ahead and she moved up the stairs. She loosed Ethan's hand to open the door, sighed, took a breath, and turned the knob as if it was the most difficult thing in the world. The click of the door handle drew Hattie's attention.

"Are you Ann?" The middle-aged seamstress got up somewhat slowly from the seat drawn up to her sewing machine, a true wonder of modern technology. "And Sol, on my word, Sol Eichas!" Hattie clapped her hands in delight when she spotted him and the children behind Ann. "Are these your children? Sol, they're precious in God's sight, and mine, too! How wonderful that they've arrived!" She switched her attention right back to Ann. "That you've all arrived. Come in, come in!"

"I'd love to, but I can't," Sol told her. "I've got to get Ethan and Sarah settled in my room and most likely fed, if I remember correctly." He smiled down at Ethan and the boy agreed quickly.

"I'm real hungry, Pa!"

"Nellie wants you to know that she's taking my Aunt Ivy who is also Levi's Aunt Ivy out to the farm to reacquaint with Rachel, Miriam and Esther. I told her I'd see Miss Ann over here."

"Just Ann."

The sharp note in her voice made Sol turn, surprised. "Well. Sorry." He glanced at Hattie, but she wasn't looking at him. Her attention was trained on the solemn woman, and Sol didn't miss the worried furrow lining her brow.

"Sol, before you go, if you could walk Ann's bag into the back, that would be lovely, and I do believe children in my day enjoyed an odd biscuit or two." Hattie retrieved a tin as if wondering, opened it wide and held it out. "I wonder if that's still the case?"

"I like them a whole lot!" Ethan grinned up at her, eyes bright, and his curly, brown hair in a mess.

"Then you should have one, I believe!" Hattie's smile matched his, and when Ethan had picked out the biggest cookie he could find, she held the tin lower for Sarah.

Sarah shrank back into Sol's side. She didn't return Hattie's smile, or reach for the treat. She looked tired, ornery and overwhelmed by the entire affair. "Ethan, can you take one for Sarah, too?" Sol asked. "She might like one once we get settled."

"Sure, Pa!"

"Ann, I'll set these here and let you remove your wrap. You can hook it right back there, just inside the door, so handy, don't you think?"

In all that time, the woman hadn't loosened her cloak, nor had she moved. She stood silent and still, as if wondering how she'd arrived at this place.

"Handy. Yes." She pulled in a breath and reached up to undo her cloak, but then she didn't undo it. She stared, straight ahead, her hands raised, and one silent, single tear dripped down her cheek.

Sol had the sudden urge to either run or offer assistance, but he had no clue how. He turned to Hattie for help, but she was moving to the living quarters herself. "Thank you for seeing Ann over, Sol, I'm that beholdin'. I'll be glad enough when this leg heals proper, but in the meantime I'm much obliged for the kindness of neighbors."

"And friends," Sol reminded her. He took her cue and ignored the woman's plight, but he did it reluctantly. His father used to say that if a stray animal longed to be saved, it should wander into Sol's path, and there was truth in those words. He liked to forge, and he liked to fix, and that included folks and critters, too, but he had enough fixing on his plate right now. He lifted Sarah back into his arms and guided Ethan through the door. "See you soon, Hattie. Nice meeting you, Miss." He stumbled over the mistake and corrected himself, stumbling again. "Ann, I mean. Nice meeting you, Ann."

She nodded slightly. Her gaze settled on the children, then jerked away, and Sol left, pretty sure that Miss Ann or Ann or whoever she was, was way too sensitive and tentative to make it on the prairie. The prairie took guts and gumption, and Sol had plenty of that.

He was sorry that Tillie Aldrich spouted off in front of his son, but Sol would show the boy that faith in God, hard work, and devotion paid off. He had no room in his life for sour. He'd come west to embrace the sweetness of independence, and he had every intention of doing exactly that, with his children at his side at long last.

"Now, Ann."

Ann swiped the dampness from her cheek and moved forward.

"Have a seat right there and we'll chat."

Ann didn't want to talk. She didn't want to answer questions about what had been and what was lost. If she could, she'd find a potion that wiped away all memories, because she couldn't think of the good ones without crying, and she couldn't think without crying, so maybe not thinking at all would just be better. She moved forward and took the seat reluctantly.

"Hems."

"Excuse me?" Surely she heard wrong. She faced Hattie more directly.

"Jean Ellen assured me that your hand-sewing skills are of solid note, and dress hems are a constant source of aggravation." Hattie raised her hands. "I'm quick on the machine, but my fingers, truth to tell, aren't as nimble as they once were, and a machine hem is fine on undergarments, but on a gown, a hem should not be noticed." She finger-tapped the table to punctuate the last four words. "Invisibility is the goal, and a fine hand with a blind stitch sets the pace."

Ann took a moment to wrap her head around the conversational turn. "I'm good at hems."

"Exactly!" Hattie smiled. "Lucky for me that Jean Ellen sent you my way because of my leg injury." She patted her left leg. "I took a misstep on the new boardwalk and gave a good twist to my ankle. It does appear to be healing nicely, quicker than I'd originally supposed, but to have you around with a hand for a turn-and-tuck hem, well, that's a problem solved, right there."

A problem solved.

Yes.

Hattie didn't want to delve into her life and her past. She wanted to talk about work. About sewing.

Ann took a breath, because that was something she could do. "It's all right that I stay here, then?" She glanced around the living area. "With you?"

"Room and board are part of the package, so yes. I love having a bit of company, although my last two assistants managed to fall in love and get married, so neither lived with me any too long. But they're now life-long friends and ready and willing to help build this town up proper."

"Well, that won't be the case with me," Ann told her softly. "But I am grateful for a chance to do a job and come west. It was always a dream of mine, to try new things."

"And there you go. You're here, I'm here, and the west is new!" Hattie pointed up front. "That's where most of the work will get done, but when Nellie's here, there's scarcely room for the two of us in front, and dresses and skirts are rather large."

"I could work back here, all alone. I'd prefer it, actually."

"Well, fine, that will work splendidly, except, of course, when it won't, but we'll figure that out as things go by, don't you think?"

Think? Ann hadn't had time to think, but she was pretty sure whatever Hattie said made sense. "We can adjust as we go, of course."

"Exactly that, dear, and now, how about a bite? Nothing major, I expect your stomach's a bit riled from the rumblings of that train, but isn't it just the most amazing invention? Why the sound of that whistle put me in mind of coming west years back, and I haven't regretted a minute of it."

Ann would never be able to say that, but she nodded

because it was expected. Lately she hated doing what was expected, but maybe out here, where the trees were different, and there were no rolling mountains and raging rivers… maybe here, the expected would be easier. Because there was nothing in Second Chance to remind her of what she'd left in Pennsylvania.

Chapter Three

"WHAT DO YOU MEAN, SAMANTHA can't watch the kids?" Sol couldn't have heard right. He peered over Ginny's shoulder to see if this was some kind of joke. Surely, Ginny's seventeen-year-old daughter would come walking out, laughing.

"We can't let her near your children," Ginny told him. "What if she's contagious? And she most likely is, the poor dear."

Sol swallowed hard. "That wouldn't be good."

"No, it wouldn't, and it might just be a bad cold, but it could be worse. She's got fever and chills. Saints alive, if those little ones came down plum sick like that, I'd be beyond vexed with myself because I'm a mother, Solomon. I know better."

Sol did too. There were plenty of child graves back in Minnesota. His ma used to say if you can raise them to school age, you've got a good shot at raising them right on through. Ethan and Sarah weren't school age, and there was no way he could take a chance with them, but what was he supposed to do? He and Levi had commitments and contracts for work.

He stared around, thinking, then stepped back as Hattie came into the store. "Sol, good morning! Oh, isn't this a glorious day?" she asked, but in typical Hattie style, she didn't wait for or need an answer. "That touch of warmth is such a gift, and I saw a peek of sun not long ago. Not enough to do much yet, but a promise, Sol." She laughed and gripped his hands firmly. "A promise, for sure. The weather will soon turn and we'll all be busy in the dirt, planting, sowing—" She spotted his expression and paused. "What is it? What's wrong? Is it the children?"

He opened his mouth to speak, but Ginny stepped right up and did it for him. "Samantha's gone and gotten sick, and she was going to watch Ethan and little Sarah for Sol but of course she can't risk getting them sick, and her so faint she doesn't dare raise her head."

"No." Hattie looked from Ginny to Sol, distraught. "Oh, Sol…" She paused, then turned as the door opened behind her. "Ann. Of course. Ann to the rescue. Ann could watch the children today. Problem solved."

Sol recognized the somber woman from the train, and the last thing he had in mind was letting a grumpy person rescue him or his marvelous children. He was just about to say he'd keep the kids himself and hang Levi out to dry, when the woman's eyes went wide.

Pain.

He saw the look and it kind of broke his heart to see it, because he knew that kind of pain first-hand.

"I couldn't." The woman— Ann— stepped back, bumping the now-closed door. "I, I…" She bit her lip and shook her head.

"Hattie, I'm sure Levi would understand—" Sol began an appeal, but Hattie wasn't the sort to look toward excuses. He'd figured that out when they first met.

"Well, he would for a day or so, but land sakes, Sol, you can't be thinking Levi took hold of all those orders thinking he'd be doing them himself?"

Well, no, he hadn't thought that at all. But he'd also figured he had all this babysitting stuff arranged. And Hattie's helper looked just as concerned about watching Ethan and Sarah as he was about letting her watch them. "I'll go talk with him."

"I declare, if you leave it to a man to come up with the

common sense of a given situation, you'll be waiting far too long." Hattie set her hands atop her thick hips and went toe-to-toe with Sol. "We have the perfect answer right here. Ann and I can mind the kids at my place for the day, you can get your work done, and we'll have a bonnie time of it. You can't leave Levi to tackle the spring rush of orders, and I've got work to get back to, myself. Ginny." She swung about as if the day was settled, and Sol was pretty sure that in her mind, it was. "I've a need for some plain white cotton for undergarments, nothing fancy, but good quality."

"How many yards, Hattie?"

"Well, Joy Thurston isn't a small woman, and we're talking a full petticoat, though I hope she has sense enough to stay clear of hot stoves. Maybe ten yards, give or take, and that way I've got extra on hand. And five lengths of white shirting, as well. The rail has decided all workers not in uniform should wear white, not blue, which is fine for me because I get more business, but it's a raw shake for the men who need to replace shirts before they're worn out."

"Pa?"

Sol turned at the sound of Ethan's voice.

"Can we come down now?"

"I believe your question is a little late since you're already down," Sol replied, but he couldn't hold back a smile.

"Well, it took so long, and you said you'd be just a minute to get the girl, and we waited a lot of minutes, so I wanted to make sure no injuns or anything got you."

"Indians, and there are no hostile natives here," Hattie told him. She stooped a little and tapped a finger to her chin. "I expect you're getting just about old enough to prepare for school, aren't you, Ethan?"

"I think I am," he told her, looking every bit as serious.

"Well, it's a good thing I still have some fine supplies at my place for a youngster who likes to learn."

"I wike to wearn, too. I wike it a very wot." Sarah peeked

out from behind Ethan. "I know a wot of things."

"I bet you do, darling. Well, Sol, why don't you take the kids and Ann to my shop and get them settled. I'll be along a little more slowly, and Hi can bring my things by later on, can't he Ginny?"

"He'd be happy to, Hattie. And Sol, I'm right sorry about Samantha, but I'm so relieved to have Ann on hand." She directed a smile to the somber woman. "Perfect timing."

There was nothing perfect about this timing, nor anything that could remotely be called good, but Ann swallowed her fear and followed Sol Eichas and his kids out the door.

She could make a run for it. She mentally measured the distance between the mercantile and the depot, but just as her feet felt ready to fly, five little fingers reached up and threaded themselves with hers. "I fink it will be fun to be wiff you, Miss Ann."

Those fingers, so small.

The voice, like a breath of fresh spring air, bright and light and full of life.

Sarah clutched hold and fairly danced down the outside steps. "It feels good to be outside, Pa! I don't wike being all cooped up wike Aunt Iby's chickens!"

"But sometimes you need to be indoors and mind a grown-up, Sarah Joy. Children need to mind and be watched."

"I don't need so much watchin'," declared Ethan. "Opa said I'm 'bout sized for workin', and that's what I aim to do."

"Did he, now?" Sol asked the question mildly, but Ann heard something fiercer in the question. "I think you'll be fine helping me out on the farm, Ethan. But not on your own, not for a while. Right now you'll be working with your father."

"But Opa—"

"Opa isn't here and it's my job to keep you safe." Sol squatted and looked carefully into each small face with an expression of such love that Ann could almost cry, seeing it. But what didn't make her cry these days?

She swallowed a sigh and tried not to mind Sarah's tiny hand tucked in hers.

"I'll make decisions and you need to listen to me, both of you. This is a big land out here, and grand enough, but there are dangers on farms and in metal shops. Do you hear me?" He looked from one to the other, stern.

"I do, Pa!" Sarah smiled up at him, all sweetness and light, but Ethan rolled his eyes.

"I mean it, son." Sol stood and palmed the boy's head. "I know you're headstrong, but if you do dangerous things, you're going to have to be watched more closely and I guarantee you won't like that."

The boy grumbled and sulked, but when they got to Hattie's shop, he smiled. "At least we have really good cookies here! Aunt Ivy's cookies are dry, like old biscuits. Miss Hattie's were real good. Like my Ma's."

Sol's face shadowed. Ann read the loss and the sorrow, jumbled like a bowl of mixed beans. Blended flavors and textures, that's what his creased face made her think of, but then Ethan skipped up the steps and paused.

He looked around. So did Sarah. And when Sol cleared his throat, she realized they were waiting for her. "I need to let us in, I guess."

It felt odd to let folks into someone else's house, but she'd come West feeling odd, so this wasn't much different. And when the two children hurried through to the small living area, she remembered how tough it was to keep children busy and content in small quarters.

How could she do this?

Why would she do this?

This wasn't what she came west for, this wasn't part of the deal, but when Ethan saw a pack of sticks on Hattie's counter, he laughed out loud. "We can play sticks, Sarah!"

"Sarah's small for that game," warned their father, but not in a tired voice. It was a gentle voice, filled with warmth. "Don't take advantage of that, son."

"I won't." Ethan smiled a promise, but Ann was pretty sure he'd best his sister every chance he got. "I don't have to do numbers, do I?"

"Numbers are good practice. Letters, too. If Miss Ann doesn't mind."

"Just Ann, please."

"Ann, then."

"I saw a chalkboard over beyond that window curtain, and perhaps a slate pencil is there, too?"

Sol moved back, reached around and nodded as he withdrew the small slate and the rose-toned pencil. "Here you go."

"I expect Hattie makes notes on this with ink being so costly these days."

"Makes sense, ma'am. Are you sure you're okay with this, Ann?"

She wasn't one bit sure, she was almost one hundred percent certain she'd rather be most anywhere else besides this room, trapped with two small children, but when she looked up, his sweet, gentle face made her heart pause and her tongue stammer.

Kindness and concern softened his rugged features. When he dipped his chin in question, as if he really cared about her answer, something warm and sweet flowed through her. It felt strange and at odds because she'd been cold as stone for so very long.

But not now, not here, with him looking down and her looking up. "It's fine."

"Okay." He bent and kissed the children goodbye, then turned. "I didn't bring a lunch for them, I can have something made up by noon or thereabouts."

"That's fine, too."

"Okay, then."

"We'll see you at lunch."

"All right." He hesitated, then shoved his hat onto his head and walked out, carefully closing the door behind him.

And there she was, in a strange house, an unfamiliar room, with someone else's children staring up at her, wondering what she'd do next.

Ann was wondering the very same thing.

Chapter Four

WALKING AWAY FROM THOSE CHILDREN was one of the toughest things Sol had done since coming to Second Chance last year.

He didn't know that woman. He hadn't planned on his children spending their day cooped up in a sewing shop, littered with pins and needles and what all. He strode into the smithy, ignored Levi's greeting, changed into his work apron and growled.

"Good heavens, man, I thought having your kids nearby would be pleasing to you." Levi sent him a mildly amused look, pretty strange for a man who'd spent most of his adult life grumpy. Then he'd gone and found himself a spunky wife and all of a sudden Levi Eichas was walking around town with a goofy grin on his face. "Trouble already?"

Sol shook his head, then nodded, then shrugged.

"Well, which is it?"

"I had everything fixed, and then Samantha went and caught sick and couldn't watch the kids and now they're up the road at Hattie's with a perfect stranger minding them, and her not looking any too happy about the situation."

"Well that makes two of you, then," Levi replied cheerfully. "They're barely out of your sight, Hattie's door is about four hundred feet away. If she needs you, she can practically hail you from there without even opening a door."

"But what am I going to do?" Sol straightened up, squared

his shoulders and faced Levi. "I should have thought this through more carefully. It's time to move to the claim and that means trying to mind the kids on the claim while I work the claim and work here."

"It's a tough row, either way," Levi agreed. "If they're in town, there's danger. If they're on the claim, there's danger. Either way, you need a woman, Sol. You ever thought of marrying again? Not to be nosy," he added, but then shrugged. "But watching kids and a farm and a job in town is about a job too many no matter how ambitious the man."

It was, and his father had scoffed at his ability to juggle all this before he left the previous year. Sol had ignored the older man's warning, and set off on his own. With reality facing him, he had absolutely no idea how to make this work. He planned to stop by the hotel to buy lunch for the kids, but Nellie had entered the shop a quarter hour before noon. She heard his plan and stepped right in. "I've got food right here, Sol, follow me. Fresh bread, Hattie's jam, and here's a sugar cake, made by Miriam just yesterday. I'll cut away the scorch mark, she's none too good with that stove when calves are dropping, and the kids will like it just fine. And milk, I've got some in the pitcher in the cool room." She moved to the back of the little apartment Levi had fashioned onto the building, then bustled back. "Miriam will bring me milk tomorrow when she brings Ivy back to the train and I just need a splash for Levi's coffee."

"And yours," Levi reminded her.

She made a face, a face Sol remembered like it was yesterday instead of four long years back. "I've lost my taste for coffee. It smells funny."

"The coffee does?" Levi looked astounded. He sniffed his coffee, sipped, then frowned. "It tastes just fine, Nell. Are you catching a cold? That can make things smell off."

She glanced from him to Sol. She hesitated, and Sol got the message. "I'll give you two a minute."

"A minute? For what?" Levi scraped a rag to his forehead, looking perplexed.

Sol stepped outside, and when he heard Levi's whoop of delight, he took time then and there to say a prayer, a solid one.

He'd been so excited to have a family. He'd walked around with his chest puffed out, so sure of who he was, where he was going and what he was doing.

And when everything went all right with Ethan, Sol honestly never gave a thought to not having more children. Why would he? He had a strong, beautiful wife, so sweet and kind. A small parcel of land, sectioned off his father's holdings. And a son, a beautiful boy, burly and bright.

Later he couldn't imagine being so cavalier about something as dangerous as pregnancy. Sure it was natural. He'd been farm-born and field-raised, he understood the workings of life and procreation and was a big proponent. Being in love with his wife and making love with his wife hadn't just been *good*.

It had been amazing.

And then the smiling midwife handed him a tiny, squalling bundle, Sarah Joy, and his heart was full. So full. "A girl, this time." She'd nodded as if approving a job well done. "So nice, jah?"

It was. He'd held Sarah and showed her off to her big brother who didn't seem overly impressed. And then he'd walked out to the kitchen and showed Sarah to the aunts, careful to hold her just so.

They'd preened over the amazement of it all.

And then the midwife screamed his name.

He'd almost dropped the baby.

He didn't, but only because Elsa Bean had reached right out and grabbed hold of the newborn.

He'd turned and rushed back into the first-floor bedroom, the birthing room his mother had called it.

Gone.

His beautiful, precious wife, full of life, love and laughter, a vessel of joy where ever she went, simply… gone. Just like that. And not a word of explanation from anyone, except that sometimes things just didn't go right.

His gut went tight, standing there on the chill, windswept stoop. His hands did, too, then the palms got damp.

Levi Eichas was on the other side of that door, hugging his pretty, bouncy wife because of the news she'd just shared. Better he wasn't in that room for a while because one look at his face would spoil their glee.

That wasn't his right, but after burying his beloved wife in a cemetery filled with small children and young wives, he realized he hadn't known all that much after all, because if he'd known then what he knew now, his boy would have been an only child, and he'd still have a mother.

"Sol, here's the food packed up." Nellie came out the door, smiling, and Sol had to hold back words of warning. "Levi said if you need a few minutes with the kids, go ahead. He won't need those wheel straps for a little bit."

"I'll give them a hug and kiss, but I've got a job for Phillip Dickinson I want to finish up."

"He's a good, solid customer and his wife is the sweetest thing. I wish they lived closer, I'd like a chance to see our children grow up side by side."

"Well with newfangled things coming along pretty regular, there might be a time when a dozen miles isn't a big deal half the year."

"We live in amazing times," she agreed. "I'm off to the mercantile, then back to Hattie's to work with Ann and set her up with a couple of hems." She started off, then paused and turned back. "Hems," she announced, as if women's clothing had suddenly become profound.

"Huh?" Sol had taken two steps toward Hattie's when she stopped.

"Ann's going to be hand-stitching hems on gowns, and there's no reason she couldn't do that right out at your claim, Sol."

He tried to talk but it came out more as a croak. "My claim?"

"Don't you see? Ann needs money, she does lovely hand stitching, and if she's taking care of hems, Hattie and I can take on more jobs that require the machine or pin-tucks and smocking. But she doesn't have to do her part *here.*" Hattie waved a hand to indicate their small western town. "She could do it out at your place and watch the kids. At least until Samantha's better."

Sol was a quiet man by nature, but not generally speech-less.

Right now he was exactly that, and it wasn't because Nellie's idea didn't have merit. He'd found over the winter that Nellie knew a lot, thought a lot, and decided a lot which kept Levi on his toes. Now that was all well and good for his cousin Levi, but Sol liked to make up his own mind about things, after a while.

"Sol, I can see that Eichas-born stubborn look on your face, and for pity's sake, just this once, if an Eichas man didn't have to be cajoled into seeing the common sense of the situation before it got to crisis point, that would ben-efit every one of us. I'm doing the math, Solomon, and in this case one plus one equals your kids are safe and sound on their new claim, just like they should be. With a very," she tapped a finger to his arm. "nice," she tapped him once more, even though he took a step back. "woman," she fin-ished. She'd stopped tapping him, and he decided he might want to pray a little harder for his cousin Levi because Nellie Eichas was a pistol, sure as shooting.

"Nellie, you mean well, but you're asking me to take a woman out to a claim with no chaperone. I don't think this Ann or anyone else would take a shine to that idea."

"Nor would I and shame on you for thinking it, although these days folks have to do what they have to do to make it out here. I'm right here in town, and if I ride out to get her in the evening, Hattie and I can see her back home. The days are getting longer, leaving time enough to drive to your place, pick Ann up, then have her back in the morning. And you're halfway out to Levi's farm, so between the girls and us, we can make this work." The quite capable Eichas sisters worked their farm just beyond his claim.

Still he hesitated, and she rolled her eyes as she tugged her cape more snugly around her shoulders as she turned back toward the road. "Something to think on, Sol."

She said it in a tired voice that meant he shouldn't have to think on it, and he almost smiled because his wife had used the same kind of voice with him. Fairly often, as a matter of fact.

He missed Greta's pretty smile. Her light hair, tucked up but always coming loose, and sometimes coming loose on purpose, into his hands. And yes, he missed her funny scoldings, too, because she didn't have a mean bone in her body and the scoldings were more funny than exasperating.

He missed her.

Nellie's news had stirred up an old pot of mixed regrets, and as he strode toward Hattie's, Nellie's advice hit a nerve, but he wasn't ready to have someone just slip into their lives, taking their mother's place.

You were okay with it when it was Samantha, an inner voice scolded. *Why not Ann? What's different about her?*

Samantha was a child. A teenager, sure, but a girl, still. This Ann woman with the soulful eyes and the tired brow and the fragile mouth...

She needed caring for. He could see that right off, but he saw something else, too, when she looked around Second Chance. She was eyeing a new beginning, just like him, and that made her vulnerable. Or maybe he was the vulnerable one.

Either way, he wasn't about to spread talk or rumors by having her out to the house, or have his children cared for by a stern, unsmiling person. There'd been plenty of that with Aunt Ivy around. Now it was time to embrace a new beginning. He clutched the little sack of food tightly and bounded up Hattie's steps, nearly plowing a railroad man over in his rush.

Hattie looked up as he strode in. She looked surprised, then a little exasperated, but she nodded toward the back. "They're right in there, Sol."

The thick curtain separating the front from the living space had been drawn shut. He stepped up to it, then stopped in his tracks.

"Like this?" Ethan's voice pitched up with excitement from beyond the tightly woven door. "Just like this, Miss Ann?"

"Exactly like that."

Her voice surprised him. It surprised him so much that he stood there on the near side of the curtain like a perfect ninny while she talked.

"Your 'E' is perfect and the t is fine, but that h resembles an 'n' that forgot to grow a leg! Try this, instead." Silence filled the air for a few seconds, then Ethan laughed.

"I did it!"

"And so you did."

He turned toward Hattie to see if she was as surprised as he was.

Nope.

She looked pleased but not one bit surprised, and that meant she'd expected Ann to rise to the occasion. But then, Hattie McGillicuddy expected the best out of everyone, so maybe she wasn't the most reliable indicator. But come to think of it, she hadn't been wrong once in the months he'd known her, so maybe *he* was the doubter. He opened the curtain a little. "Ann?"

She turned his way quickly and for a moment her hopeful look made him see a different woman. A different Ann. Younger. Softer. More approachable. And the minute he thought that, he scolded himself internally for thinking it. "I brought some lunch by from Nellie. Like I said, I never thought to pack one this morning."

"But you did now, and it's perfect timing." She crossed the room with a polite stride. Her expression had gone wan again, but for those few seconds he'd seen the beauty within her, and that wasn't his overactive imagination working.

The woman was downright lovely when she put a smile on her face, and for just a moment he wondered what he could do to see that smile re-appear. She took the small sack from his hands and set it to one side. "Thank you, Mr. Eichas. Did you want to visit with the children?"

"Sol. Please."

She frowned before her face relaxed. "Sol." She said the simple name softly, as if testing it on her tongue.

"I appreciate the offer, but I can't stay. We're swamped up the road."

"It's a thrill to have so many orders, isn't it?" Hattie offered from her post at the machine. "There's a comfort in gainful employment that helps soothe the weariest soul."

"Keeping busy and seed money for the farm, two good things. Everything is going all right?"

Sarah jumped up to hug him, spilling the button box she'd been sorting. She stopped, clapped her hands to her mouth and looked downright scared to death. "I'm sowry! I'm sowry! I'm sowry!"

Sol moved forward from his side of the room.

So did Ann. She got to Sarah first, and crouched low, her dull skirt fanning the floor. "It gave us a start, didn't it? But it's just buttons, after all, Sarah. Easily spilled and easily picked up."

Sarah stared at her. So did Ethan. Then Ethan glanced up at Sol and the sight of his father seemed to make him breathe easier. "Aunt Ivy didn't like it when we dropped things. And she really doesn't like loud, 'noxious children.'"

"No, she doesn't." Sarah added the words in such an earnest tone that Sol was sure she'd heard the scolding terms far too often.

"Well, there is some truth in the pleasantry of quiet children, but no one can be constantly quiet, can they?" Ann asked gently.

Ethan shook his head. "No, ma'am."

"And," she started tossing buttons back into the large, red tin. "I expect there was far too much inside time over the winter and that's taxing on children and grown-ups alike. So perhaps people's feelings got worn and frazzled as time dragged on."

Sarah didn't really understand her reasoning, but Ethan did. He nodded earnestly. "I can't wait to get outside and play! My Pa has a farm and we can play on his farm soon, can't we Pa?"

Timing and reality combined to push Sol to a decision he'd been loath to make. "We need to move out to the claim, for sure. Room to run and dig and jump and play." He'd loved growing up with the freedom of property around him in Minnesota. He shifted his attention to Ann. "If we can arrange transportation, would you consider coming out to my claim daily and watching these two while I work, Ann? You could do your sewing out there, if it suits."

She'd just picked up a handful of buttons.

She didn't move them to the box. She knelt there, face down, the clutch of buttons motionless for several ticks of the clock. And then she nodded, slowly, as if saying yes to his simple request bore momentous consequence. "If Hattie doesn't mind, I think that would be good for the children."

"Sewing is sewing," Hattie announced from her machine. She waved an easy hand. "You not only have my permission, you have my blessing, Ann. Those two could use some good old-fashioned time outdoors, couldn't they?"

"Yes," agreed Sol.

"Yes," echoed Ann. She and Sol helped Sarah pick up the last of the buttons, and when they were done, she handed the button box to Sol. He stood, set the box down, then took her hand to help her up.

She stood as well, facing him, her small hand clasped in his.

Uncommon beauty. He didn't know why he hadn't seen it before. Pale skin, wide, brown eyes, not too dark. Long lashes, too, and just enough honey tones in her hair to match the same in her eyes and it was a few long seconds before he realized he could be rightly accused of holding her hand.

He dropped it like a hot potato fresh from the Franklin stove and stepped back. "I'll be getting on. Levi's going to help me move things out to my claim tonight. It's not fancy." He hesitated, because maybe Ann thought she'd be working in a normal house. "I bought it last fall and the long winter left no time for fixing, but once we're out there, I'll take some time each day to make a difference."

"There is rare beauty in humble beginnings."

Did she believe that? One look at her confirmed it for Sol, but he'd been out to the claim and there was nothing rare or beautiful about it. Still, it was nice for her to say so. "Nellie said she'd drive you out in the morning."

"That's a kindness, much appreciated."

"I'll see you then." He tipped his hat and started for the door. Her voice stopped him.

"Possibly before then, unless the children are spending the night?"

He turned, embarrassed, because of course he had to come back for the children.

"And actually, even though there's a quick wind, we're going to take a walk after a while. It's not good to be cooped up, day after day. We'll walk later on and I'll bring them by the shop, if that's all right?"

"Fine, yes, thank you." He turned for the door, then swung back and smiled at her, then the kids. "And I most likely would have remembered them eventually."

Ethan laughed and Sarah smiled up at him.

He nodded good day to Hattie and strode out the door and up the street. It had all been handled without duress, and now Ann would ride out and back each day.

He thought of the unimproved farm and winced, but she hadn't seemed to mind the notion of simple. But her idea of rare beauty might be a sight different from the actuality of Sol's farm.

Chapter Five

"HERE WE ARE!" NELLIE DIRECTED the horses up a small dirt lane to a shack that couldn't rightfully be called a house by anyone's standards. "Now, I promise you once things start to green up, it all looks much better out here. Right now it's endless brown and gray but with that spring sunshine everything will change. At least that's what Hattie's promising me, I came out in the fall so I can't swear to the veracity of her claims, but she's as honest as the day is long." She and Ann climbed down and she led the way to the back of the wagon. "In this trunk are the dresses for hemming, but I also put some scraps we had at the shop, thinking that maybe a few tacked curtains would brighten this place up. What do you think, Ann?"

She loved curtains, so she nodded. "Curtains have a way of framing everything we see."

"And you have a way with words," Nellie exclaimed. "Ann, have you ever thought of writing things? I don't have an imagination to save my soul except with fabrics and trim, but you paint pictures with words. I know there weren't spots for women writers back east with their fuddy-duddy ways, but out here the sky is the limit, Ann!"

Writing?

Ann shrunk into her cloak a little further.

Nellie handed her the box, and lifted the smaller tote bag. "I've always felt that God hands out some pretty nice talents to both men and women, and when old thoughts and rules stand in the way of progress, we need to change both the thoughts and the rules. Sol, good morning!"

"Ladies." Sol crossed the narrow brown turf quickly. "Here, let me get these and bring them into the house." He took the satchel from Nellie and reached for the wooden box.

Ann held tight. "I'll bring this along, you've got enough there."

"The good Lord handed out broad shoulders to man for a reason, Ann. I don't mind."

He looked down at her, hiked his brows and almost smiled, so then she almost smiled back. "Where are the children?"

He nodded toward the far side, and just then she heard their voices. "The necessary is back there aways, and they were checking out that poor excuse for a barn."

"Well, now that you're here and the days are getting longer, we can fix things up once the seed is in," Nellie assured him. "And when you're ready to do that barn raising, Sol, you know we'll all pitch in and then we'll call that shed what it is."

"A barn raising?" Ann asked.

Sol nodded. "Me and Levi planned it out over the winter. Of course there won't be a minute to do it until the first crop is in. That's the breathing time around here."

"Did you have barn raisings where you lived?" Nellie asked.

Ann nodded as the kids raced around the side of the house. "It was common enough."

"Well, maybe you'd help with the cooking side of things," Nellie suggested as they followed Sol into the dark shack. "If there's enough of us, we could make a difference that day. Do you cook?"

"I do, yes." The thought of making a difference seemed unexpectedly nice, but looking around Sol's shack told a different story. Sol followed the direction of her gaze. "I expect you're not seeing too much rare beauty about now, are you?"

The children rushed in, gathering around him, chatting of this and that, and Ann looked their way. "I am, actually."

She didn't miss Sol's smile as she set the crate on a solid, well-made table. "Light's a problem in here," he told her, "but I'll bring back lamps from the mercantile tonight so tomorrow will be better."

"That would be good." She reached up and undid her cape. He pointed to a hook and she hung it there. "Light is important for raising cheerful children."

"And for cheerful grown-ups, too," Nellie agreed. She minded the children outside while Sol showed Ann around, and with the miniscule size of the house, that took all of two minutes. "Ann, if you're set, I'm going to head back to town. Sol, why don't you come with me this morning? Then you and Levi can bring the rest of the things tonight, and Ann can ride back to town with him."

"Sensible plan." He bent and hugged each child in turn. "You be good for Ann, okay?"

"We'll be so good!" Sarah promised. Ethan promised, too, but not with the same level of confidence.

Like Robert, she thought, or rather, let herself think. *Such a boy, nodding agreement while plotting adventures.*

Regret stabbed like it always did, but seeing Ethan's expectation lightened the jab this time.

"We'll get on, then. See you all later."

"Bye, Pa!"

"Bye!"

They dashed out and waved until Nellie's wagon was hidden by a swell of land, then turned her way. "What now?"

That was the question, wasn't it? She looked around, and took them each by the hand. "First, we're going to scout for danger."

"Scout?" Ethan widened his eyes. "Like for Injuns?" His gaze darted left, then right with a mix of fear and excitement. "For real?"

"Indians, not 'injuns', and no. People may be different, but difference doesn't make them dangerous and I've known many a native in my time. No, our scouting will be for sharp things. Places that kids might find where they can get hurt. Our job is to hunt for those places and then avoid them. That's how early scouts mapped the west," she told them. "They went up and down rivers and drew pictures."

"I'm not a good drawer." Sarah lifted sad eyes her way.

"I am," Ann told her, "so we'll hunt up places right now, and then we can draw on the slate boards I have."

"You brought them?" Ethan gripped her hand tightly. "I'm so glad!"

"Miss Hattie said it was of supreme necessity, and I'm pretty sure no one argues with Miss Hattie."

"Or Aunt Iby." Sarah frowned, glum. "She gets grumpy."

"She gets grumpy really fast," noted Ethan. He reached up and gripped Ann's hand and part of her heart. "But you don't."

Those words.

A small child's confidence in her.

Be still her heart, his sweet gesture fissured the rock-hard armor she wore. She'd been grumpy for so long, she couldn't remember not being that way.

That's because you won't remember the 'before'... There was much to be joyful about then. Two children, two hearts that loved you unconditionally. And a husband, flawed, but kind in his own manner.

She couldn't think of that. Not yet, anyway, and who knew when? But being here, holding Ethan's and Sarah's little hands, made her want to be not grumpy. And that hadn't happened in recent memory. She held Sarah's hand and let Ethan dash around as they checked out the claim.

The creek ran diagonally through the back side, and as she studied that, she wondered why the original owner put the claim shack in front of the creek. In a bad spring or a logjam, water would run right into the house, and rushing creek waters were nothing to be taken lightly with small children around.

She made a note to discuss that with Sol, and hoped he wouldn't take offense.

"Ann, look here!" Ethan lifted a rusted pitchfork. "I scouted it, just like you said!"

"Clever boy." She took the pitchfork and put it in the lean-to attached to the ramshackle excuse of a barn. "I'm wondering how your pa is going to work this land."

"He's mighty smart," declared Ethan. "No matter what Aunt Tillie said, our pa knows what he's doing!"

Did he?

Most likely he understood the farming aspects, but the setting of a household was no job for amateurs. Food needed to be preserved at the right times in the proper ways. Storage was vital for maintaining a year-long supply.

Dark clouds dimmed the sun. She took the children inside the small shack. She'd brought bread from Hattie and a jar of jam from Nellie's pantry, and as she looked around the small place, she began a list of things Sol might need. It seemed cheeky to do it. She had no idea what his financial situation might be, but there were certain items crucial to the children's well-being, and when the wagon pulled up several hours later, with a milk cow walking behind, she struck one item off the list.

"You bought us a cow?" Ethan cheered as he charged toward the wagon. "Is she ours, Pa? Can we name her?"

"We can, and she's due to have a baby, and we'll name that, too." He ruffled Ethan's hair, then lifted his gaze to Ann as Levi climbed down from the other side. "You got on all right, then?"

Ann nodded from the door. "Fine, actually, although there are a few things we might discuss."

He gave her that half-smile again as he carried a bench to the door. "When a woman says she might want to discuss something, a smart man takes heed and listens, real quick."

Heat flooded her cheeks. "I don't mean to be presumptuous."

"Presume away, Ann." He set the bench down, noticed the list and whistled softly. "That's quite a list."

She kneaded her hands together, hoping she didn't offend. "I don't mean to imply that you can't take care of the children, Sol, it's just that coming out here at the end of winter means there are few provisions."

"And I wasn't here to put things up last year, and a man who's lived on his father's farm, might not be schooled in how things get done."

"Some are and some aren't," she told him as Levi led the cow to the small penned area behind the shack. "A good many mothers put provisions on their daughters and neglect to train the sons. But then what do you do if that woman is no longer there?"

He worked his jaw, then grimaced slightly. "I can't deny your words, but I'm not exactly pleased that you're echoing what my pa said back in Minnesota. He said I'm biting off more than I can chew with the jobs and the kids, but I can't see raising these two in town." He scrubbed a hand to his chin. "I love the image of them running on the farm, well." He looked over her head and grinned. "Not a farm that looks like this, exactly, but when we've made some improvements, it can be their legacy. And a legacy takes time."

"It does, but children get hungry daily," she supposed. She lifted her cape off the hook as Levi moved their way. "I hope you don't think ill of me. I didn't mean to insult, but to be able to exist out here, you have to have some essentials."

"The lesson of the prairie," Levi noted as he stepped through the door, then leaned it shut to block the draft. "Get stocked and stay stocked. That way if blizzard or flood hits, you've got provisions. Especially the first year when nothing's put by."

Sol exchanged a quick look with Levi. "Should I have waited to bring the kids here? Been more established?"

Levi began to answer, but Ann put a hand on Sol's arm. "Oh, no. I think they were dreadfully unhappy before, and being with your very own parent is best. But they have needs you must see to quickly. And you might want to consider setting the house above the creek, if that's possible. Sitting downslope like this seems to be inviting disaster in a bad spring or if there's a logjam."

"We'd need a bridge to cross it, then." Sol noted. "And that's no easy task to build or upkeep. But I see what you're saying, Ann, so maybe setting the house across the road might be a smarter plan. There's a rise just there." He pointed southeast. "And this could be cropland and pasture land with the creek for water."

Levi noticed the list in Sol's hand and smiled. "And that's the best help you could ask for right there, Sol. Someone who knows what you need and writes it down for you."

"It is," he admitted, and when he aimed that smile her way, Ann tucked her shoulders back a little taller and prouder than they'd been in a while. "Ann, what about this? Instead of coming out here with Nellie tomorrow morning, why don't we meet you in town. If you can direct me around the mercantile, we can bring things out here and maybe get you off to a sounder start. Does that sound all right to you?"

Shopping together like a family.

They weren't family, of course, but if her knowledge could help him get things put to rights for these children, she'd gladly do it. She nodded and moved past him as the young cow bawled beyond the house. She indicated the cow with a nod. "That was first on my list, which has now been checked off. A milk cow, and then some young calves to raise for beef. And chickens. And a cat."

"The mice."

She swept the rough floor a quick look. "Tight boards and a cat work wonders."

"They surely do," Levi agreed, but then he aimed a broad smile in Sol's direction. "See you in the morning."

"I'll be there," Sol promised. "As soon as I've got supplies enough to stock those two shelves."

"Well, about that." Ann was about to leave, but she turned back and pointed well down the list where she'd written 'Additional shelving.' "Might as well make it as hard for the mice as we possibly can, don't you think?"

He didn't look one bit angry at her deduction. He looked more pleased, and maybe a little relieved, and Ann realized something for the second time in two days.

She'd come west to help stitch hems, a likely job for an avid sewer, but in two days she'd realized she had more talents needed in the west. A way with words, and the know-how to run a tight house.

Who knew such things could be considered a necessity?

Chapter Six

L UMBER FOR SHELVES.
Sol aimed the team to the lumberyard set alongside the railroad tracks. He ordered two board lengths from Seb Ward, then added a third, just in case. He'd fashioned strong metal brackets over the winter, so he paused at the shop and picked out six of them, then settled them between the wood and the wagon wall.

He steered the team toward the mercantile, then tethered them to the hitching posts with just enough grain to amuse them while he took the kids inside. He couldn't honestly say he'd ever done much shopping. He'd never seen the lack in his planning until Ann pointed it out to him. Back in Minnesota, his mother, the aunts and the girls took care of the inside work, and he'd just assumed it got done, without any real knowledge of how long it took. Ann's list illustrated a hole in his plan. He carried Sarah up the stairs as Ethan ran ahead, and when he got inside, there was Ann.

His heart stutter-stepped. When she turned his way, his smile was automatic and inspired hers in return, and that made his heart dance a little skip-hop again.

He handed her the list.

She handed it right back and looked discomfited. Reason enough to hand it right back to her and raise his hands. "You have me convinced that this is more your realm than mine, and I have to say that I was married for over four years, and didn't do much in the way of shopping in that time, unless it was to pick up feed and seed or parts. Before that, only if my mother needed things from town and made a list, which I then handed to Mrs. Gruber, Ivy's sister-by-marriage. If you know what you're doing, Ann Hazel, I'd be obliged if you just went ahead and did it."

"You're serious?" She looked surprised, but a little intrigued, too.

"Most assuredly. And appreciative of the help, yet again." Her cheeks flushed when he said that, and the brighter color suited her real nice. "You point and I'll carry. While watching the children, of course."

"All right." In no time at all they had a half-full wagon of supplies, including seed sacks and the hefty bill that went along with it, but as Sol counted out the money, it made perfect sense.

No more eating at the little hotel restaurant. If Ann didn't mind setting bread each day, they could eat off provisions and then garden produce. They wouldn't be able to store meat until winter, but beans and smoked meat would suffice for a while, with maybe some fresh fish from time to time. With care, they'd get by, and that was the toughest thing, the first year. He hated spending money on supplies because lumber for fixing the barn and moving the house would be dear, but the funds from the sale of his Minnesota property were untouched. That would be their investment, and his weekly pay from Levi would more than cover their needs. Now if there was only time to get things done in a proper manner.

"The climate here is not unlike what I knew in Pennsylvania."

"No?" Sol had never been east. "Did you farm there, Ann? Or did you live in the city?"

"A farm, all my life. My father's and then—"

He navigated the horses to follow the right bend in the rode, sloping up, toward his claim, then realized she'd stopped. When the horses were headed straight and true again, he glanced her way.

A quick tear slipped down her cheek. Then another and another.

"Are you all right?" He whispered the words so he wouldn't panic Ethan in back. Sarah was snugged on Ann's lap, and when he whispered, she looked up and saw what he saw. "Don't cwy, Ann." She reached up and snugged her arms around Ann's neck. "It's all wight. Don't cwy."

Ann dropped her face to the little girl's hair, and Sol was pretty sure the child's entreaty had only made things worse. Much worse.

His heart broke, seeing her like that, because he'd seen himself like that after burying his wife. What words could he say, with a wagonload of this and that being chugged home? Not much, and as Sarah clung tight to Ann, the woman held her just as snugly, and Sol got a new dose of reality.

His children deserved to be loved by two parents. His children deserved to be cherished daily, while he was working a field or in town, fashioning strapping and tools for the push west.

He glanced to the right again, then hurriedly brought his attention back forward.

He'd loved his wife. He'd been attracted to her a decade past, he'd courted her, married her and had children with her. The thought of bringing someone else into his life, his home without the depth of that love seemed so wrong.

But it wasn't just *his* life, now.

"There's our place, Pa! I see it, we're almost home!"

It was *theirs*, too, and his first job was to them, wasn't it?

He rolled the wagon up to the front of the house and drew the reins tight to pause the horses. He set the brake, jumped down and rounded the wagon quickly. Ann held Sarah out, into his waiting arms, but once he set his daughter down, he turned and reached back to help Ann.

She looked surprised and embarrassed. Redness rimmed

her eyes, and her left cheek still bore the streaks of tears.

He took her hand, a strong hand. A woman's hand, not a girl's. And when she stepped down, he said, "Mind the wheel, Ann." Not as if she didn't know to do that, but because he wanted her to be careful.

She stepped down and he didn't release her hand. Ethan jumped off the wagon bed and followed Sarah toward the necessary, and that made her smile, an odd thing to smile about unless…

He faced her more squarely so she couldn't quite look away. "You had children."

She kept her gaze trained on the path Ethan had taken. "A boy and a girl."

Her face and voice said the unspeakable, and Sol did the only thing he could do. He pulled her into his arms and held her. "Ann. Oh, Ann, I am so sorry." Did she cry more?

He wasn't sure, but he held her like that until she pulled back and stepped away. When she did, the thought that he'd wanted to go right on holding her took him by surprise. She dashed her hand to her face, then scolded herself. "You'd think a smart woman of fabrics would remember to carry a hanky, and of course I forgot to grab one today."

"Here." He withdrew the one he had stuffed in a pocket, and was glad it was unused because that wasn't always the case. He started to hand it to her, then stopped. Instead, he cupped her chin with one hand and gently wiped her eyes, her cheeks. And then he handed it over while she looked at him, right at him with the pain and longing he knew too well. "Life isn't easy, is it?" he whispered.

"No." But just then Sarah and Ethan came racing back down hill, laughing and she took a deep breath. "But it *is* good in so many ways, Sol. Two of them, right there."

He believed that, too. "I don't know how I would have gotten through without them and God."

His words made her frown, but then she stood straight, shoulders back and said, "I think we need to get things into the house so you can get to town and help your cousin."

"True." He put the brackets in place on the wall and had the long shelves installed quickly. Three was one too many for the small house, but he set the other board inside the barn because a good barn needed shelving, too. He put the seed sacks in the metal bin he'd fashioned over the winter to keep the precious seed safe from vermin, and when they'd carried everything inside, the small place looked cramped and crowded, unsuited for children.

"The lamps will help." Ann lit the first lamp as he added small logs to the wood stove. "Light chases the gloom of clouds by the simplicity of its being."

"That's a cheerful way of looking at it," he said, as a new band of thick gray clouds pushed their way east. "Our home here will be a sight more friendly in time, I hope."

She sent him a curious look.

"Once the weather's full broke and I have time to fix things proper."

A mouse chose that moment to cut a diagonal path through the tiny house, and Sol's guilt rose. How could he leave a delicate woman and two small children in these conditions?

"We're going to spend this day organizing and getting things set up properly," Ann told the children, as if mice parading near her skirts wasn't a big deal. "And when your pa gets ahead on his work in town, he's going to help us fix things up."

Ann said 'us', and he felt good, hearing it.

"I like fixing things," Ethan announced. "It's one of my favorite things. And climbing. Can we plant a climbing tree, Pa? Like we had back home?"

"We sure can, but it's not likely to be climbing size in time for you. There is a proper tree stand up above the creek and when the weather's fine, we'll go up there and let you have climbing time, okay? But it's not a place you go to alone, Ethan Eichas. You hear?"

"I won't, Pa! I'll stay close, like you said, leastways 'til I know my way about."

"And even then." Ann put her hands on her hips and held the boy's gaze tight. "We scouted for safety yesterday, Ethan, but the best way to keep safe is to follow directions. When a grown-up tells you to mind, you need to do it, at least until you're of an age to see the dangers."

"Yes'm."

The boy seemed impressed by Ann's stance, or maybe humbled was a better word and Sol couldn't deny a sense of relief. Ethan's impetuous nature at a tender age was a recipe for trouble.

Once again the thought of a mother for his children seemed not just sensible, but necessary. Was he stupid to think re-marriage should be a love-based relationship? It felt selfish to think that way. Shouldn't the children's needs be put first and foremost? "I'll head back to town. Tomorrow I'm going to use some of the chicken wire to set up a pen for a flock. There won't be enough to eat for a while, but in time, we'll have all the chicken we want."

"With dumplings, Pa!" Ethan's eyes grew round at the thought as Sol bent and kissed them both goodbye. When he stood and turned, Ann was there, right there by his elbow, and he'd be lying if he said the thought of kissing her goodbye didn't occur to him.

He didn't, of course, but he did look deep into her eyes and smiled. "Thank you for being here, Ann. For making a difference."

His words pleased her.

Color bit her cheeks and the winsome smile softened her features. "Well, we have our work cut out for us today, that's for sure!"

Capable hands.

He left, smiling, knowing his children were in capable hands and while that might not have been his primary thought when he first laid eyes on Greta long years back, the warmth of Ann's capable hands made him feel secure about going off to work, and that meant a great deal, too.

They'd sorted, organized, shelved, dusted, wiped and refilled the water kettle for hot water later in the day. She couldn't do too much about the mice, but Ann had learned a long time ago how to put a house in order. She hadn't cared much about it for a while, but that wasn't from lack of knowledge. Just lack of interest, swept aside by grief.

She was plenty interested today, and when Sarah napped on the small cot set up for the two children, she and Ethan set dough rising for bread. "We're going to let it rise right here," she told him and put the greased loaves up above the stove. "They'll rise quick and won't dry out with that nice bacon grease we used on the outside of the loaves. And when they bake, they'll have a lovely, rich crust and flavor."

"My grandma used to make us jam," he told her, once she set the loaves up. "If you're here this summer, can we make jam, Ann? I'll be your big helper."

Would she be here come summer?

Ann weighed the question as they cleaned up the wooden board she'd used for kneading the bread.

She'd only been here a few days, and already the thought of leaving these two children went beyond a bother, but she didn't dare make promises she couldn't keep. She'd never done that with her own children, until that last, fateful day, when she promised she'd see them for supper.

That wasn't your promise, broken. It was an accident. A tragic accident.

She pushed the annoying thoughts of her conscience aside. Their father should have known better. Taking two children out in a boat alone was a reckless act.

Nothing he hadn't done a dozen times before, and something they loved, to go fishing with their father, her conscience prodded. *Maybe you're not so mad at him as you are at yourself for going to town that day.*

She set Ethan to working on simple sums and then a book of primer words, and withdrew a gown from the box. The hem was already turned and basted. She couldn't sit on a chair and sew without the dress brushing the rough floor, so she settled onto the table.

Ethan laughed, then clapped his hand over his mouth when Sarah stirred. "You're sitting on the table, Ann!"

"Shh." She positioned the skirt onto her lap and poised the needle just above the side seam. "If you wake your sister, I can't get my work done, and yes. The chair is too low, so I'm making do. That's a good thing, you know. Learning to make do."

"That's smart."

"Well, thank you." She worked doggedly on the hem, using a single thread and a blind-stitch while Ethan studiously copied his words, erased them and copied again. She sounded them out with him, and when he suddenly looked up at her and said, "'S-H-E' she! And 'H-E' he!" she cheered him on softly.

"Clever boy, yes! *She* ran to the well. *He* ran to the well. He saw a cat. She saw a cat."

Ethan traced the words in the small book as she recited the old sentences by heart. "I can do this!" Excited, he practiced the words again and again, turning the pages, and copying the letters. She'd never seen a child this young take such joy in learning to read, and when Sol arrived home at the end of the day, Ethan raced for the door and threw it wide. "Pa! I can read! I can read you this book, Pa, all by myself! Ann showed me the letters and the words and I can read!"

"Not even six, yet?" Sol aimed a doubtful look toward his son. "Maybe you've read the book so often, you know it by heart, eh?"

Ethan frowned, confused. They came through the door as a clap of thunder rolled across the plain. "You don't think I can read, Pa?"

Sol was about to give his opinion when Ann lifted one of the slate boards. "Ethan, what does this say?"

"He saw the cat." He read the words slowly, with a fierce look of concentration, and when Ann erased that and wrote another sentence, he read that too.

Sol stared at him, then her, then the book. "You can read, son?"

"I said so!" Ethan grinned up at him, a little boy who hadn't even gotten his first big teeth yet. "Ann taught me! She knows a lot of things!"

Ann laughed, but when Sol turned his gaze to hers, the laughter turned into something softer. Sweeter. Gentler, and maybe even more exciting. "You taught him to read."

She brushed off her part. "A willing student is a great help."

"A clever mind is a gift, but if never offered opportunity, it stagnates. Ann, I don't know how to thank you." He held her gaze, and so doing, won another little corner of her heart, too. He lifted his right hand and cradled her cheek. He'd held her gaze with sweet intensity, but now his attention wandered to her mouth, and then her lips. It settled there, as if wondering, and darned if she wasn't wondering the exact same thing.

But she hadn't come here for this, had she? She had a home back east, and lonely graves in need of tending. But the warmth and feel of Sol's broad hand stirred thoughts. Sweet thoughts.

A wagon lumbered up the drive. "That will be Levi." She kept her voice soft on purpose. He'd offered to come by for her earlier that day.

"It's mighty wet out," said Sol, just as softly, as if thinking it would be nice for her to just stay there, cozy, warm and dry.

Levi didn't knock, not with the rain and all. He came right in as Ann stepped back. "We'd best get a move on before the road muddies up."

She started to turn his way, then remembered her cloak. She crossed to the hook, took it down and wrapped herself in it, with the hood up, then turned.

Ethan was showing Levi his new skill, Sarah was waking up from her nap, and Sol had eyes for her. Just her.

A buzz of anticipation raced somewhere from the vicinity of her toes upward, and set her mind to all kinds of things she'd pushed aside over a year-and-a-half before. The sight of sleepy Sarah, Ethan's excitement and Sol's gaze made her wish she could take a step forward into a new day, but the steady sound of the rain reminded her of how quickly all could be lost. In a blink of an eye, a storm could rage forth, and sweep it all away, and she couldn't risk going through that again.

She swept by Sol with a quick nod and hurried toward Levi's buggy. He'd put the rain curtains forward, but even with that, the storm soaked them well before they got back to town.

She shouldn't go back to Sol Eichas's holding, she realized despite the wet, chilled conditions. Sol's life offered too many parallels, too many reminders, and far too many temptations.

Going back to his claim enticed her to move forward, but if she did that, how could she reconcile what had gone before? How could she justify leaving the only thing she had left of the life she'd loved, the final resting spots in the German Evangelical cemetery?

Would you deny their father? A man you once loved?

Oh, her heart ached at that thought, because had she loved him? Or had he wooed her with promises as empty as his industry? What did a young woman, scarcely eighteen, know of a forever vow? Was it her mistake *then* that caused the children's deaths later?

Or was it as so many said, sometimes things just happen. She'd been asking 'why' for so long, that the revolving list of questions was like a mental gear, just another part of the action, now.

Levi pulled up tight to the walkway bordering Hattie's shop. He started to get down, but Ann jumped to the walk and waved him off. "Go get you and the horses dry, Levi, and thank you so much for the ride."

"A quiet one," he observed in his steady way. "A bit different than traveling with my wife."

His observation almost made her smile as she hurried into the shop, because Nellie would be the first to say she didn't believe in thinking a thing to death. She acted, then reacted. A part of Ann wished she could claim that logic, because having these thoughts spinning through her mind was making her plum crazy.

She hurried into the shop and peeled her cloak off, first thing.

"Let's hang that right up!" Hattie moved pretty ably for a woman with a bad ankle. She whisked the cloak out of Ann's hands and laid it over a chair not too far from the fire. "It will dry there. What a ride back that must have been."

Ann sent her a blank look, because she'd barely noticed the ride.

"Unless our mind is engaged someplace else, of course." Hattie moved to the stove. "I've got stew here, perfect for a wet, chilly night, and I'm glad you had sense enough not to bring a gown back in these conditions."

She'd totally forgotten the gown she'd finished today, and when Hattie looked her way, she fumbled for words. "The green one is done, and it's very nice. The ivory and blue is for tomorrow."

"Perfect. Does it work all right with your schedule with the kids, Ann? I don't want to mess that up for you."

"Which is odd," Ann noted, "because the dresses are the

intended job, whereas the children were an unexpected addition."

"Of course." Hattie bobbed her head firmly. "And it's so nice of you to do it, dear, it's truly a blessing how it all worked out, don't you think?"

"Amazing." She murmured the word, and when Hattie shot her a quick look, Ann got the idea that maybe the perfect timing surrounding her coming and Sol needing a caretaker for his children, and a pile of dresses with no hems wasn't an accident.

Of course that was ridiculous, but in some odd way it didn't feel ridiculous. She carried the two bowls of stew to the small table, then took a half-loaf of bread from her satchel. She unwrapped it and set it on the bread board.

"On my word, that smells amazing!" Hattie leaned forward and inhaled deeply. "Ann, you made this?"

"Two loaves, which means Sol and those children won't starve tonight," she offered wryly.

Hattie paused. She caught Ann's gaze and held it. "Did you just make a joke, Ann?"

"I may have."

"Oh, how nice!" Hattie flipped open a napkin and beamed. "A sense of humor is such a gift around children, and it is a dire necessity around men."

"Were you married, Hattie?" She hadn't asked a thing about her employer in the few days she'd been here, and that probably seemed rude. Funny, she hadn't cared to ask the first day. Today she did.

"I was, to a kindly man, rather old-fashioned, but I worked on him until he saw the light," Hattie declared. "And it was a good marriage in so many ways, not the kind of thing I'd repeat at this age, but wonderful in its time. And there were, of course, my two blessings, gone too soon."

Ann's hands paused. She swallowed hard, eyes down.

"I don't know how I got through those first days,

months, even years without them when the fever took them. Everything about me ached, and I couldn't see my way out of a fog with a dozen flaming candles, I was that lost."

Ann choked down air, not daring to speak.

"But then one day I heard a woman talking of opportunities for women, and places in the west, and how a woman could start her own business and get through her own day with no one shaking their finger her way, and that whole conversation just lit up an idea in my head! I took care to sell my place, then I tucked my money in a safe spot, pulled a hat on my head and headed west, and haven't looked back."

"Wasn't it hard?" Ann couldn't do anything but whisper the words around a lump in her throat.

"Painfully hard," Hattie admitted. "I felt like I was abandoning my family, but I'd learned one thing in that grieving, that when life bowls you over, it expects you to get back up again, and not look back, but gaze forward. And God brought me here, to South Dakota. The minute I laid eyes on Second Chance, I knew it was the place for me, and I was right. A growing town, a growing prairie, and good women coming west to chart their own course." She set the butter over on Ann's side of the table. "But it's different from person to person, I suppose."

Ann gripped her fork. She couldn't pick it up, and she couldn't put it down. She sat there, fork in hand, and took a breath, then glanced up. "I had two children, also."

Hattie lifted kind eyes to hers. She blinked once and Ann saw the truth. "You know."

"Jean Ellen told me. Yes."

The fork felt heavy, too heavy to hold. She set it down. "I haven't been well since."

"It takes the heart right out of us, to bury a child. And it happens all too often."

"Coming here felt wrong."

Hattie nodded.

"But not for you, you said you wanted to come here."

"Oh, I did. And I'm glad I did," Hattie told her. "But leaving my family back in the cool soil of Massachusetts felt like I was turning my back on them. Like I was abandoning what I'd had and leaving them on their own. But of course that was the devil's own way of thinking."

Ann frowned. "You consider it sinful to miss your children?"

"No." Hattie shook her head firmly. "But it's wrong and ungrateful to turn your back and say no to life and love and the holy Father in heaven. It's wrong to brush off the blessings I'd had for years and dwell in the pit of despair. Once I saw the selfishness in that, I knew I had to become unselfish again. And so I did."

"Grieving isn't selfish," Ann argued. "It's normal. It's what people do when they lose someone."

"Oh, you're absolutely right." Hattie put a light smearing of butter on her bread, sighed and added more, then topped it with a generous dash of salt. "It's not up to me or anyone else to tell a body when enough is enough, but it came to me that while God had called my two blessed children home, I had been given a chance many never get. I had them with me for years. I knew their laughter and their joy and their sorrows and their tears. They changed me, and even though that sadness was wicked deep, I had to turn it for good sometime. And so I came here, and started a business that allows me to help this one or that. Depending, of course."

Turn it for good…

Hadn't Peter talked of being harassed by evil in his epistles? And how to turn it around?

And the good Lord himself had bowed the wretched spectacle of his crucifixion into the blinding light of resurrection, and washed a world anew. "I don't know how to begin again," she confessed softly, eyes down. "Somedays I don't know if I should."

"Oh, darling Ann." Hattie reached over and laid a hand atop Ann's and just that warmth and support strengthened Ann's shaky resolve. "You already have. Now you just have to keep walking that path."

She squeezed Ann's hand lightly, then scolded, "And if you let good bread like this go to waste, that's a shame. I've never had better, Ann, and you know what? Miriam Eichas makes cheese out at their place and that cheese is a perfect match for this bread. A body could eat for a week on toasting cheese and bread, and be happy for it! I'll speak to Levi about ordering some directly."

"I've made cheese," Ann told her. "We had a New York cheesemaker move his factory to Pittsburgh, and what a fine group of cheeses they produced. I copied some of them."

"Well, clever girl, maybe you can share tips with Miri, she's got a knack that's for sure, but she's having a hard time keeping the general store stocked." Hattie smiled at her.

"And cheese can't be hurried," Ann noted. "It needs and takes its own sweet time to work up proper."

"So it does."

Ann wasn't sure if it was Hattie's smile or the talk of mundane cheese, or doing and trying new things, but the stew suddenly smelled marvelous. She took a bite, and then another, and couldn't remember the last time stew, or food in general, tasted this good. And Hattie was right on another thing, too. The bread she'd shaped with Sol's young son provided a perfect balance.

The rain beat the roof with relentless vigor. The wind picked up, howling this way and that through the night. But when Ann finally lay down to sleep, she found undisturbed slumber for the first time in long months, and the simple joy of that gave her a lighter step come morning.

Chapter Seven

A NN HAD FASHIONED CURTAINS ALONG a
wooden rod over the two windows, then drew them
back to bring in the light. Sol hadn't thought it would
make much sense, to put up cloth to cover the windows,
only to uncover them, but when she was done, he had to
admit it looked kind of cheerful.

He met with Levi to plan the house and barn. He
bought a team of oxen, then discovered the upper pen
wasn't strong enough for oxen, which meant he'd re-build
a stout fence, too.

He went to the lumberyard and ordered the supplies he'd
need for the rebuilding once planting was done, including
four glass windows. They seemed a little frivolous for the
price, but the thought of looking out, over his own land,
made him plunk down his money.

He came home to a simple but solid supper every night,
and with Ann's bread, he was able to take a lunch to work
each day, saving dimes and nickels along the way. Rumor
had it a bank would be coming to town soon, and another
church was plotting a building on Harrison Street.

Levi was right. Second Chance was growing, and he was
in the right place and time to grow along with it, but
the more he thought of the sweetness of spring and new
growth, the more he thought of Ann.

He hated to see her go each night, and that made him
feel guilty.

He was delighted to have her arrive each morning, and

when the children ran to her, all he could think of was how Ethan used to run to Greta. And yet…

He sighed as he guided Sugarfoot and Tansy to pull the plow through the second field. When he looked up, Ann and the children were coming his way. His breath caught. His pulse picked up, seeing her smile and the children's joy as they skipped furrows, laughing and falling in the clods like a pair of young pups. When she drew near, he couldn't help himself.

She handed him a jug of tea.

He took her hand instead of the tea, and when she looked startled… *and pleased*… he nodded toward the children's antics. "Look what a difference you've made, Ann Hazel."

She blushed, and that blush was an invitation. He tipped her chin up. He smiled into her eyes, then let his gaze drop to her mouth on purpose. He knew what he wanted. What he needed. And when this woman was around, his thoughts wandered to what could be on a pretty steady basis now.

He kissed her. He kissed her long and slow and deep, wanting nothing more than to go on kissing her. His body shielded them from the children's curiosity for now, but his feelings for Ann went beyond baked bread and good codfish gravy. They went straight to love and protection, long cozy nights and sun-drenched days.

"Sol." She pulled back and she was right to do it, he knew that, but he wasn't ready to let her go. Not quite yet.

"I've been puzzling over that for weeks, Ann."

The blush rose higher and went deeper.

"I think of you in the morning." He kissed her right cheek. "In the evening." Then the left, and he might have lingered a little extra there. "And at night."

She dipped her chin, embarrassed, but he smiled and rubbed his scruffy face along her hairline. "And every moment in between. I hate to have you leave at night, and I hate that I wake up alone every morning, which means one thing, Ann."

She gave him an earnest look and nodded. "You should get a dog. Of course."

He stopped outright, and when she laughed, it was the prettiest laugh he'd ever heard. He grabbed hold of her waist, lifted her and swung her around. "You're funny, Ann."

"Put me down!" She giggled when she said it, and he'd never heard her giggle or truly laugh before. He liked it.

"I think I won't," he mused, with her still in the air. "I think if I hold you like this you'll giggle and laugh and maybe kiss me again, and then." He sent her a mock serious look as the oxen stirred their feet, wondering what to do. "And then I will put you down for it seems my team is getting fractious."

"They could run," she whispered, and wriggled to loosen his grip.

"They could," he whispered back, and drew her closer. "I'm still waiting for the laugh."

"And not the kiss?"

"I left that ambiguous on purpose, but I'd not be refusing your kiss if so offered, Ann. What say you?"

She answered him by pressing her lips to his and lingering there. When he finally set her down, he almost missed the firm ground. She started to tumble into a furrow, but he held tight and drew here back to the flat, grassy topsoil. "You're blushing."

She rolled her eyes, embarrassed.

"And beautiful."

"Sol."

"Shh." He put one finger to her lips and shook his head. "We've no big need for words right now, do we, Ann? You've stolen my heart and the hearts of my children."

"Have I?"

He lost himself in those pretty brown eyes. "It's so."

She sighed.

"Pa, what are you guys doin'?" Ethan's voice hailed them.

"Look how far we've gotten!"

"Too far." Ann pulled back and cupped her hands to her mouth. "Come back here right now, both of you."

"Aww…" Ethan clomped back, head down.

Sarah tried, but what had seemed fun a few minutes before was more like punishment now. She made it across four furrows, fell and burst into tears.

"Hang on, Sarah-girl. I'm coming." Sol's big strides made short work of getting to her. He hoisted her and pulled her close to stave her tears. "There now, you're all right, not hurt, just unnerved."

"I'm all dirty." Sarah blubbered the words, swiping messy hands to wet cheeks, smearing dirt this way and that.

Ann had a clean hanky waiting when he drew up beside her. She wiped Sarah's face down and took her from Sol. "Let's get you back up to the house for a bit of clean up and a rest, all right?"

Sarah tucked her face onto Ann's shoulder. Ann glanced up at him, still flushed, but kept her attention on Sarah. "There, there." She patted the little one's back and started moving forward. "Come along, Ethan. Let's get Sissy tucked down and do some lessons."

"On a fine day like this, I should be helpin' my pa," Ethan grumbled. He sent a dark look Sol's way. "There's a lot to be done on this claim, you said so, Pa."

"And we'll work at it day by day, son. Mind Ann, now and get some schooling out of the way. That way when I've got work for you, you can jump right to it."

Chin tucked, the boy didn't look one bit happy, but Sol didn't give in. Following directions could be life or death for children on a farm, and more so for children on the prairie. Land swells didn't look like too much to the grown eye, but children had gone missing too often across the heartland, straying too far and unable to find their way home. When claims lay so far apart, danger lurked in the shadows. He thought of his mother's warning again, that getting children to school age was a feat. And he thought of Ann's sadness, the loss she'd faced back East.

His father thought his move west with kids was foolish, and more than one person back home had agreed. He'd show them it wasn't rash, it wasn't one bit impetuous. His success with the children and the land would be proof enough, in time.

He went back to plowing, thinking of the future, and wanting Ann's kisses to be part of that plan.

Nellie pulled up to Sol's claim shack the next morning. Sol was taking his horse into town, and Ann was taking his kids to the Eichas farm so that she and Miri could share cheese-making skills again. They'd conferred the week before and just the thought of working on a project with another woman lightened her step. Nellie paused the gelding just south of the door. Sol walked the children out to the small buckboard. Ethan scrambled into the back and Sol lifted Sarah up, into Ann's arms. "Make sure you both mind Ann and your cousins," he warned them. "There are big animals at Levi's place and some big equipment, too. No climbing or monkeying around farm tools, you hear?"

"Yes, sir."

"I won't, Pa!"

He turned his attention to Ann. "If they don't mind, it's all right to make them play on the porch. Or stay in the house."

"We'll be good, Pa, we're not babies!"

"So good, Pa!" Sarah promised.

"Miri and I will keep track of them as we work, and if they don't listen, we'll keep them in the house."

"And I'm staying right there," Nellie assured him. "We'll be fine."

"It's not that I don't trust you," Sol began, but Ann didn't need to hear reasoning where children were concerned.

"Better safe than sorry," she agreed, her hands light but firm around Sarah. "They were good the last time I took them there, Sol. I expect they'll be good again."

"And the current abundance of milk is calling for more cheesemaking, that's for sure," Nellie added.

Sol stepped back, and once Nellie stirred the horses forward, he mounted his horse and rode toward town.

"I'm not a baby," Ethan told them from the cradle of the wagon. "I know how to be careful."

"You do," Ann agreed. "But a good pa is always looking out for his youngsters, isn't he?" She tried not to mean that personally, but she knew full well how one poorly thought decision could change a family.

"I guess."

"Nellie, thank you for doing this." Ann turned her way. "I know I'm taking you from work."

"It's a pleasure, actually, and with everyone planting on their claims, and you taking over hems, Hattie and I are caught up and have shirts pre-made for coming orders. She said she's never been so well-stocked and prepared in her life, so that's good!" Nellie directed the horses left, toward the homestead. "And if things go the way I think they might, I'd love for this big family to do all kinds of things together." She angled a saucy, knowing look Ann's way. "Cheese-making is just the beginning, I expect."

Miri hurried out of the house just then, and waved a towel their way. "You were able to come, wonderful! I thought with such a fine day that if the kids played outside, you and I could share our methods. It's so much easier to do it in person, don't you think?"

."I am in full agreement," Ann told her.

"Is Esther here?" Nellie asked from the bench seat.

"She's not," Miri replied. "She's over at the Tompkins claim putting together some kind of new barn door sys-

tem with Old Elmer. He had it in his head, Sol fashioned
the slide, and you'd think he'd just invented the wheel the
way they were carrying on. She'll be back later."

"Good." Once Ann and the children climbed down, Nellie directed the wagon toward the far side of the barnyard.
"I'll set the horses out and I can help with the children
while you ladies make cheese. And I'd be greatly pleased to
not have to come near the smell of it at this stage, if that's
all right?"

"Nellie." Ann looked up, excited. "Are you in the family
way?"

"I am, and smells have become my most ardent enemies."

"I've got the first curds draining, come see my set-up in
the near barn, Ann. It's like a second kitchen. Levi took
the time to do it. It keeps the mess out of the house, and it
gives me temperature control all year long."

Ann doubted her words until she realized that the back
of the foremost barn was cut into the side of a swell. Once
through the door, the temperature dropped. "Cool and dry,
this is a perfect setting, Miri."

"A blessing, for sure." She showed Ann around. Kettles
and strainers, muslin and string, and blocks of clean, fresh
wax shelved above. They set one tub of milk on to clabber.
Then they sliced an already gelled and cooled pot into
curds. They drained the curd, poured it into a cheesecloth
sack and hung it to drain. They were just about to manage
a sack of dried curd, when Nellie's voice interrupted them.
"Ann? Miri? Is Sarah in there with you?"

"No." Miri crossed and opened the door. "We haven't
seen or heard either of them, Nellie."

Uncommon fear grabbed Ann's gut. *Stay calm. Children
are small and generally found quite easily. Stay calm.* "Where
was she last, Nellie?"

"Right on the porch, playing with Ethan, but then he
chased off to use the necessary and I was in the house. By
the time he got back, she wasn't there."

Miri set the kettle off the heat of the small wood stove. "Let's find her."

They hurried back toward the house. Ethan was on the porch. He looked worried, and when he spotted Ann, he raced her way. "I lost Sarah, and I promised Pa I'd take good care of her!"

Chill coursed up her spine. This little child shouldn't be concerned with watching Sarah. That was her job, and she'd failed. "Sarah!" She called the girl's name, hoping she'd hear and come dashing out, laughing. "Sarah, come back here!"

The Eichas farm was much more elaborate than Sol's holding. Two solid barns blocked much of the view. Cattle fencing separated pens, but there were gates with easy gaps, certainly big enough for a small child like Sarah to fit through. Ann turned in a half circle and began calling her again. "Sarah! Sarah! Where are you?"

No answer came.

Her heart clutched tight. Her brain went instantly to the worst possible outcome. "I'll go this way." Nellie hurried toward the back of the house.

"And I'll head toward the road." Miri ran that way.

Ann took tight hold of Ethan's hand. "Come with me, Ethan."

"But then no one will be here if Sarah comes back." His voice went low, soft and scared. His tone begged for everything to be all right.

"You can't stay here alone, Ethan."

"I can." He jerked loose, folded his arms and stood, legs spread apart, a miniature of his father. "I'm not little, I'm big, I can read and everything, and if Sarah comes back here and we're all gone, she'll be a scare-baby."

The two sisters kept calling Sarah's name, their voices growing fainter as they moved farther afield.

What could she do? What should she do? She snapped her fingers and re-took Ethan's hand because there was no way she was letting the boy out of her sight. "Let's check the barns. Sarah's curious."

He nodded and didn't argue.

"And that way if she comes back, she'll hear us because we'll be right here, okay?"

He glanced around, unsure, but let her draw him forward. "All right, Ann."

They crossed the yard. Ann called the girl's name repeatedly.

Nothing.

They went through both barns and the lean-to shack.

No Sarah.

She couldn't cry. She wanted to, but she didn't have the right to break down, not yet. Esther rode in a few minutes later. She went to swing down from the horse, but Ann raced across the barnyard toward her. "Esther, stay up top. Sarah's missing, and we haven't been able to find her."

Esther's eyes went round. She glanced around, then brought her gaze back to Ann. "What can I do?"

"Ride to town. Get Sol and Levi and anyone else who's available. And tell them to hurry, it will be dark in a few hours."

Esther tapped the horse's hip and rode off, her body bent low over the horse's neck, like one of those jockeys she'd seen at the local track outside of Pittsburgh.

Ann hated to send her. She hated to admit that she'd messed up her job. She knew Nellie would feel bad for not seeing Sarah wander off, but Sarah wasn't Nellie's job. Not really. She was Ann's, and Ann had put a small child in danger.

Nellie and Miri had circled toward one another. They hurried back toward the barnyard. When they drew close enough, Miri took Ann's hand. "We're going to saddle up and go farther. I don't know how a child that size could get that far, but with every passing minute she could be getting farther and farther away from us. Can you and

Ethan stay right here in case she finds her way back?"

"Of course." That's what she said, but every ounce of her being longed to be out there, beating the bushes, searching through scrub brush, trying to find Sol's precious daughter.

Sol.

How would she face him? What could she say? There were no words to explain her neglect, especially after her personal loss. Shouldn't that have been a valuable lesson? That children must be treated like prized gold, more valued than the greatest pearl?

And she'd walked away, leaving the children in someone else's care to make cheese.

Her chest heaved heavy. Her throat went tight. Miri and Nellie were hurrying toward the second paddock when a sound made them both stop dead in their tracks.

"Ann? I'm so firsty. Can I have a dwink of water, pwease?"

Ann turned, heart pounding.

Sarah came out the door of the farmhouse, rubbing sleepy eyes. She looked at Ann, then Miri and Nellie, then Ethan. "Eaffen!" She smiled, seeing him. Her eyes went wide and she skipped toward the steps, happy as could be. "Oh, Eaffen, good! You're back! We can pway!"

"Sarah!" Ann raced across the farmyard. She leaped up the steps and gathered the startled child into her arms. "Oh, Sarah, darling where were you?"

Nellie crossed her arms, sheepish. Miri did the same. They exchanged looks, then climbed the steps. "Do you think she was in the house that whole time?" Nellie asked. "Oh good heavens, I am beyond embarrassed to have caused all this ruckus. I did look for her," she declared, but she sounded as if there may have been a spot or two she missed. "Sarah, where were you?"

"I found the sun!" Sarah told her. "Behind the l-long curtain and the big chair, and it was so warm and nice. I wike playing in sunbeams the best. They're my favowite thing to pway in."

A sunbeam.

She'd found a cozy warm corner, curled up and fell sound asleep.

Ann held her close, embarrassed that she hadn't gone inside and checked the house more thoroughly. Nellie and Miri had no children. They didn't know the likely, and sometimes *unlikely* things kids did.

She should have known. She should have checked. And now Sol and Levi would race out here, bent on finding a child who had never been lost.

But she *could* have been lost, and Ann had to own that reality. Maybe it was an honest mistake. And perhaps they were rash to jump to conclusions, but she'd come to a solid conclusion during the long search.

She wasn't meant for this. Not anymore. Not when the thought of something happening to a small child on her watch struck her dumb with fear.

Horses came into view over the small swell beyond the main paddock. Dust from the horse's hooves obscured the identities, but as they drew closer, Levi, Esther, Sol and four others pounded their way. As the lead horses turned into the lane leading to the farmyard, they slowed.

There was nothing to do but move forward, the well-rested girl snug in her arms.

"You found her! Oh, thank God!" Sol shot off his horse, and the others followed. "Sarah, honey, what were you thinking?"

"Sol."

He took Sarah from her, clutched the girl to his chest and turned grateful eyes to Ann. "I'm so glad you found her."

Ann fought for words of admission from two directions. Her culpability in making something else more important and the foolishness of not checking the house thoroughly. She started to speak, but then Nellie sashayed right up to the group, grabbed her husband's arm and announced, "All is well that ends well, I say."

"Endeth gut, alles gut." Levi's nod said he found wisdom in the words.

"Just how my mother used to say it," Nellie agreed. She faced the others and looked genuinely apologetic, but not one bit desperate. Of course Ann felt desperate enough for all of them. "We are so sorry we had to sound an alarm," Nellie told the gathered riders. "The least we can do is offer all of you some of Rachel's biscuits before you ride back to town."

Mr. Towner waved a hand of refusal. "No need, Nellie, it's just good to know the child is all right. They do bear close watching on these spreads, don't they?"

"Oh, indeed!" Nellie agreed wholeheartedly, and it wasn't an untruth, but Ann was somewhat amazed at how smoothly the dressmaker wriggled them out of looking downright foolish. "Thank you so much for rushing out here. Are you sure about the cookies? I can set coffee up, too, we are so grateful!"

"Best get back to it." Sebastian Ward, the lumberyard owner, turned his horse around first. The others followed, walking the horses for a cool-down after pushing them all the way to the Eichas farm. In the end it was Sol and Levi left standing there, with the little girl snug in Sol's arms.

"On my word, I've never felt so stupid in all my life." Nellie dropped the pretense of cheer and fell into Levi's strong arms. "How am I going to take care of this little baby, Levi Eichas, if I can't mind a child for a few hours? Maybe I'm not meant to be a mother, have you given that one bit of consideration while you fashion your wood to absolute perfection? Raising children is hard, hard work, and I now suspect that I am not cut out for the endeavor! Only now is a mite too late, don't you think?"

"What?" Levi hiked his brows toward Miriam, then Ann. "Nell, now don't go getting yourself all worked up, I meant what I said. Kids get into scrapes all the time. It's part of growing up."

"She didn't get into a scrape," Nellie wailed. She pushed back from Levi's arms and pointed to the house. "She fell sound asleep in the house, nestled up in a sunbeam, and I didn't have sense enough to check for her. I got everyone riled up, poor Ann is beside herself, half the town came racing to our aid, when none was required because I wasn't smart enough to look behind a chair. Oh, Levi, what kind of mother will I be, with not a lick of common sense as to the ways of children?"

"She was in the house?" Sol looked from Ann to Nell and back. "All this time?"

"Yes." Ann spoke softly, because as bad as Nellie felt, she felt worse. "She'd curled up to play and dozed off, and we created quite the ruckus, looking for her."

"You must have been so worried, Ann." Sol's gaze, sweet and tender. His eyes, full of understanding, as if it was all right that she'd mucked up the day.

It wasn't all right.

None of this was all right, but she didn't dare cave here and let her emotions show. She needed to leave, be on her own, make some kind of sense of what happened.

Her heart had gone chill.

Her nerves had spiked a fever.

Her brain had refused to work, she'd been absolutely addled in a time of need.

"I need to go home." She said the words softly, as if to herself, but Sol heard them. He nodded, gathered the children, and with him on his horse, Levi drove them back to Sol's place. Ann paused long enough to gather her cloak and wrap it around her, in spite of the pleasant day.

She picked up the box of finished gowns, plunked it into the wagon bed, and when Levi drove her into town, she let him carry it into Hattie's place.

"Ann, I know Nellie is truly sorry by what happened today." Levi held his hat in his hands and twisted it, nervous. "Please don't take this too seriously."

She lifted her gaze to his. "As if the loss of a child could be anything but grievous." She whispered the words. "Goodbye, Levi."

He studied her, then grimaced, as if knowing her plan. "Go with God, Ann Hazel." He turned and walked out the door.

She wrote Hattie a quick note, threw her meager possessions back into her worn satchel and when the four-forty train heading east pulled out of the small, Second Chance depot, Ann Hazel was on it.

Chapter Eight

SOL'S HEART ACHED.
  He hadn't thought it possible to care so much about a person in a few weeks' time, but he did. And his children did, too. It was 'Ann, this' and 'Ann, that', until he was pretty sure he'd go crazy fielding their questions.

Samantha stepped in to help with the children, and she was a sweet girl, but it wasn't the same.

Ethan stopped working at letters and numbers. He demanded to play and Samantha was of the mind to let him.

Sarah took a turn toward whininess and self-indulgence, and was that because of her age or because Samantha took care to let her do as she pleased?

Sol didn't know, but the clarity of the situation wasn't lost on him. He'd brought his children here for a strong, warm, Christian upbringing. By default, that wasn't happening and he didn't have a clue what to do about it, so he went through his days, chin down, consumed with worry, and wondering if his father was right about raising a foolhardy son, after all.

He stopped by the inn, bought a loaf of their fresh bread, and tried not to compare it to the superior texture and taste he'd enjoyed while Ann was in town.

Go get her.

He swiped a hand to his neck in frustration.

He'd heard that small voice a dozen times, at least, but today the words were stronger. Louder. And when he looked back straight, if that wasn't Hattie McGillicuddy aiming his way like a big ship in full sail, and him with nowhere to duck.

"Sol! Just the person I wanted to see!"

He stood still, the paper sack of bread clutched in his hand.

"And as I thought, you don't look one bit good," she went on, sounding decidedly too cheerful about his lack of good appearance. "Now here's what I'm thinking."

He tried to dodge left, but she moved to her right.

He tried the opposite, but Hattie was too quick and not small, and she cut him off again, without even looking like it was deliberate. "About Ann," she said, and that got his attention right quick.

"Did you hear from her?"

She rolled her eyes and shook her head. "No, she's as stubborn and bone-headed as they come, and yet not the kind of woman who gives her heart carelessly, I believe."

"Gives her heart?" Sol made a wry face. "I'd best be getting back to work, Hattie."

"As I was saying." She fell into step beside him, ignoring his obvious ploy to be alone.

"Ann not being a careless one, it must have weighed heavy on her to have Sarah disappear like that. Children can be a blessing and a vexation all in one, of course, but after Ann's loss, I expect the thought of losing a child while doing the mundane struck deep. Which means a man who is interested in such a rare find like Ann Hazel, would do himself and his children and I dare say his community well to ride back to Pittsburgh and bring her back where she belongs."

"Ride to Pittsburgh? Hattie, are you out of your mind?" He stopped right there and put his hands on his hips, because the very thought was ludicrous. Wasn't it? "I've got two children and a business and a farm. A man can't just up and leave his responsibilities to take off cross-country after a woman who left without word or bother."

"Well, there was plenty of bother," Hattie corrected him. "And as for the word, sometimes it's a good thing to have a woman of few words, as my late husband and Levi Eichas would attest because their fate brought no such thing. But in Ann's case, I expect she had some sweet words with you, over time?"

Heat rose, thinking of their words. Their teasing. That kiss. He scrubbed a hand to the base of his neck again and said nothing, but this was Hattie, and he didn't need to.

"I thought as much, and I've got it all arranged if you've got a mind to take a few days to ensure faith, hope and love the rest of your days. The sisters will take the children, the seed is in, Samantha will stay at your place to see to the animals and the garden, and Levi said if having you go east to fetch yourself a wife wiped that scowl off your face, he'd be glad of a double load for a week."

"Levi said that?"

Hattie hemmed and hawed, then said, "I may have embellished his sentiments slightly, him being a man of few words, but his meaning was clear enough. What say you, Sol Eichas? Are you enough in love with this woman to head east and state your case? Because if you're not, then it's best to leave well enough alone, I expect."

Enough in love? Was he in love?

The truth in the matter came in hard and strong. "Hattie, you mean well, but—"

She raised a hand, brushing him off, and turned. "Not a problem, Sol, at all, I misjudged and that's an error on my part, not yours. I'm sure Ann will do just fine back east." She began walking away, moving more slowly than she had before.

"Hattie, I—"

She kept walking, toward the mercantile, like their conversation was over, but how come it didn't feel over?

He chased after her, the sack of bread swinging from his

hand. "Hattie, listen."

She paused.

"Ann and me, we've both got water under the dam. We've both buried those we love. And on Ann's part, she's mighty mad at God for all that's gone wrong in her life."

"A serious question, for certain, one that is made better by knowing a man of conviction."

"Except that each of us must take God as our own in our own way, our own time," he told her. "What kind of marriage can occur if one believes and the other does not?"

"Wretched," she declared, and thumped her little cane with some alacrity. "But it's plain as the nose upon your face, Solomon, that Ann's faith is just as strong and true as yours, for pity's sake."

"It is?"

"Solomon." She put her hands on his arms and met him eye-to-eye. "A body can't be mad at something they don't believe in, can they? The sheer ludicrousness of such a notion amazes me. If Ann didn't believe in God, then why would she be mad at Him?"

He hated that she made sense. That in some weird, confounded way, Hattie's logic was, well… logical.

"When a body feels lost or let down, anger is an understandable reaction. So we can't judge a person on a natural consequence, we look to the heart and soul of that person to be their claim. And Ann Hazel's claim is of a loving, God-fearing woman who came home one day to horrific circumstances. I expect we'd all get a little shaken up in such a time."

He heard her, and she made sense, and he couldn't believe he was actually contemplating the idea of riding east to claim his beloved. What if she wouldn't have him? What if he came away the fool? What if—

"He who hesitates is lost," she told him softly. "You're a thinker Sol, but now and again, a man needs to put doing first."

His father had set that example for him, time and again. That sometimes a man just needs to jump in and get a job done. Like now. He shoved his hand through his hair and nodded. "I'll do it. I'll go home, get a change of clothes and catch the four-forty."

"And I'll ride with you and see to the children until Rachel comes by for them. And what fun they'll have at the Eichas place, cows and horses and baby pigs and chicks." She grabbed his arm and started walking with him.

"Didn't you have business at the mercantile?" he asked.

She squeezed his arm like a proud mother and shook her head. "My business is complete. For today, that is," she added, smiling. "Of course, God willing, there's always another day, isn't there?"

"God willing." He drove the team home, unhitched them, and brought a single horse back to town after kissing his surprised children goodbye. He didn't dare tell them the purpose of his mission. If he failed, they'd be broken-hearted all over again. Levi took charge of his horse, and at exactly four-forty that afternoon, Solomon Eichas headed east toward one thing or another, but what he hoped and prayed was that this trip would bring him his destiny for the rest of his days: Ann Hazel.

Chapter Nine

THE LONG, LONELY RIDE EAST gave Ann time to think. Too much time.

But by the time she walked the final half-mile to her old home, her search for some sort of truth came clear.

Memories swamped her as she approached the small, clapboard house, quaint and improved compared to Sol's meager shack.

Silent, she stood in the small yard bordered by overgrown fields. Her gardens, once a pretty frame for a family home, lay untended for two seasons. Her paths, unwalked, had grown thick with greens. The barn lay empty but for field mice.

Nothing of what she'd loved remained because the hearts that beat in time with hers were gone. All gone.

She put her satchel inside, threw open a few windows, then came back outside.

She pictured Adele and Robert running and playing, then realized she'd said their names in her head. Usually she'd kept them as a unit, 'the children', unable to deal with the pain of recognition.

But now she remembered them as individuals, running, laughing. She could hear their voices, light and carefree, two lives full of hope, work, fun and love. And like Sarah and Ethan, Robert was older and bossier, but Adele didn't shrink from standing her ground as needed.

They were good children. Loved and cherished and disciplined.

But Robert and Adele were gone, and Sol's children weren't. They were here on earth, alive and in need of a strong, loving hand and sweet laughter.

She put cool hands to her warm cheeks, cheeks warmed when she thought of Sol and his kindness, his humor, the strength in his hands and the depth of his kiss.

She'd run, foolishly.

She'd had all that time on the rail to think of it, and how she wished she'd taken Nellie's cue and made light of an exasperating situation.

Could she do that? she wondered.

Could she learn to be normal again? To not take things too seriously or over-react?

You could try. Nothing is achieved without trying, is it?

The quiet voice within her nudged her forward.

Clean out your gardens, sell this spot and go back to where you now belong. Go back west, like Hattie and Nellie before you. Go home, Ann.

She surveyed the grounds around the house, changed into an old work frock and got to work. By the next week, the yard looked better, the paths were cleared and the old Hazel home had the appearance of love.

She walked to town with the thought of listing her small farm, but a neighboring farm owner met her halfway. When she explained her mission to him, John Richards made her an offer on the spot, an offer she accepted before doubts had a chance to creep in and take hold.

Within a few days the local lawyer had drawn up an agreeable contract, they both signed, money changed hands, and Ann Hazel was free to board the train west once more.

"Are you heading straight back, Ann?" John asked once the business was accomplished.

"The mid-day train tomorrow," she told him. She gazed around. "There's much to miss here, John, but much to look forward to, as well."

"The Lord giveth… and he taketh away." John spoke softly, for he had two small graves in the Evangelical cemetery as well.

"Blessed be the name of the Lord." She ended the verse gently, with no rancor. While her heart kept hold with a disappointment that would never fully disappear, her shoulders lay ready to take on new responsibilities and new love.

She wasn't the first or last to have lost a child or a spouse. She'd spent an inordinate amount of time blaming her husband for something that was just what folks had said. An accident. She rued the long seasons of angst and lost time, but this summer would hold a different newness, if Sol was willing.

She woke early the next morning, packed the satchel and a trunk, a sure sign that she wasn't coming back, then walked toward the old resting grounds. She crossed to the far left side and knelt. A cool, smooth stone stood before her. It was blank, her fault for never contacting the stone smith to carve the names, but she'd taken care of that yesterday. Soon Jonah's name would be inscribed in the center, with Robert to his right and Adele to his left, tucked in the curve of their father's arms.

As it should be, she knew. As it should have been all along. She leaned her cheek down to the center of that cool, smooth stone. "Forgive me, Jonah. Please forgive me."

The stone warmed beneath the press of her cheek. She knew it meant nothing, simply warmth from her body transferring to the stone, but she could imagine it as Jonah's kiss. His blessing. And maybe, too, his apology for what went wrong.

She stood, laid her hands on the grave marker one last time, then walked back toward the house. It wasn't a short walk, but a good one. As she came in sight of the farm cottage, a buggy approached from town. She glanced up at the sun, but knew it was too early for John to come by and give her the ride he'd offered. She waited, not wanting to impede the horse's progress, so when the horse and buggy pulled into her yard, she stood still, surprised.

And then she was more surprised when Sol Eichas jumped down from the buggy seat.

Her heart soared.

Her palms grew damp.

She stood like a rock as he faced her across the short expanse of yard, and then he opened his arms.

Oh, how she ran to him! Swift, like the deer of the field in early spring! And when he caught her up in his arms, he held her close. So close. His face in her hair, then against her cheek, and then his lips, busy with hers. He kissed her long and full and when he was done, he loosened his hold just enough. "I've come to fetch you home, Ann. If you'll have me. It is my sincere wish that you *will* have me and be mine forever."

"My beloved spake, and said unto me, rise up, my love, my fair one, and come away."

He smiled, recognizing the words from the second Song of Solomon. "For, lo, the winter is past, the rain is over and gone," he whispered back. His hands cradled her face. His gaze searched her features, as if memorizing every one, and then he smiled. "The flowers appear on the earth; the time of the singing of birds is come, and the voice of the turtle is heard in our land." He leaned down and feathered a kiss to her mouth, a kiss so gentle and yet so full that she remembered much of what had been forgotten in grief. "May I take you home with me, Ann? Back to a somewhat harsh land, not so pretty as this? Not yet, anyway."

She leaned into his kiss and fluttered her lashes against his skin. "Yes." She pulled back slightly and indicated the trunk and bag set just outside the door. "I'm ready."

He stared at the trunk, then her. "You meant to return."

She shook her head quickly. "Not at first. At first I meant to run, but then I realized I was tired of running and tired of sadness and tired of anger. And I thought of how Christ's mother must have felt, watching her son on that last, long walk to the hill. And then everything went clear, as if I could finally see that being a mother, or a parent or a spouse didn't come with a promise of forever, but a promise to love forever. And I saw the difference."

He pulled her into his arms again and held her. Just that. The loving embrace of a man who loved her enough to travel a great distance to find her and fetch her home. "I love you, Ann."

Oh, those words. Such sweet, beautiful words. She felt the nub of his jacket beneath her cheek, the scent of mint and spring wood fires and she hugged him back. "I love you, too. And I have a ticket on the two-fifteen train. My farm is sold, my bags are packed and I've said my goodbyes. Let's go home, Sol."

He gave her one last kiss, then looped his arm about her shoulders and started moving toward the stoop. "That's a fine idea, my love." He picked up the trunk onto strong, broad shoulders.

She lifted her bag.

They loaded them into the backseat of the buggy, and then he turned and helped her step up, between the wheels. "Mind the step, Ann." He said it softly, out of habit, perhaps, or just out of simple, loving care.

"I will, Sol."

She settled into the seat and placed her hands in her lap. He climbed in beside her, tapped the reins lightly, and the well-trained horse stepped smartly, making the turn, and heading back up the road, toward town.

She didn't look back. There was no need. She would carry the image of that first place and that first family in her heart and mind forever.

She looked forward, just as the good Lord intended, knowing that weeping had its time of endurance. And now was the promised time of joy.

Epilogue

"YOU ALL NEED TO STOP fussing so."
Ann addressed the gathered group, but as she'd found since the day she arrived in Second Chance, these women had minds of their own and used them. They paid not a whit of attention as Nellie adjusted the little bustle on her gown, Esther set up finger sandwiches using Ann's homemade bread and Miri cut slabs of cheese into delightful triangle shaped pieces. Esther and Hattie then arranged Hattie's famous biscuits around pots of homemade strawberry jam, and Macy Barber, the minister's wife, had offered to mind the children during the outdoor ceremony.

"This isn't a first marriage for either of us, and it's probably best with the least bother. Don't you think?" She tried to curb the hint of wistfulness, because in truth, she was enjoying the anticipation, but a twinge of guilt ran neck in neck with the joy.

"Oh, hush." Nellie refused to be deterred, as usual. "If we're to become a family of new brides, in a new town, we get precious little enough to make a big to-do over, and a wedding, no matter what the number, is nothing to be taken lightly."

"Simple truth from a not-so-simple woman," Rachel remarked. "I do believe that little bit of salt added the best flavor to this icing. And what fun to make special cakes and treats to celebrate a marriage."

"Keep that in mind in case any one of us ever captures a

husband." Esther's dry tone said she thought that unlikely and when the sisters exchanged rueful looks, Ann knew the others agreed.

"Well, Miss Esther." Hattie didn't look up, she kept placing biscuits with a dexterity that put many a younger woman to the test. "With so many new folks coming in, I'd say your chances of wedded bliss have greatly improved this season." She finished that tray while Esther decorated the platters with sprigs of mint leaf and fresh blossoms. "Four claims have been bought in the past week, a new church laid out, a bank being installed on Main Street, and two new buildings going up just west of the wagon shop and smithy. Never in my years here have I seen a groundswell of so many coming so quickly. We've survived drought and naysayers and are now a state of the union. I'd say prospects are looking up. And to have the school board mentioning Rachel as a possible new teacher for next year's term, change seems to be finding us even whether we seek it or not."

"Opportunities couldn't have looked much worse than they did," Miriam teased, laughing. "This time of year, when this farm is so busy, and so much to be done, it doesn't weigh on me in the same manner as long, cold months of winter. And there's not much dreaming allowed then, but plenty of thinking, I'll say."

"Time-ticking-away-thinking," Rachel noted. She finished frosting the grand cake and set it aside. "The food is ready, tables are set up outside, and I hear wagons approaching."

"It's time." Ann said the words as flutters of anticipation warred with the nerves dancing up her spine. She turned slightly. "Thank you. Thank you all for what you've done, and for what you're always doing." She paused, thinking, then said, "I came here so empty and lost, unknowing. But being here, I found not only myself, again. I found Sol and those precious children I tried so hard to ignore on the voyage! I found peace with the past I battled daily. And I found you. All of you." She hugged each one of the ladies in turn, and Ann had never been too much of a hugger before. Now she wanted these women to understand the difference they'd made in her life. "Thank you."

A tap on the door averted tears. Ann turned.

Sol walked in, looking tanned and fine and good. He saw her and crossed the room quickly and took her hands. "You are beautiful Ann. So very beautiful."

A blush crept up from somewhere around her toes, wending around her like a blanket on a winter's night.

He squeezed her hands lightly, then, in front of all the ladies, he drew her close and kissed her. "Thank you for saying yes, Ann." He held her gently against his chest, against his heart. "Thank you for coming back. We wouldn't make it out here without you. We wouldn't want to make it out here without you. I love you."

Two of the ladies sniffled. Ann wasn't sure which ones because she kept her gaze on Sol. Only Sol. She returned the gentle pressure of his hands and couldn't help but smile up at him. Her beautiful, beloved, slightly stubborn Solomon. "Come, my beloved, let us go forth into the field; let us lodge in the villages."

He grinned recognizing the sweet text of his namesake. "Set me as a seal upon thine heart, Ann," he paraphrased gently. "Your husband. Your beloved."

He took her hand and tucked it through his arm, and when they stepped through the screen door Levi had fashioned for the Eichas farmhouse, the guests clapped softly, sharing their joy.

Behind them, a row of buckboards and buggies sat waiting. Horses had been turned out in the nearby pasture. Ethan and Sarah spotted them. They raced forward, despite Macy's attempts to keep them close. Those precious children came their way clean and sweet, filled with life. Ann bent low and captured them into her arms.

They smelled marvelous and they both talked at once, filling the air with childish excitement. With innocent love.

Reverend Barber motioned them forward. His wife stepped up to take charge of the children, but Ann waved her away. With one arm tucked through Sol's, she clasped Ethan's sturdy hand. Sol took her lead and gathered Sarah into his left arm. Together, they approached the minister, as one. As a family.

Will Barber's smile of understanding blessed their choice, and as they recited words of old, Ann was filled with thoughts of new. A new home. A new life. A new family.

Nothing would ever replace what had gone before, but for her and Solomon, it wasn't about replacing.

It was all about a new beginning. Another time, another chance. And this one was in Second Chance, South Dakota.

Home.

FROM THE PEN OF
Hattie McGillicuddy,
SECOND CHANCE, SOUTH DAKOTA, NOW A STATE:

ANOTHER HELPER GONE!
Ann Hazel came to town ready to leave, but with the good Lord's timing, a fine man, needy children and a chance for a new beginning, she's decided to stay, but not without a bit of drama and a bigger slice of travel! Surely the age of the railroad has offered choices never before seen by modern-day women, and I can only think that adds to our influence, which is, of course, a good thing.

The wedding was lovely, and with Nellie expecting a most welcome child, and Macy looking a bit wan again, and the likelihood of Ann and Sol increasing their family, I have two items on my agenda: Our lovely, growing town is in need of a skilled midwife, and I've sent Jean Ellen word about that very thing, with word to make haste!

And those Eichas sisters have a fine hand at running that growing farm, but three such lovely ladies should at least be seen now and again, and I believe I've got an idea worth considering. Of course, it's in God's hands, now as ever, but in all my days on His green earth I've found a bit of prodding now and again is generally all right.

Business remains strong, the rise of catalogues makes a small business like mine a bit uneasy, but the current population still prefers the personal touch on their items, and the craze of ordering sight unseen hasn't swept the nation as yet. Knowing women as I do, I doubt it ever will.

Hattie McGillicuddy, in the year of our Lord 1890

DEAR READERS,

I love delving into history. I love looking back to see what it took to thrust this great country forward, and it's amazing, isn't it? I'm a total softie compared to these brave women who sacrificed so much to risk a chance at love and life, women and men who clung to faith through the rigors of settling a new land.

I hope you loved Ann and Solomon's story. I hope you enjoyed the glimpse into a past that helped form a future we're blessed to enjoy today. And I hope you fall in love with Hattie McGillicuddy and the young brides and grooms surrounding her in the growing town of Second Chance, South Dakota, a place of fiction based on the reality of history.

God bless you and yours, and thank you so much for taking the time to read this. You honor me with that gift of time. I love hearing from readers. Drop me an email at *loganherne@gmail.com* stop by my website *www.ruthloganherne.com* and friend me on facebook or Twitter.

And be prepared for more stories from Second Chance, South Dakota because when Hattie McGillicuddy is running the show, you know that things are happening!

Links to my other books are available after the next delicious recipe for Ann's homemade white bread… a clear favorite on the prairie back then and here in Western New York today!

With love,

Ann's Homemade Bread

¼ cup warm water to start the yeast

2 Tablespoons of yeast

¼ cup sugar

1 Tablespoon salt

Mix these together. Let sit for a few minutes while you check the children or make a cup of coffee or tea. Or ponder the beauty of life.

Add in:

3 Tablespoons shortening (lard or butter can be used, but shortening was Ann's favorite)

2 2/3 cup very warm water

8-9 cups of flour, mixing in until a stiff dough is made. Not too dry. Not too wet. Just kind of sticky.

Ann would have turned the dough onto a flour-dusted board and kneaded it repeatedly, but if you have a dough hook on your mixer, that's a wonderful invention!

Dough should be smooth and elastic.

Set dough in greased bowl, grease the top to avoid drying and cover with a clean towel. Let rise in a warm place until about double. If you forget and it gets bigger, the world does not end. I promise. If your oven has a "proof" setting, wonderful! If not, we set ours near the wood stove or in really warm car mid-summer. ☺

Punch down dough. (little children with freshly washed hands are great at this)

Cut dough in half. For loaves, each half can be rolled out into a 9" x 18" rectangle. Then roll the dough up from short side, tuck the ends under (like wrapping a present) and settle into an 8" x 4" loaf pan. Grease dough top lightly, let rise until dough is above the pan.

Bake at 400 degrees for about 25-35 minutes until loaf

is golden brown and bread sounds a bit 'hollow' if you tap it. Turn out onto cooling rack. Brush with butter to keep crust soft.

For cinnamon rolls or bread, coat rolled out dough with butter, then sprinkle liberally with cinnamon sugar. Roll up same as above. For rolls, then slice the roll into 1" sections. Set the "pinwheels" into a greased cake pan, a little space between each one, leaving room to rise. Bake at 400 degrees until deep gold on top.

GLAZE WHILE WARM.

Glaze:

1 cup powdered sugar

Enough water to form medium-thick glaze. If too thick or too thin, simply add more water or sugar. Drizzle over cinnamon rolls while warm.

For a cinnamon bread loaf, follow the instructions above, but tuck the ends and place into a greased loaf pan. Let rise until above the pan, then bake at 400 degrees like the loaves above.

Turn out of pan while warm and brush loaf with butter. Then glaze, if desired.

Other books by
Ruth Logan Herne

Ruthy's Amazon Author page and books:
http://amzn.to/1v26FHw

INDEPENDENTLY PUBLISHED BOOKS
Running on Empty
Try, Try Again
Safely Home
Refuge of the Heart
More Than a Promise
The First Gift
From This Day Forward
Christmas on the Frontier

FROM WATERFALL PRESS/AMAZON
Welcome to Wishing Bridge
At Home in Wishing Bridge

FROM WATERBROOK PRESS/PENGUIN/ RANDOM HOUSE
Back in the Saddle
Home on the Range
Peace in the Valley

LOVE INSPIRED BOOKS
North Country:
Winter's End
Waiting Out the Storm
Made to Order Family

MEN OF ALLEGANY COUNTY SERIES
Reunited Hearts
Small Town Hearts
Mended Hearts
Yuletide Hearts
A Family to Cherish
His Mistletoe Family

KIRKWOOD LAKE SERIES
The Lawman's Second Chance
Falling for the Lawman
The Lawman's Holiday Wish
Loving the Lawman
Her Holiday Family
Healing the Lawman's Heart

GRACE HAVEN SERIES
An Unexpected Groom
Her Unexpected Family
Their Surprise Daddy
The Lawman's Yuletide Baby
Her Secret Daughter

SHEPHERD'S CROSSING SERIES
Her Cowboy Reunion
A Cowboy Christmas (with Linda Goodnight)
A Cowboy in Shepherd's Crossing
Healing the Cowboy's Heart (July 2019)

FROM BIG SKY CONTINUITY/LOVE INSPIRED BOOKS
His Montana Sweetheart

FROM SUMMERSIDE PRESS
Love Finds You in the City at Christmas

FROM BARBOUR PUBLISHING
Homestead Brides Collection

**FROM ZONDERVAN/HARPER COL-
LINS**
All Dressed Up in Love

Contributing author
"Mysteries of Martha's Vineyard"
Available at Guideposts.com
A Light in the Darkness
Swept Away
Catch of the Day
Just over the Horizon (June 2019)